Shattering the Void

Zora Stone

Copyright © 2025 Zora Stone

All rights reserved.

No part of this publication may be copied, reproduced, distributed, or transmitted in any form or by any means—electronic, mechanical, photocopying, recording, or otherwise—without the prior written permission of the publisher, except in the case of brief quotations used in reviews or other noncommercial purposes permitted by copyright law.

This is a work of fiction. Names, characters, places, and events are either products of the author's imagination or used fictitiously. Any resemblance to actual persons, living or dead, or actual events is purely coincidental.

Print ISBN: 978-1-971405-08-7

Published by: Smut by Design

www.zorastone.com

Now that I've ruined you... let me put you back together again.

Previously in the Ether Chronicles

A quick refresher before we dive into void and vengeance

Welcome back, beautiful chaos-loving readers! Ready to watch everything fall apart again? Here's what you need to remember before reality starts bending:

Crown of the Mist: Bree discovered she's the last Source, magic is real, and her creepy landlord Phil got exactly what he deserved (ash, specifically). Five childhood friends finally admitted they'd been in love with her forever. A magical crown chose her. Things were looking up.

Into the Ether: Thane arrived—dangerous, deadly, and completely unprepared for Bree to accidentally rebuild an entire sanctuary around herself. Refugees showed up. Powers manifested. Everyone looked unfairly attractive while glowing slightly.

Ashen Oath: Seth betrayed her. Bree's Ether exploded. Seth turned to ash. She entered the Mirror Rite chamber alone and emerged... different. The mirrors weren't broken anymore. Neither was she.

Veil of Echoes: Things got properly complicated. Riley—Bree's mirror self, everything she fears becoming—stumbled out of the shadows, hollowed out by Ethos's feeding. He'd used Riley up searching for magic that was never hers to give.

The guys warned Bree not to merge. Theo's vision made it clear: *fuse with Riley, finish Ethos's work.* So Bree did something impossible instead—she healed Riley without merging. Black and silver wove together until they balanced. Mirror-born. Whole but separate. The bond to Ethos *snapped.*

Then they discovered the truth. Bree had been trapped in the Void for a year. But outside? *Five years* had passed. Riley had been wearing Bree's face, sitting on the Council, and letting the sanctuary become a labor camp. Feeders in collars. Forced to mine Ether from veins that came from Bree's own drained power.

They found their people enslaved. Bree shattered every collar with a single wave of Ether and promised them freedom.

The Council came with an army of five hundred. Ethos came to finish what he started.

The battle nearly killed them all. Seth used Void powers against Ethos. Riley's healed magic raced across the battlefield, stopping people from dying. And Bree—surrounded by everyone she loved falling—pushed *everything* out. Every drop of Ether. Every thread of light.

They breathed again.

She didn't.

Welcome to **Shattering the Void.** The war isn't over. Ethos is still out there. And Bree gave everything to save the people she loves.

The question now is what's left of her to give.

SHATTERING THE VOID

(Fair warning: some voids can't be filled.)

Content Warnings

This book contains themes and content that may be triggering to some readers. Please review the following warnings before proceeding:

Emotional & Psychological Themes

- **Mass Death & Warfare** – Large-scale battle with significant casualties; feeling deaths through magical bonds

- **Forced Witnessing** – Being magically paralyzed while watching loved ones suffer and die

- **Survivor's Guilt** – Characters questioning their worth after being saved at great cost

- **Self-Sacrifice** – Giving everything to save others, including potential loss of self

- **PTSD & Trauma Responses** – Ongoing impact of captivity, dissociation, traumatic memory triggers

- **Parental Abandonment & Reunion** – Complex confrontation with estranged mother; revelations about choices made

- **Childhood Abuse Revelations** – Direct references to past abuse by a caregiver

- **Time Displacement Trauma** – Discovering years have passed while trapped; loss of family to time

Violence & Supernatural Threats

- **Slavery & Forced Labor** – Feeders in magical collars, forced to mine Ether in labor camp conditions

- **Large-Scale Combat** – Graphic battle sequences with significant injuries and death

- **Blood & Feeding** – Vampire-class feeding, magical consumption, life-force drain

- **Physical Restraint & Binding** – Magical paralysis, collars, loss of bodily autonomy

- **Near-Death Experiences** – Multiple characters severely injured; protagonist pushes magic to fatal limits

- **Predatory Supernatural Beings** – Ancient entity that feeds on life force and manipulates victims

Intimacy & Relationships

- **Explicit Sexual Content** – Detailed intimate scenes between adults (multiple instances)

- **Polyamorous Dynamics** – Multiple simultaneous romantic/sexual relationships

- **Consensual Voyeurism** – Witnessing intimate moments between partners

- **Magical Bonding** – Soul-deep connections with permanent, life-altering consequences

Dark Magic & Supernatural Elements

- **Void Realm** – Otherworldly dimension with time distortion and existential isolation

- **Magical Draining** – Being used as a source of power; Ether extracted without consent

- **Self-Sacrifice Through Magic** – Using all magical reserves to save others, with potentially fatal consequences

- **Predatory Manipulation** – Ancient being using charm and isolation to control victims

Family & Authority

- **Past Abuse References** – Ongoing impact of childhood trauma; direct discussion of abuse

- **Maternal Abandonment** – Confrontation with mother who left; complex emotions around protection vs. abandonment

- **Governmental Persecution** – Council-sanctioned hunting, surveillance, and oppression

- **Systemic Oppression** – Discrimination against Feeders, forced labor, magical hierarchy abuse

- **Power Imbalances** – Political manipulation, magical control, weaponized authority

This list is provided to ensure a safe reading experience. If any of these topics are personally distressing, please read with care and compassion for yourself.

Thank you for continuing this journey with Bree and her chosen family.
Zora Stone

Contents

1. Thane — 1
2. Theo — 7
3. Gray — 15
4. Stellan — 25
5. Rhett — 33
6. Bree — 41
7. Thane — 45
8. Jace — 49
9. Wes — 55
10. Bree — 65
11. Bree — 71
12. Theo — 81
13. Rhett — 83
14. Jace — 85
15. Seth — 87
16. Gray — 89

17.	Thane	91
18.	Bree	95
19.	Bree	103
20.	Bree	115
21.	Gray	125
22.	Rhett	137
23.	Bree	147
24.	Bree	151
25.	Thane	163
26.	Seth	173
27.	Stellan	179
28.	Wes	185
29.	Bree	189
30.	Jace	193
31.	Bree	199
32.	Gray	205
33.	Seth	211
34.	Bree	215
35.	Bree	221
36.	Bree	229
37.	Thane	233
38.	Rhett	239

39.	Bree	245
40.	Jace	251
41.	Jace	257
42.	Rhett	267
43.	Bree	277
44.	Wes	287
45.	Bree	293
46.	Theo	299
47.	Seth	311
48.	Bree	319
49.	Stellan	325
50.	Bree	331
51.	Bree	337
52.	Gray	341
53.	Bree	345
54.	Bree	347
Thank You		351
About the Author		353
Also by Zora Stone		355

Chapter 1
THANE

There's nothing here.

No sky. No ground. No horizon where one should end and the other begin.

Just black.

And we've been walking through it for what feels like a year.

The others move ahead of me in the darkness, barely visible even with my vampire sight. Rhett's dim blue flame flickers at the center of our formation—the only light we have, burning on nothing but his stubborn refusal to let it die.

Rhett insists it's fire. Personally, I think it's just his temper.

It's not enough to see by. Barely enough to convince me we still exist.

I stopped counting days somewhere around three hundred scratches on the obsidian shard I carry in my pocket. Time doesn't work here anyway—days stretch into weeks, hours collapse into seconds. But my body knows. The way my hands shake when I try to summon power I no longer have. The fact that I can't remember what her voice sounds like anymore.

That's the worst part.

Not the hunger, not the cold, not even the certainty that we might never escape.

It's that I'm forgetting her.

The exact cadence of her breath when she slept. The way her Ether curled when she was afraid but trying to hide it. The softness in her eyes right before she let herself trust me—really trust me.

It's slipping away, piece by piece, and I can't stop it.

We've tried everything.

Spells drawn in blood that Theo picked up somewhere. Rift-tears forced open with raw power we couldn't afford to spend. Bargains whispered to things that live in the spaces between breaths. Every door we make, the Void eats. Every escape route closes before we can follow it through.

Even Stellan's calm has cracked—which I didn't think was possible. Apparently the Void has stronger opinions than I do.

I caught him three turns of Rhett's fire ago — what passes for night here — whispering to something in the dark. Bartering bits of his soul like spare change in exchange for a way out.

"Please tell him I need him," he'd said, voice raw in a way I've never heard from him before.

I didn't interrupt. Desperation makes equals of us all.

And I don't know who the fuck he was talking to. Maybe he's as lost as I am.

Gray crouches ahead in his dire wolf form, motionless except for the subtle shift of his shoulders. Hunting. He insisted before his shift that he could find her this way—track her through instinct where logic failed us. That was months ago. Now he either can't shift back or won't. I'm not sure which possibility is worse.

Wes sits behind Gray, thinner than he should be. We all are, but it shows on him worst—hunger etched into every line of his face. He feeds on memory now, on ghost-impressions of emotion that cling to the things we carry. If you catch him staring too long at someone, check your nostalgia—he might be sipping it.

It's not enough. It's never enough.

Jace talks to the echoes because silence is worse. His voice drifts over from the far edge of our makeshift camp, one-sided conversation with things that sometimes answer and sometimes don't. I don't stop him. Madness is just another tool for survival here. Sometimes the echoes answer. Honestly, they're better company than most of us.

Theo sleeps.

He always sleeps too much or not at all. When he's awake, his eyes are unfocused, seeing things the rest of us can't. When he's asleep, he dreams the same thing every time.

Bree's face, turning away.

Stellan sits beside Rhett's fire, statue-still. He conserves everything now—words, movement, even breath. The only time he stirs is when Wes starts to fade too far, and then Stellan moves with eerie precision, offering just enough of himself to keep Wes from unraveling completely.

I don't ask what it costs him.

I already know.

We walk toward the faint pull in the dark, following the only thing that ever changes—small shifts in pressure, variations in the oppressive weight of nothing. They might mean we're still inside time. They might mean nothing at all.

But it's all we have.

Every once in a while the air shifts and I swear I smell her—vanilla, ozone, heartbreak—but it's just the Void mocking me.

The ground trembles.

Subtle at first—barely perceptible. But I feel it through the soles of my boots, and my head snaps up. The darkness around us shivers, the oppressive black bleeding silver, like ink remembering how to be light.

Then a sound breaks the silence.

Sharp. Ragged. Too loud.

Theo.

I'm moving before I've finished the thought, crossing the camp in three strides. He's sitting up, chest heaving, eyes wide and wild in the dim firelight.

"What did you see?" My voice comes out harsher than I intend, but I don't soften it.

Theo's gaze locks on mine, and for the first time in months, there's something other than despair in his expression.

Hope.

Fragile and desperate, but real.

"She's alive," he gasps.

The words hit me and I can't catch my breath. I feel the others stirring, moving closer. Rhett's fire flares brighter. Gray abandons his hunt and turns toward us. Even Stellan lifts his head.

"Bree?" Wes's voice cracks on her name.

Theo nods, frantic. "I saw her. Not—not like before. Not a memory. A *vision*." He presses his palms against his temples, breathing hard. "She's chained. Surrounded by mirrors. But she's breathing. The air around her moves again."

"Where?" Rhett demands.

"I don't—" Theo shakes his head. "Deep. Deeper than we've gone. But she's *here*, in the Void. We can reach her."

For a moment, no one speaks.

The ground trembles again, stronger this time. The silver threads through the darkness multiply, spreading like cracks in ice.

The Void is reacting.

Because she is.

"Move." My voice cuts through the shock, sharp and decisive. "Gather everything. We leave now."

"Thane—" Jace starts.

"*Now.*"

They scatter, trained by months of survival to obey without question when my tone leaves no room for argument. Weapons pulled from makeshift sheaths—mirror-glass daggers, chains forged from scar-metal, anything that can hold an edge in this place.

Rhett extinguishes the fire with a flick of his wrist, plunging us into darkness relieved only by the faint silver glow threading through the Void.

I turn to Theo. "Can you track it?"

He nods, already moving. "This way. I can feel her now—like a pull."

Gray falls into step beside him, senses sharpened. Wes follows close behind, steadier than he's been in weeks. Jace and Rhett flank the group, weapons ready. Stellan brings up the rear, silent but present.

And I take point.

Because if there's a door, I'll kick it open. If there's a wall, I'll tear it down. If something stands between us and her, I'll rip it apart with my bare hands.

The Void shifts around us as we move, shadows curling and retreating. We're not the same men who fell into this place a year ago.

We're something harder now. Sharper.

Desperate enough to burn the world if it means bringing her home.

The silver light grows stronger ahead, and for the first time in months, I let myself believe.

If the world's still out there when we break through, we'll fight our way back to it

If it isn't, then we'll make one.

Chapter 2
THEO

The silver veins pulse through the dark like exposed nerves, and my head throbs in time with them.

We've been walking for hours. Maybe days. Time's a joke here, but exhaustion isn't.

The vision hits again—third time since Thane gave the order to move. I don't fight it anymore. Fighting just makes it worse.

A horseshoe.

Right...

Suspended in black water that isn't water, turning end over end. Silver script covers the curved surface, glowing like the eyes of the creatures Gray hunts. I can read it this time—shapes that feel like words, though not in any language I know.

Luck. Warning. Path.

The horseshoe spins faster, and I catch the reflection in its surface: not my face, but something with too many eyes, watching back.

Then it's gone.

I stumble, reach for nothing. The Void doesn't offer handholds.

"You good?" Jace's voice cuts through the dark, closer than I expected.

"Fine."

"You look like you're about to puke."

"I'm *fine*."

I'm not fine. I haven't been fine since we fell into this place. But I'm functional, and that's all that matters.

The visions haven't stopped—they've sharpened. Every step we take toward Bree, they get clearer. Louder. More insistent.

And I'm done pretending they're just fragments.

Gray's massive dire wolf form moves ahead of us, white fur catching the faint silver glow. He still won't shift back. Can't or won't—no one's asked, and he can't answer. Just hunts, tracks, moves forward like that's all he has left.

Wes walks behind him, hollow-eyed and too thin. We all are, but it shows most on him—hunger etched into every line of his face. His hands shake when he thinks no one's looking. Rhett keeps close to Wes, heat flickering under his skin like he's trying to burn away the cold that's eating all of us from the inside.

And Stellan—

Stellan drifts at the back, lips moving silently in the dark.

Again.

I've been watching him for the past hour. The whispers started faint, barely audible over the sound of our footsteps on stone that shouldn't exist. But they've gotten louder. More desperate.

"Please," I hear him murmur. "Just a little longer. I need—"

He cuts off when he notices me looking.

The silence stretches.

I'm done with silence.

"Stellan," I say, voice flat. "You wanna tell us who the fuck you keep talking to?"

Everyone stops.

Gray's head swings toward us, silver eyes reflecting nothing. A low growl rumbles from his chest—warning or question, I can't tell.

Jace turns, one hand on his blade. Wes looks between me and Stellan like he's not sure if he should intervene or run.

Thane's gaze locks on Stellan, cold and unreadable.

"Can't imagine it's normal," I continue, "having friends in the Void."

Stellan's expression doesn't change. "Lonely men talk to echoes, Theo. You should know—you've been muttering prophecies for months."

"That's different."

"Is it?"

"Yeah." I take a step toward him. "Because my visions don't answer back."

"If he's got a book club in here," Jace says, "I want the reading list."

No one laughs. He shuts up.

"I'm saying," Stellan replies, voice smooth and controlled, "that when you spend enough time in the dark, your mind fills in the gaps."

"Bullshit," Thane says quietly.

The word instantly makes everything fucking awkward. Good.

Stellan's jaw tightens. "Excuse me?"

"You heard me." Thane moves forward, deliberate and unhurried. "We've all been listening to you for weeks. That's not your mind filling gaps. That's you begging someone—or something—for help."

"You don't know what you're—"

"*Please tell him I need him*," Thane interrupts, voice dropping into a perfect mimic. "Your exact words—three turns of Rhett's fire ago. I was two paces behind you; sound carries in here."

Stellan goes still.

The silence that follows isn't empty. It's the kind of silence that comes right before something breaks.

"You've been spying on me," Stellan says, voice low and dangerous.

"I've been surviving," Thane counters. "And part of that is knowing when someone in my group is keeping secrets that could get us killed."

"Oh, that's rich coming from you—"

"Stop."

The word shears through the ringing in my ears. We all turn to look at Wes.

He's staring at the ground, arms wrapped around himself like he's trying to hold his own shape together. His hands are shaking. His jaw ticks.

"I can't keep the starving saint act," he says, voice raw. "And I know I'm not the only one barely holding it together."

His eyes lift, meeting each of ours in turn. "But if Stellan has a way out—if he knows something we don't—then we need to hear it. Now."

The truth of it settles over us like ash.

Stellan's mask cracks.

Not much. Just enough.

I see it in the way his shoulders drop, the way his hands unclench at his sides. The way he looks at Thane and says, voice tight, "You're an ass."

"Frequently," Thane agrees. "Now talk."

Stellan exhales slowly, like he's been holding that breath for months.

"I wasn't talking to the Void," he says finally. "I was talking *through* it."

"Through it to what?" Jace demands.

Stellan's gaze flicks to me, then away. "To someone who might actually be able to get us out of here."

Before anyone can respond, the vision slams into me again.

Harder this time. Sharper.

The horseshoe spins in black water, and now I see more—chains attached to darkness. And at the far edge of my vision, something moves. Something massive and wrong and *alive*.

Silver eyes in the dark. Dozens of them.

But not watching us.

Waiting.

I gasp, stumbling backward. Jace catches my arm before I fall.

"Theo? What did you see?"

I shake my head, trying to clear it. "Something's coming. Not hunting—answering."

Stellan goes very still.

"You called them," I say, looking at him. "Didn't you?"

His expression shifts—surprise, then something almost like relief.

"Not called," he says quietly. "Asked."

"Asked *what*?" Rhett's voice is tight with restrained fire.

"For reinforcements." Stellan's eyes meet mine, steady now. "The Void isn't empty." He exhales. "It never has been. And some of the things that live here…" He pauses. "Some of them remember me."

The silence that follows is heavier than before.

Thane's the first to break it. "You've been here before."

It's not a question.

Stellan nods once. "A long time ago. Before any of you knew what the Void was. Before Bree." His voice drops. "I barely made it out. But I didn't make it out alone."

"What does that mean?" Wes asks.

"It means," Stellan says, turning to face us fully, "that I know someone who knows how to navigate this place. I know what hunts here. I know what can be bargained with, and what should be avoided at all costs."

He looks at each of us in turn.

"And I know who owes me a debt."

Gray growls again, deeper this time. Insistent.

The horseshoe flashes in my mind, but fainter now—like it's retreating, waiting. Not a warning. Not luck.

A marker. A path they'll recognize when the time comes.

"What did you ask for?" I press.

Stellan's quiet for a long moment. Then: "Protection. Passage. A way to find what we're looking for without being hunted by everything else in here."

"And they agreed?" Thane's voice is skeptical.

"They owe me," Stellan repeats. "But it'll come with a price."

"What kind of price?" Jace asks.

"The kind I'll pay when the time comes." Stellan's expression closes off again. "Not before."

The weight of that sits on all of us.

Rhett's fire flickers brighter. Wes straightens slightly, hunger momentarily forgotten. Gray's massive form shifts, and he lets out a short, sharp bark—the first sound he's made in weeks that isn't a growl.

But it's Thane who speaks, voice cold and measured.

"Then you better hope they remember you fondly."

Stellan's mouth curves into something that's almost a smile. "They will. I made sure of it."

The silver veins pulse brighter, and I feel the Void shift around us—not threatening, but *aware*. Like it knows something's coming.

Like it's been waiting for this.

"We keep moving," Thane says, voice cutting through the moment. "Toward Bree. If your reinforcements show up, they can catch us on the way."

No one argues.

We start walking again, but the silence is different now. Not empty. Not exhausted.

Expectant.

I drift to the back, watching Stellan ahead of me. He's not whispering anymore, but his fingers trace the inside of his wrist—checking for something that should be there but isn't.

The horseshoe doesn't spin in my mind anymore. It's settled. Waiting.

Everything in this place waits for something.

I speed up until I'm walking beside him.

"The things in my vision," I say. "The ones with the silver eyes. What are they?"

Stellan's jaw tightens. He's still processing—I can see it in the rigid set of his shoulders, the way his hands flex and unflex at his sides. Anger. Irritation. Resignation, maybe, that he has to explain at all.

He doesn't look at me when he finally answers.

"Nightmares," he says quietly. "They're called Nightmares."

Chapter 3
GRAY

I can't shift back.

I won't.

I'm not sure I even remember how anymore.

The wolf doesn't speak, doesn't think in words the way the man does. It just *is*—instinct and sensation, hunger and purpose stripped down to their most basic form. There's clarity in that. Safety.

Because if I shift back, I'll have to face what we've done.

What I've done.

How long we've left her here.

The world feels different in this form. Sounds sharper—every footstep echoes like thunder, every breath a windstorm. Smells thick with rot and magic, everything tasting like failure on my tongue. The silver veins that pulse through the Void carry a scent like lightning and blood. They started appearing shortly after we fell into this place. Thin threads at first. Now they're everywhere—brighter, thicker, pulsing like exposed nerves. We don't know what they mean. Just that they keep growing.

The others talk around me sometimes. Voices echoing like ghosts, words I don't bother trying to parse. They've stopped expecting responses. Stopped reaching out to touch my fur or check if I'm still in there.

Good.

I don't deserve their concern.

I tried to shift back once, weeks ago. Maybe months. I don't know or care anymore. But I tried, and instead of bones breaking and reforming, I heard her scream. Not a memory—something worse. Like the Ether itself was reminding me what I'd failed to prevent.

I haven't tried since.

Sometimes I see flashes—not visions like Theo's, but sensory echoes that hit me in ways I don't think I can ever come back from. Her scent in phantom bursts: vanilla and ozone and whatever it is that makes her, *her*. The ghost of her touch on my fur. The sound of her breathing when she slept, steady and safe and *alive*.

I'm convinced they're guilt hallucinations.

The Void playing with what's left of my sanity.

Because she can't be here. We would have found her by now. We would have—

I shake my head, a very human gesture in a very inhuman body.

Keep moving. That's all there is. One paw in front of the other, tracking fading hope through endless black, pretending the cold doesn't reach all the way to bone.

Stopping means remembering.

Remembering means breaking.

And I can't afford to break. Not when they need—

The silence presses in, a living thing.

Then the scent hits me and steals my breath.

I freeze mid-step, every muscle locking down. I manage to pull myself together. My nose lifts, nostrils flaring as I pull the air in deep.

No.

It can't be.

But there it is, threading through the cold and rot and emptiness like a lifeline I don't deserve to grab.

Vanilla. Ozone. Heartbreak.

Her.

The others are saying something behind me—questions, maybe, or curses—but their voices blur into static. The world narrows to that single thread of scent, impossibly warm in a place that shouldn't know warmth at all.

It's probably another trick. The Void has fooled me before, dangled phantom traces of her just to watch me chase nothing.

But...

This time is different.

This time, the scent carries *presence*. Not memory. Not ghost.

Real.

The wolf surges forward before the man can think to question.

I bolt.

Behind me, shouts—my name, sharp and urgent. Rhett's voice, maybe Thane's. But they're already fading, swallowed by the rush of blood in my ears and the desperate, animal need to *find her find her find her*—

The silver light veins through the darkness like roots guiding me home. The scent strengthens with every stride, pulling me like a leash I'd willingly wear for the rest of my life if it meant reaching her.

My paws hit stone that shouldn't be warm. The air shifts, thickens.

And then the darkness opens.

A chamber.

Massive. Ancient. Obsidian walls rising into shadow, shards of light embedded like broken mirrors catching and throwing back silver glow. The air hums—not sound, not quiet, but *pressure*. Like the Ether is trying to wake but can't quite manage it.

The silver veins converge here. All of them. Threading through the floor, the walls, pulsing brighter as they lead toward the center of the chamber. Toward her scent.

I move forward, alert, because I know in my bones I was never meant to be here.

At the center—

My legs give out.

Bree.

Bound in silver chains.

Sitting against the obsidian wall, head bowed, dark hair falling forward to hide her face. Barefoot. Too thin. The chains loop around her wrists, her ankles, her throat—delicate but absolute, glowing faintly with the same light as the veins threading through the Void.

Where her bare feet touch the floor, the silver veins begin. Spreading outward from that single point of contact like roots, like cracks, like something alive drinking from the source.

Ether leaks from her like smoke. Silver threaded with black—alive, but wrong. Suppressed. Contained.

The smell of her nearly breaks me.

It's *real*.

She's *real*.

A sound tears out of me—half howl, half sob. Mourning and relief tangled into something that hurts worse than either alone.

And beside her—

Seth.

Collapsed on his side, one hand stretched toward Bree like he was reaching for her when consciousness left him. His chest barely moves. Too still. Too pale.

Footsteps thunder behind me. The others catching up, skidding to stops that echo through the chamber.

"Holy shit," Jace breathes.

Rhett's fire ignites, blue flame casting harsh shadows across the obsidian. "Bree—"

"Don't." Thane's voice cuts sharp. "The chains. They're silver."

"So?" Rhett demands.

"So they eat magic." Thane moves forward slowly, silver eyes scanning the bindings. "Touch them wrong and they'll drain you dry."

Theo's eyes are glowing, distant and horrified. "She's been here the whole time. Chained. Alone."

"Not alone," Wes whispers, staring at Seth. "He's—is he alive?"

I'm already moving.

The wolf doesn't care about silver or magic or consequences. It only knows one thing: *she's here and she's hurting and I failed her but I'm here now—*

I reach her in three strides, close enough to see the rise and fall of her chest. Close enough to smell the corruption threading through her Ether, sweet and rotten like fruit left too long in the sun.

The chains hum when I get close. Warning. Threat.

I bare my teeth.

The silver burns when my jaw closes around the first chain. Pain lances through me—not heat, but *absence*. Like the metal is drinking the wolf out of me, replacing fur with void.

"Gray, stop!" Thane's hand closes on my scruff, yanking me back. "You touch those chains too long and they'll kill you."

I snarl, twisting in his grip.

"I know." His voice drops, quieter. Steadier. "I know. But we need you functional, not ash."

Rhett steps forward, fire coiling around his hands. "Then we burn them."

"They're warded," Stellan says from the entrance, voice tight. "You burn them, you burn her."

Silence.

Heavy and helpless.

Then Bree's eyes flicker open.

Just for a moment. Just long enough to find mine.

Green eyes, dulled with exhaustion but *aware*. Recognition flares—brief and bright and devastating.

Thin threads of Ether reach out from her—silver mist so faint I almost miss it, brushing the air like static. They stretch toward me. Rhett. Jace. Wes. Theo. Stellan.

Not Thane.

I don't understand why, but there's no time to question it.

The moment the threads touch us, the world *stops*.

Everything goes silent. Still. Like the Void itself is holding its breath.

Then something snaps into place inside my chest—so profound, so *final*, that my legs nearly give out again.

Not painful.

Chosen.

That's the only word for it. She's choosing us. Here, now, dying and chained and barely conscious—she's *choosing us*.

The warmth floods through me, burning away a year of cold and emptiness and guilt. A connection that goes deeper than bone, deeper than blood. I can feel her—not just her presence, but *her*. Her exhaustion. Her fear. Her desperate, fragile hope that we're real.

Around me, the others make sounds—Rhett's sharp inhale, Jace's choked gasp, Wes's broken sob. Theo staggers, pressing both hands to his chest like he's trying to hold something in. Stellan goes perfectly still, eyes wide and unguarded for the first time since I've known him.

We're hers.

She made us hers.

Even here. Even now. Even like this.

"Welcome to the club," Thane says quietly from behind me, voice rough with something that might be relief. Might be grief. Probably both.

Her lips move. One word, barely audible:

"Gray."

Not a question. Not relief.

Apology.

Like she's sorry I had to find her like this.

The sound that rips out of me this time is pure anguish.

Her eyes close again, consciousness slipping away like water.

I press my nose to her hand—the only part of her I can reach that isn't wrapped in silver. Her fingers are cold. Too cold.

But her pulse beats against my muzzle.

Alive.

Behind me, the others are arguing—Rhett demanding they break the chains anyway, Stellan insisting there's a better way, Theo muttering about visions and keys and time running out.

I don't listen.

I just stay there, nose pressed to her hand, breathing in the proof that she's real.

That we found her.

That we're not too late.

"We're not leaving her here," I think, the words human-shaped even if I can't speak them. *Not this time.*

Thane's hand settles on my head, steady and certain.

"We're not leaving her here," he says, voice carrying to the others. "But we're not moving her until we know how to break those chains without killing her."

He looks at Stellan. "You said you have help coming. You said they know how to navigate this place."

Stellan's expression is unreadable. "They do."

"Then we wait for them." Thane's voice goes cold. Sharp. "And pray they get here before whatever's keeping her like this notices we found her."

For a moment, no one moves.

Then Stellan nods once. "They're coming. We just have to hold position until they arrive."

"How long?" Rhett demands.

"I don't know." Stellan's voice is tight. "Time doesn't work the same for them."

"Fine." Thane doesn't look away from Bree. "Rhett, Jace—secure the perimeter. Wes, check Seth. See if he's salvageable. We hold here until Stellan's reinforcements show."

Commands. Purpose. Direction.

The group scatters into motion.

I stay where I am, nose still pressed to Bree's hand.

Her pulse beats steady against my fur.

For the first time in forever, the Void smells like home. Her. Alive. Mine to protect.

Home, I think. *You're home now.*

Even if she can't hear me.

Even if I don't deserve to be the one to find her.

I'm not leaving her again.

Chapter 4
STELLAN

No one speaks—there's nothing to say.

We've arranged ourselves in a rough circle around Bree and Seth—silent sentinels keeping watch over the broken and the unconscious. Gray's massive wolf form is curled at Bree's feet, nose pressed against her ankle like he's trying to will warmth back into her. His eyes haven't closed once.

Seth lies motionless a few feet away, chest rising and falling in shallow, uneven breaths. Alive, but barely. Wes checked him twice already, hands shaking so badly he could barely find a pulse.

No fire. Rhett tried earlier, but the flames guttered out almost immediately, swallowed by the same pressure that made the air feel thick and wrong.

The only light comes from the silver veins pulsing through the floor and threading up the obsidian walls, and the silver flames flickering in sconces along the perimeter. The veins are brighter here, more concentrated. All of them converging on this chamber like arteries leading to a heart.

Leading to her.

I study the pattern, tracing the lines with my eyes. They spread outward from where her bare feet touch the floor, branching and splitting until they disappear into the dark beyond the chamber walls.

I've heard of this before.

The realization hits cold and certain, settling in my stomach like a stone.

I kneel, pressing my palm flat against one of the veins. It pulses back—faint but rhythmic. Not random. Not ambient magic.

Feeding.

My hand jerks back.

"Stellan?"

Thane's voice cuts through the silence, sharp with suspicion.

I don't answer immediately. Just stare at the veins, watching them pulse in time with Bree's shallow breathing.

I've heard stories. Old ones, passed down through Feeder lines when the Council wasn't listening. Tales of places where the something in the Void learned to drink power directly from a Source without touching them. Where simply *being* was enough.

The chains are just holding her in place.

Ethos is feeding on her.

Ethos is the something those stories were talking about.

Horror crawls up my throat.

"Stellan." Thane's tone hardens. "What do you see?"

I stand slowly, brushing ash from my hands. "A theory. An old story."

"Elaborate."

"These veins." I gesture at the pulsing silver threads. "They're not part of the Void's natural structure. They're hers. Her Ether, pulled from her just by being here. Ethos is feeding on her, using her power for something."

Jace swears under his breath. Rhett's hands twitch, and I notice—

Heat.

Faint, but there. His palms glow with warmth that wasn't there before. My stomach drops as the second realization hits.

"So he's draining her," Theo says quietly. "Just by her being in the Void."

"Yes," I say, but my eyes are still on Rhett's hands. On Wes, who's stopped shaking. On Jace, who looks less gray than he did an hour ago.

They're feeding too.

All of us. Bonded to her, pulling from the Ether that saturates this place now. Not from Bree directly—thank fuck—from what she's already given. The silver veins pulsing through the floor and walls, the ambient power soaking the air.

It's passive. Automatic. Our bonds drinking from the source she's become.

Just like Ethos.

The horror of it settles like ice in my chest. They didn't choose this. Don't even realize it's happening. But they're feeding nonetheless, growing stronger while she drains away. It also explains why Thane didn't end up like the rest of us being here.

"Her Ether is being used by Ethos for something," I finish quietly. "The chains are just keeping her in place. The real drain…" I touch the vein again. "His reach is everywhere here."

Wes makes a sound halfway between a growl and a sob. His voice is stronger now—the bond feeding him even as we speak. "Can we stop it?"

"Not here." The words taste like ash. "As long as she's in the Void, it'll keep taking from her. The only way to stop it is to get her out."

"Then what do we do?" Rhett demands, fire sparking in his palms—not struggling now, but *there*. Real flame growing stronger by the minute.

Fed by her, just like everything else in this cursed place.

I'm quiet for a long moment.

Then Theo's voice cuts through, flat and exhausted and done with my evasion.

"You said you've been here before." He stares at me across Bree's unconscious form. "So start talking."

The demand hangs in the air.

I could deflect. Redirect. Change the subject like I've done for centuries.

But we're out of time, and they deserve the truth.

Most of it, anyway.

"I was lost here once," I say finally. "A long time ago. Before the Council. Before most of you were born."

"How long?" Thane asks.

"Centuries."

Silence. Heavy and disbelieving.

"How did you get out?" Jace's tone is carefully neutral, but I hear the edge underneath.

"I made a deal." I look at the veins again, remembering. "With Ethos."

Silence. Sharp and horrified.

Thane's silver eyes go cold. He already suspected, but hearing it confirmed is different.

"What did you give him?" Rhett asks quietly.

"That's not part of this story."

The silence that follows is tense, but I don't elaborate. What I gave Ethos stays between me and the dark.

"He betrayed you," Theo says softly. Not a question—a certainty drawn from whatever fragments of vision he's catching.

I nod once. "The deal was simple: my freedom in exchange for..." I pause. "Something he wanted. But Ethos doesn't honor bargains the way you'd expect. He sent me to the outer edges of the Void. The parts where nothing survives. Where even the darkness is afraid to go."

"Why there?" Wes asks.

"To die, probably." My mouth curves into something bitter. "Or to be forgotten. Either way, it was meant to be the end."

"But it wasn't," Gray says.

"No." I look at Bree's unconscious form, remembering those years in the dark. "I was dying. Magically starving. There was nothing to feed on out there—no fear, no connection, no life force. Just... emptiness. It doesn't kill you quickly, but it hollows you out until there's nothing left but desperation."

I pause, choosing my words carefully.

"That's when I found them."

"The Nightmares," Theo breathes.

I exhale slowly, choosing my words carefully.

"There are things that live in the Void. Most of them hunt. Some of them feed. A few of them... remember what they used to be."

I pause, letting the weight of that settle.

"I thought I was hallucinating at first." The memory is vivid even now. "Creatures that looked like myths—like unicorns pulled inside-out and remade in shadow. Black as the Void itself, but when the light hit them right, they shimmered silver. Two horns instead of one. Eyes that glowed like molten mercury."

Jace's blade stills in his hand. "You're describing dream-steeds."

Theo looks at him, eyebrows raised. "How the hell do you know that, Jace?"

"Hey, I read too, you know." Jace shrugs, but there's an edge of defensiveness in it.

"That's what they are." I meet his gaze. "Nightmares. They feed on fear and terror, but they were something else too. Something majestic. Wild."

"And you just walked up to one?" Rhett sounds skeptical.

"I collapsed in front of one." The truth is far less heroic than they probably imagine. "Hollowed out by hunger, barely conscious. Should have been trampled, or possibly consumed. But one of them…" I shake my head. "It didn't kill me."

"Why not?" Wes asks.

"Because I offered it something it wanted more than my death."

"What?"

"Order." The word tastes strange after all these years. "Purpose. A reason to exist beyond hunger and fear."

Thane's silver eyes narrow. "You taught them to serve you."

"I taught them to survive." I meet his gaze. "They were going feral, consuming each other when there was nothing else to feed on. Magnificent creatures eating themselves alive in the dark."

"So you gave them structure," Theo murmurs.

"I gave them discipline. Rules. A way to exist that didn't end in self-destruction." I look at the veins pulsing through the floor. "It took years. But eventually, they trusted me enough to help me find a way out."

"How many?" Thane's voice is cold. Calculating.

"Enough."

"That's not an answer."

"It's the only one you're getting." I turn to face him fully. "Their leader eventually grew strong enough to tear open a way back to the mortal world. A few dared to follow me through. The rest stayed behind—too afraid of what waited outside, or too changed by the Void to leave."

My jaw tightens. "I promised them freedom, someday. They swore they'd ride for me again if I ever called."

Understanding ripples through the group.

"That's the debt," Rhett breathes.

I nod. "That's the debt."

"And you're calling it now." Thane's voice carries no judgment. Just cold assessment. "For her."

"For all of us." I gesture at the veins. "Ethos is using her Ether the way the Nightmares once used fear."

Silence stretches taut as wire.

"Can Ethos be stopped?" Thane asks finally.

I stand, brushing ash from my hands. "That's what we need to find out."

"How?"

I meet his eyes. "We get her out of here first. Then we deal with him."

The veins flicker.

A tremor runs through the stone beneath our feet—subtle at first, then stronger. The silver light pulses brighter, faster, like a heartbeat accelerating.

Theo's head snaps up, eyes going distant. When he speaks, his voice is hollow.

"They heard you."

I feel it too—a shift in the air, a change in pressure. Something moving through the dark, drawn by my voice carried through the Void's twisted pathways.

Something answering.

Gray lifts his head, a low growl rumbling in his chest. Sharper now. More alert. The wolf growing stronger with every passing hour.

Rhett's fire burns steady in his palms—blue flames that would've been impossible when we first arrived. "How long?"

"I don't know." I stare at the veins, watching them pulse.

"Could be hours," Theo murmurs. "Could be minutes."

Jace's blade appears in his hand, reflecting the silver light. "And when they get here?"

I don't answer immediately.

Because the truth is, I don't know what they've become in the centuries since I left them behind. I don't know if they'll remember our pact or if the Void has twisted them into something unrecognizable.

I don't know if calling them was salvation or suicide.

But it's too late to take it back now.

"When they get here," I say quietly, "we'll find out if the dark remembers its debts."

The veins pulse brighter—steady, certain.

And somewhere in the distance—faint but unmistakable—I hear hoofbeats.

Chapter 5
RHETT

The hoofbeats are louder now.

Not just sound—pressure. Each one reverberates through the obsidian floor, up through my worn boots, into my bones. Rhythmic. Relentless. Like a heartbeat that doesn't belong to anything living.

My fire responds before I can think, heat prickling under my skin in answer to the wrongness of it all.

"They're here," Stellan says quietly.

I look at him, standing perfectly still at the edge of our makeshift circle around Bree and Seth. His expression is calm—too calm. Like he's bracing for something he both dreads and needs.

"You sure about this?" I ask, voice rougher than I mean it to be.

He doesn't answer. Just watches the darkness beyond the silver flames flickering in the sconces.

Gray lifts his head from where he's curled at Bree's feet, ears flattening against his skull. A low growl rumbles in his chest—warning or fear, I can't tell. Maybe both.

Wes shifts closer to Seth's unconscious form, dark eyes tracking something. "Something's wrong with him."

I follow his gaze.

Seth's chest still rises and falls in shallow breaths, but there's something else now. Faint tendrils of black smoke seeping into his skin—so thin they're almost invisible.

"What the hell is that?" Jace breathes.

Theo steps closer, eyes going distant the way they do when he's Seeing. "Two energies. They're not fighting." He pauses, frowning. "They're... feeding him."

"Feeding," I repeat flatly.

What the fuck.

Stellan kneels beside Seth, careful not to touch him. His gray eyes track the silver and black weaving through Seth's body with clinical precision.

"He's bonded to her," Stellan says quietly. "The bond formed in the Void. It adapted him." He looks up at Thane. "He's feeding from both sources now. Her Ether and the Void itself."

Silence.

"That's not possible," Thane says, but there's uncertainty in his voice.

"It shouldn't be." Stellan's gaze returns to Seth. "But the Void doesn't follow rules. When a bond forms there, the magic changes. Adapts to survive." He gestures at the black threading through the silver. "He's feeding on Void energy the same way we're feeding on her Ether."

My stomach turns. "So he's feeding the same way we are? From what's already been taken?"

"Yes," Stellan says quietly. "We're all drinking from the ambient power soaking the air, the veins pulsing through the walls. It's passive. Automatic." His gaze shifts back to the black smoke seeping into Seth's skin. "But Seth's feeding from both—her Ether and the Void itself."

He pauses, watching the black and silver weave through Seth's unconscious body. "No one survives that kind of balance for long. Light and shadow don't share a body without cost."

The hoofbeats grow louder. Closer.

The silver veins pulsing through the floor flare brighter, and I feel the temperature drop—sharp enough to make my breath fog.

Gray's growl intensifies. He's on his feet now, hackles raised, positioning himself between Bree and whatever's coming.

"Easy," I murmur, but my hands are already heating, blue flames dancing across my palms.

My eyes find the chamber entrance—the threshold we crossed to get here. We walked right into his space. His territory.

The thought comes slower than it should. A year of exhaustion catching up all at once.

"Is no one worried about this?" I ask, voice tight. "We're in his chamber. What happens when he comes back?"

Stellan doesn't look up from Seth's unconscious form. "He knew we were here the moment we stepped through the threshold." His voice is flat, matter-of-fact. "He would have been here already if he was coming."

The words should be reassuring.

They're not.

Because if Ethos isn't coming, it means he doesn't need to. It means whatever's happening here—whatever he's doing to her—he's already won.

Jace's blade appears in his hand, reflecting the silver light. "How many Nightmares are we talking about?"

"Enough," Stellan says, and there's something hollow in his voice. Something that sounds like grief.

The hoofbeats crescendo.

Then—silence.

The kind of silence that makes your ears ring. That feels like the world is holding its breath.

The silver flames in the sconces gutter and die, plunging us into darkness lit only by the veins pulsing through the floor and the faint glow of Seth's corrupted bond.

I feel it before I see it.

A presence. Massive. Wrong in a way that has nothing to do with magic and everything to do with instinct screaming predator.

Then the darkness moves.

Shapes emerge from the black—tall, powerful, graceful in a way that makes my skin crawl.

Nightmares.

The name fits.

They're massive—easily seventeen hands at the shoulder. Black as the Void itself, coats so dark they seem to absorb light rather than reflect it. But when they move, silver shimmers across their flanks like moonlight on water.

Two horns curve back from each skull. Not delicate like a unicorn's—brutal, elegant, deadly. Their eyes glow molten silver, tracking us with intelligence that's too knowing to be animal.

Smoke curls from their hooves with each step, dissipating into silver mist that clings to the ground.

There are seven of them. Maybe more in the darkness. It's hard to tell where one ends and the next begins.

My fire flares hot enough to make the air shimmer, but I hold my ground.

The lead Nightmare steps forward, and I get my first clear look at it.

Bigger than the others. Scars across its flanks that shimmer silver against black. Eyes that burn with something ancient and patient and terrifying.

It moves toward Stellan first, those molten silver eyes fixed on him.

When the voice comes, it bypasses sound entirely—flowing directly into my mind like cold water.

You called, Master. We answer.

Stellan's breath catches. His hands shake.

Then the Nightmare's gaze shifts.

Past Stellan. Past all of us.

To Bree.

The creature goes utterly still.

The Source.

It's not a question. It's recognition, reverence.

The massive head lowers, and its front legs fold, bowing to the obsidian floor.

One by one, the other six follow—massive creatures bending their forelegs, horned heads dipping low in perfect synchronization. Smoke wraps around Bree like a shroud, and the veins pulse brighter in response.

The first in generations. We felt her waking across the realms.

The lead Nightmare's attention returns to Stellan.

You called. But not for you. For her.

Stellan's composure shatters.

His breath comes in ragged gasps, shoulders shaking. He sinks to his knees like someone cut his strings, and the sound that tears from his throat is raw—years of control breaking all at once.

"Please." His voice cracks. "I've kept them alive this long. I've kept them moving. But I can't—" He presses both hands to his face. "I can't save her. Please. Help her."

The words come broken, desperate. Nothing left of the elegant, controlled man who's led us through a year of hell.

Just someone who's finally, completely, out of options.

I move before I think, dropping to one knee beside him. Not as a rival. Not as someone competing for Bree's attention.

As someone who just watched another man break.

The lead Nightmare is silent for a long moment, silver eyes fixed on Stellan's bowed head.

Then, quietly: *We will guard what remains.*

"Can you stop what's draining her?" Stellan asks, voice barely above a whisper.

We cannot break what feeds the Void. But we can hold the line until you find a way.

"That's not good enough," I snap, fire flaring.

The Nightmares shift, smoke curling thicker from their hooves.

But Stellan holds up a hand. "It has to be." He looks at the lead Nightmare. "Just... keep her safe. Keep the darkness from taking her until we can get her out."

"Please," he whispers.

The single word lands like a prayer.

The Nightmare inclines its massive head. *For you, we hold the line.*

The Nightmares move as one, forming a perimeter around Bree and Seth. Their presence fills the chamber—not threatening exactly, but absolute. Like they've claimed this space and nothing will move them from it.

"You really think they can save her?" I ask quietly.

Stellan's hands are shaking. "No." His voice is barely audible. "But they can keep the dark from taking her before we do."

The hoofbeats have faded to a slow, steady rhythm—matching Bree's heartbeat. Matching the pulse of the veins.

I look at her, then at Seth, then at the black smoke still seeping into his unconscious body.

"What happens to him if we shatter the Void?" I ask.

Stellan's silence is answer enough.

He doesn't know.

None of us do.

But the Nightmares have formed their circle, and the darkness feels just a little less absolute than it did before.

For the first time since we fell into this hell, hope has a shape.

It's just wrapped in smoke and shadow, carrying debts we don't understand and a cost we haven't paid yet.

The lead Nightmare's silver eyes find mine across the chamber.

And I swear I hear a voice—not words exactly, but meaning—whisper through my mind.

Fire cannot burn what's already ash. But it can light the way home.

My flames gutter, then steady.

Yeah.

We're getting her out of here.

Chapter 6
BREE

The world comes back in pieces.

Sound first—the low thrum of something heavy moving, steady as breath. Then warmth. Not much, but enough to make me realize how cold I've been.

A voice murmurs nearby, too low to understand. Another answers. The words blend together, deep and soft, like waves hitting stone.

Light filters through my lashes—silver and black, pulsing like veins beneath skin.

I'm still in the Void.

My body tenses on instinct, but the panic doesn't come. Not this time.

Because something's different.

The realization should terrify me. It doesn't.

Then the smell hits me.

Smoke. Fire. Leather. *Them.*

The air isn't biting anymore—it hums. Low, warm, alive. The kind of magic that doesn't hurt to breathe.

I force my eyes open.

Shapes come into focus slowly: Gray's wolf form curled near my feet, motionless but watchful. Rhett kneeling beside someone—Stellan, maybe. Jace standing guard with a blade that catches the silver light. Theo's hands pressed together like he's praying. Wes leaning over Seth, his expression torn between fear and something else.

And beyond them—

Creatures.

For a heartbeat I think I'm dreaming them. Massive, horned silhouettes rising out of the mist. Smoke rolling from their hooves. Silver eyes burning like stars.

But the Ether doesn't recoil.

It stretches toward them.

I can feel it—those invisible threads inside me loosening for the first time in forever, touching theirs, recognizing something ancient and familiar at the same time.

Then a voice flows through my mind.

You are safe now, my queen.

Not a question. A vow.

Movement everywhere—heads turning, bodies shifting. All of them looking at me at once.

Gray's wolf form lifts, ears forward. Rhett's hand stills mid-gesture. Stellan's head snaps up from where he's kneeling. Jace's blade lowers. Theo's eyes widen. Wes goes perfectly still.

They heard it too.

I've forgotten what their presence feels like.

My chest aches with the effort of breathing, but the fear doesn't come. Just warmth spreading slowly through my ribs, my pulse syncing with the rhythmic sound of the men around me.

Rhett moves closer to me, firelight catching the worry in his eyes.

"Bree?"

I want to answer. I think I do. But the world tilts again, and the silver light folds over me like a blanket.

The last thing I feel is warmth—real, impossible warmth—seeping through my bones.

Then nothing.

Chapter 7
THANE

The chamber settles into an uneasy stillness.

Bree's unconscious again, her chest rising and falling in shallow breaths. The Nightmares hold their perimeter—creatures I never thought I'd see outside of myth, let alone standing guard over someone I've failed to protect. Their presence fills the space like pressure before a storm, and I can't decide if they're salvation or just another variable I can't control.

I lean against the obsidian wall, arms crossed.

If we survive this—when we survive this—we need to move fast. Get them somewhere defensible. Figure out what the year in this place has done to all of us. What it's done to her.

Theo moves.

No warning. No announcement. He just crosses the chamber and drops to his knees beside Bree.

"She doesn't deserve this," he says quietly, reaching for the chains wrapped around her wrists. "I won't sit here and watch her die."

"Theo—" Stellan starts.

Too late.

Theo's fingers close around the silver metal. "I see you," he whispers.

Light flares—blinding, searing—and Theo gasps, muscles locking. The chain burns through his skin, but he doesn't let go.

His eyes glow white-silver, Sight fully open. Patterns overlay the chains, intricate and alien, pulsing with the same rhythm as the veins in the walls.

"I can see it," he grits out. "The pattern—"

Seth's eyes snap open.

He sees Theo struggling. Sees Bree trapped.

Seth moves—shoves Theo aside hard enough to send him sprawling.

Black smoke surges from the Void, wrapping around Seth's wrists and hardening like gauntlets. He grabs the chains with both hands.

The heat strikes the smoke and gutters out.

Seth pulls.

The chains scream—metal shrieking like something alive and dying. He tears them apart, silver dissolving into ash.

For one heartbeat, his eyes go completely black.

Then they fade back to normal.

Seth staggers backward, staring down at his hands. The smoke is gone. His skin is unmarked. He looks confused. Horrified.

"What—" His voice cracks. "What did I just do?"

No one answers.

Bree gasps—a sharp, desperate sound—and her body arches off the obsidian floor. Silver light flares around her, brighter than it's been since we found her, and the veins pulsing through the walls react, some of them flickering from silver to black and back again.

The Nightmares shift, smoke curling thicker from their hooves.

Stellan moves first, dropping to his knees beside her. His hand hovers over her shoulder, then settles gently. "I'm here." His voice cracks. "We're here. We've got you."

But the black threading her Ether remains, woven too deep to fade on its own.

Theo pushes himself upright, hands burned raw, skin blistered and red. Rhett presses a hand near the worst of it, heat sealing the edges. The skin still weeps.

The veins in the walls writhe.

Not subtly. Visibly. Like serpents trapped beneath stone, twisting and coiling as the silver light flickers faster.

Some of them turn black.

The temperature drops so fast my breath fogs.

"He knows," Stellan says quietly.

Seth's still staring at his hands. "What?"

"Ethos." Stellan's gray eyes lift to meet mine across Bree's unconscious form. "He knows the chains are broken."

"Then we make a stand here," I start to say. "In his chamber—"

"No." Stellan's voice cuts sharp. "We can't fight him here. This is his domain. His power."

Movement catches my eye before anyone can argue.

The familiars appear—shadows slinking free from the obsidian glass. The fox, the raven, and the serpent uncoiling from Seth's wrist. All three move toward the chamber entrance.

Their forms begin to glow faintly, silver light tracing through the darkness like breadcrumbs in the black.

Waiting.

"They're showing us the way," Theo says quietly.

The veins in the walls writhe faster, some flickering black. The temperature drops.

Gray moves without hesitation—noses beneath Bree's shoulder, wedging his body under hers until she's draped across his back. Then he's already walking, following the lights.

The lead Nightmare's voice flows through our minds. *We hold the chamber. Follow the lights, bonded ones. We will find you when the path clears.*

Theo moves toward Seth, hands still raw and weeping. "Come on."

Seth blinks at him, still disoriented. "You—I shoved you—"

"You freed her." Theo's voice is matter-of-fact. "Move."

The familiars pulse brighter, drifting deeper into the Void.

And we follow them into the dark.

Chapter 8
JACE

The Void is lying to us.

I don't trust it. The air's warmer—not much, but enough that my breath doesn't fog anymore. The familiars slip ahead through the dark—black smoke shaped like foxes and ravens, glimmering silver only when they move. They light nothing, but somehow still show the way.

I don't buy it.

Gray carries Bree steady on his back, massive paws silent on the nothing of darkness. Seth walks beside him, hollow-eyed, but upright. The rest of us trail behind in varying states of exhaustion and barely-contained panic.

But we're moving. We're breathing. For the first time in what feels like years, we're not running from something that wants to eat us.

So obviously, something's about to go catastrophically wrong.

"On a scale of one to doomed," I say to no one in particular, "how screwed are we right now?"

Rhett glances back, fire flickering faintly around his knuckles. "You'd know. You keep the scale."

"Fair point."

Wes's stomach growls—loud enough that everyone hears it.

He presses a hand to his ribs, looking embarrassed. "Sorry."

"Don't apologize for being alive," I say. Then, because the silence is worse than the fear: "When we get out of here, first order of business—pancakes. None of that thin-as-paper garbage. I want stacks that violate the laws of physics."

Theo doesn't look back, but his voice carries. "With blueberries. She likes blueberries."

The mention of Bree settles something in the air. Like acknowledging she's still with us—unconscious, corrupted, but *with us*—makes it real.

"You flip them, I'll light the stove," Rhett mutters.

I grin. "Last time you lit something we lost half a kitchen."

Gray huffs—a sound that might be wolf laughter if wolves could laugh.

Stellan walks at the front with Thane, both of them scanning the darkness like they're waiting for it to remember we're trespassing. But even Stellan's shoulders have dropped an inch. Even Thane's stopped looking like he's three seconds from ripping someone's throat out.

Hope is a dangerous thing.

Especially here.

The familiars pulse brighter, leading us around a curve where faint traces of color bleed into the black. Not much. Just enough to remind us what isn't Void.

"Feels weird," I say quietly, "walking toward light for once."

"Don't get used to it," Rhett replies.

I wasn't planning to.

Theo slows.

Just a step. Then another. His eyes go unfocused—that thousand-yard stare that means he's Seeing something the rest of us can't.

"Theo?" Wes moves closer, concern sharpening his voice.

Theo doesn't answer. His hands start shaking.

"Shit." I step forward, but Stellan holds up a hand.

"Don't interrupt it," Stellan says quietly. "Let it finish."

Theo's breathing goes shallow. His lips move, forming words I can't hear.

Then he gasps—sharp, like surfacing from deep water.

The vision snaps.

Silence.

"Theo?" Rhett's voice is careful. Controlled. "What did you see?"

Theo blinks hard, eyes still glowing faintly silver. When he speaks, his voice is rough. Shaken.

"A year." He swallows. "We've been here at least a year."

My stomach drops.

"The sanctuary," Theo continues, words tumbling faster now. "Riley's on the Council. With them. Like she belongs there."

Thane's expression goes cold. "Riley."

"And the Feeders." Theo's hands clench into fists. "Our Feeders. The ones who came for refuge—they're not free anymore. They're chained. Mining."

"Mining what?" Stellan's voice is deadly quiet.

"The veins." Theo looks at him, and there's something broken in his eyes. "The same silver Ether veins from here—from the Void. They're spreading through the sanctuary now. They turned it into a mine."

Rhett swears—low, vicious.

Wes looks like he might be sick.

Thane goes utterly still. When he speaks, his voice is lethal. "They enslaved Feeders. My people came to Bree for sanctuary, and the Council put them in chains as soon as she was gone."

His silver eyes blaze. "I will burn that Council to ash."

"Wait." Wes looks between Theo and the rest of us. "Why didn't you see any of this before? You've been having visions this whole time."

Theo's quiet for a moment. "Maybe because it wasn't a possibility before. The Sight shows what could happen, what might happen. If we never believed we'd get out…" He looks at the familiars leading us forward. "Maybe now we do."

"Zira?" Stellan asks, and for the first time since I've known him, his voice cracks.

Theo closes his eyes. "Restrained. Overseeing the work."

Stellan goes perfectly still.

The kind of still that comes right before violence.

"Then we get her back," Wes says, quiet but absolute. "We tear it down."

"With what?" I hear myself say. "We're half-dead, Bree's unconscious, and we've been gone a *year*. They've had time to fortify. To plan. To turn everything she built into—"

"Into a weapon," Thane finishes. His silver eyes shift to Bree's unconscious form draped across Gray's back. "Against her."

The familiars pulse brighter, impatient, pulling us onward.

No one moves.

"And then pancakes," I say.

Everyone turns to stare at me.

I shrug. "What? We save the world, we liberate the sanctuary, we overthrow the Council—and then we make pancakes. It's called having priorities."

Rhett's mouth twitches. Almost a smile.

Wes exhales something that might be a laugh.

Even Theo's expression softens just slightly.

"Pancakes," Stellan repeats flatly.

"Blueberry," I confirm. "With real maple syrup. None of that fake nonsense."

"You're insane," Thane says.

"And yet here we are, following smoke foxes through hell because they told us to. So who's really the crazy one?"

The tension breaks—not shatters, but cracks enough that we can breathe again.

Gray shifts Bree's weight, then starts walking.

The rest of us follow.

The corridor opens ahead, light rippling faintly at the edges. The familiars drift faster now, shadows streaked with silver, like they're close to something.

I glance at Theo. His eyes still glow faintly, Sight not quite faded.

"We're running out of time," he says quietly.

"Then let's stop walking like ghosts."

The air feels lighter. My chest doesn't.

You can't joke away a vision like that. Can't laugh off the image of our people in chains, the sanctuary we'd bleed for turned into a mine, Riley sitting with the Council like she belongs there.

But if I stop joking, I'll start thinking.

And if I start thinking, I'll remember that hope is dangerous.

That walking toward light in the Void probably means we're walking into a trap.

That a year is long enough for everything to fall apart.

So I keep my mouth shut and follow the shadowed shapes ahead, silver glinting where they move.

Pretending they know where they're going.

Because if I stop pretending, I might start believing we don't.

Chapter 9
WES

The corridor of mirrors stretches before us, endless and identical. Each one gleams in the dim light, their surfaces rippling like disturbed water. The hunger hums low under my skin, restless. I've never felt magic like this—thick enough to taste, thin enough to starve on.

Why didn't it feel like this in the Ashen Oath Chamber?

The sight makes my chest tighten with something close to recognition.

I've seen this before. In Bree's memories, bleeding through the bond when she was trapped while we wandered through this place trying to find her. In Seth's fragmented accounts of how he found his way out. I never told the others. I couldn't. I needed something just for me in the endless darkness.

"They're all the same," Jace mutters beside me, his hand tight on one of his blades. "How the hell are we supposed to know which one—"

"That one."

Stellan's voice cuts through the murmur of unease. He's stopped ahead of us, staring at a mirror with an ornate frame carved with twisting horns that curve inward like a crown.

The horned mirror. Bree's.

My throat goes tight. I can feel it even from here—the faint hum of her Ether clinging to the glass like perfume that won't fade. It smells like her. Vanilla and something that makes my chest ache.

"That's the one Seth came through," Stellan says quietly. His gray eyes are fixed on the mirror. "The one we found her standing in front of that morning."

Rhett moves forward, drawn like we all are. "So we go through that one."

But the familiars glide past it without stopping.

My chest tightens—wrong, that's wrong—but they keep moving, deeper into the corridor. Their shadow-forms flow like water around the base of Bree's mirror and continue down the row.

"Wait." Theo's hand shoots out, catching Rhett's arm. "They're not stopping."

The familiars pause several mirrors down. Their shapes thicken, almost solid, like they're waiting for us to catch up.

"Why aren't they taking us through hers?" Jace's voice is tight with suspicion. "If that's her mirror, why—"

"Because she's here," Stellan says, his gaze shifting to where Bree lies unconscious against Gray's back. "They're taking us somewhere else. Somewhere safe."

Thane steps forward, his silver eyes narrowing as he studies the familiars. "They're following something. An instruction."

"From her?" My voice comes out rougher than I mean it to.

"She's alive." Theo's words are certain. "The familiars are hers. They wouldn't lead us wrong."

The familiars pulse once—impatient—and drift closer to the mirror they've chosen. It looks identical to all the others. No horns, no ornamentation. Just smooth glass reflecting our exhausted, filthy faces.

My hunger twists, sharpening. I can feel the pull of the mirror the familiars chose, but it's different from Bree's. Her mirror hums with silver light, with warmth. This one feels neutral. Like a doorway rather than a destination.

Stellan's gaze cuts to me, sharp. For a moment I think he'll argue. Then he nods once. "They're hers. They won't lead us wrong."

Thane moves first, stepping up to the mirror. His hand hovers over the glass, and I watch his jaw tighten as he makes contact. The surface ripples outward from his palm, liquid and impossible.

"Together," he says. Not a command. A vow.

Rhett's hand lands on my shoulder. Jace crowds close on my other side. Gray adjusts his grip on Bree. Theo flanks us. Stellan brings up the rear. The familiars dissolve into shadow, pouring through the glass ahead of us.

Thane steps through first.

Then Rhett.

Then me.

The mirror takes me like water closing over my head. Cold but weightless, and disorienting. For one terrible moment I can't breathe, can't see, can't feel anything except the pressure bearing down on my chest—

Then I stumble forward into warmth and light and sound.

My knees hit polished wood. My hands catch on something soft—carpet, thick and expensive. Music drifts from somewhere, elegant and unfamiliar, layered with laughter and the clink of glass.

I blink hard, trying to orient myself. We're not in the Oath Chamber. We're not in the sanctuary at all.

We're in someone's home.

A grand one. The kind that makes the sanctuary look like a ruin by comparison. Vaulted ceilings painted with murals of stars and moons. Chandeliers dripping with crystal. Furniture that looks like it costs more than most people earn in a lifetime.

And standing in the center of it all, wine glass in hand and a smile that could cut glass, is the most beautiful man I've ever seen.

He's tall, close to Thane's height, built like sin wrapped in silk. Golden skin and dark hair that falls in artful waves to his shoulders. He's dressed in deep purple silk that shimmers when he moves, cut to show off a body that's both elegant and dangerous. His eyes are amber, bright with amusement and something sharper.

Feeder.

The recognition hits me in a way I can't describe. I can feel what he is the way I feel my own hunger—the pull of it, the shape of his magic curling through the air like smoke.

Incubus-class.

He takes a slow sip of his wine, utterly unbothered by the fact that seven armed, filthy strangers, a massive wolf, and an unconscious woman just fell out of his mirror.

His gaze lands on Bree immediately. The amusement drains from his face.

"Well," he says, his voice rich but suddenly serious. "This is a surprise." He sets his wine glass down with careful precision. "You're early."

Jace scrambles to his feet, blades already in hand. "Who the hell—"

"Ah-ah." The man raises one finger, and Jace's words die in his throat. Not magic, exactly. Just presence. Command wrapped in velvet. "Manners, darling. You're in my home." His amber eyes never leave Bree. "And you've brought her."

Gray's ears flatten back, a low growl rumbling in his chest as he shifts his body protectively over Bree.

"Oh, but you did." The man's voice has gone softer. "Though I'll admit, I wasn't expecting you quite so soon. Or in this condition." His gaze shifts past us, to where shadows pool in the corner. "Well done."

The familiars pulse once.

Theo steps forward, his brown eyes already distant with whatever he's Seeing. After a moment, his shoulders relax. "You're not lying."

"I rarely do." The man smiles faintly. "Lying is so tedious. The truth is far more interesting." His amber eyes sweep over Bree's unconscious form again, and something that might be pain flickers across his face. "My god. What did they do to her?"

"Who are you?" Rhett's voice is tight with barely leashed aggression.

"Lord Auren Vale," he says with a shallow bow, tone dripping with practiced charm. He tears his gaze away from Bree with visible effort. "And you, my unexpected guests, are very far from where you meant to be." His amber eyes sweep over us. "Though perhaps exactly where you need to be."

Stellan moves to stand beside Thane, his gray eyes sharp. "You know who we are."

"Of course I do." Auren's voice is still distracted, his attention drawn back to Bree. "Everyone knows who you are. The Source's chosen. Her bonded." His gaze lands on me, and I feel it like a touch. His eyebrows lift suggestively. "Her lovers."

My breath catches. The way he looks at me—like he recognizes something. What I am. What I'm becoming.

"You're one too," I say quietly.

Auren's expression softens slightly. "Incubus-class, like you. Though I've had a few more centuries to perfect the craft." He glances at Stellan, one elegant eyebrow raised. "Unlike your mentor here, I don't starve myself out of misplaced nobility."

Stellan's expression doesn't change, but something flickers in his eyes.

"She needs help." Rhett's voice cracks. "Now."

Auren's attention snaps fully to Rhett, and the playful mask drops completely. "Yes. She does." He moves forward with purpose. "Bring her. I have healers on staff, and rooms prepared." He pauses, his amber eyes meeting each of ours in turn. "I've been waiting for her. For all of you."

"Waiting?" Thane's voice is clipped. Suspicious. "What do you mean, waiting?"

"I mean," Auren says carefully, "that when a Source awakens after centuries of silence, and then vanishes, people notice. And some of those people..." He pauses. "Some of us choose to care. To prepare."

"How did you know she vanished?" Thane's voice is sharp.

Auren's amber eyes meet his. "Because whoever is playing her part is awful at it." His gaze sweeps over us. "And when all of you disappeared all at once shortly after? That confirmed it. The real Source wouldn't have let you go without her."

My chest tightens.

Theo's eyes refocus on him. After a long moment, he nods. "He's telling the truth. He's... on our side."

"How convenient," Jace mutters.

Auren's smile flickers back, brief and sharp. "Oh, I like you. You'll fit right in." His expression sobers as he looks at Bree again. "But your friend is right. I've been helping organize resistance efforts since your girl first appeared. Preparing for the moment she'd need sanctuary." His voice drops. "Please. Let me help her. Then we'll talk."

"One of your people comes near her," Rhett says quietly, "and I burn this place to the ground."

"Fair enough." Auren doesn't look offended. "Then I'll tend her myself. I'm quite skilled at healing, actually." He gestures toward a sweeping staircase. "This way. Quickly."

Gray moves forward, Bree still unconscious on his back. Auren leads us up the stairs, through hallways lined with mirrors and art, until he stops before a set of double doors.

"The guest wing," he says, pushing them open. "Six bedrooms, all connected to a central sitting room. And this one—" He opens another door, revealing a room that's all soft light and cream-colored silk. "This one is hers."

Gray moves into the room without hesitation, standing next to the bed, waiting for one of us to move her. Rhett carefully moves Bree onto the bed with a gentleness that makes my chest ache. She looks so small against the white sheets. So still.

Auren moves to the bedside, his earlier playfulness completely gone. "What happened to her?"

"The Void," Thane says flatly. "She's been there for... we don't know how long."

"And the corruption?" Auren's fingers hover over Bree's arm, where black veins spider beneath her skin. "This isn't just Void exposure. This is active feeding."

My stomach drops. "We suspected."

"Someone's been feeding on her." Auren's voice is grim. "Consistently. For a while." His amber eyes lift to meet mine. "This is what we look like when we take too much, too often. This is starvation dressed as consumption."

"Can you help her?" Thane's voice is barely human.

Auren nods slowly. "Yes. But it will take time. Her body needs rest, nutrition, and most importantly—" His gaze shifts to me, then Stellan, then Thane. "She needs to feed. Not give. Take."

"We're Feeders," Thane says. "We don't—"

"She's Source." Auren cuts him off. "Her Ether is like a living thing. Right now it's starving because she's been drained dry. If she's bonded to you—" His eyes narrow. "And I can feel that she is—then you need to let her draw through those connections. Your emotions, your vitality, your love. Her Ether will know what to take."

The room goes silent.

"How?" My voice comes out rough. Desperate.

Auren's expression gentles. "Be near her. Let your bonds open. Let her feel your presence, your emotions, your—" He pauses. "Your love. If she's as powerful as I think she is, her Ether will do the rest."

His gaze shifts to the massive bed that dominates the room, and he lets out a soft chuckle. "Why do you think a tiny woman needs a bed that size?"

The implication settles over us like a weight.

"What do you need from us?" Rhett asks.

"Right now? Nothing." Auren moves toward the door. "I'm going to have food and water brought up. Clean clothes. Medical supplies. You're going to stay near her, sleep next to her." His amber eyes are serious. "And then, when she wakes, we're going to figure out how to keep her alive long enough to end the bastard who did this to her."

He pauses in the doorway, looking back at Bree's still form.

"She's going to need you whole when she wakes," he says quietly. "Not broken. So rest. Heal. Prepare." His voice drops. "Because whoever trapped her in the Void? They're not going to let her go easily."

Then he's gone, leaving us alone with Bree and the weight of everything we almost lost.

I sink onto the bed next to her, my hand finding hers beneath the sheets. Her skin is cold. Too cold.

But her pulse beats steady beneath my fingers.

Warming as my skin begins to tingle everywhere we touch.

She's feeding.

I smile, laying back. I can finally rest knowing she's here. Alive.

That I'm doing something to protect her.

Because she's everything.

Chapter 10
BREE

Warmth.

I feel it before I feel anything else. Not cold. Not the endless ache of the Void pressing against my skin.

Just warmth.

It moves through me in pulses—slow and steady. Eight different rhythms, each one humming somewhere beneath my ribs where the bonds live.

Heat that crackles. Wind that whispers. Something heavy that anchors. Light that clarifies. Emptiness that no longer feels so empty.

They're here.

I try to open my eyes, but my body won't listen. Everything feels too heavy—like I'm wrapped in something thick, stuck somewhere between asleep and awake. But the warmth keeps pulling me back, coaxing me toward the surface one breath at a time.

The air smells different. Not metal like the Void. Not dust and old stone like the sanctuary. This smells like sunlight. Like citrus and something rich.

Silk against my skin. Cool sheets.

I'm not in the Void anymore.

The thought cracks something open. Relief so sharp it almost hurts.

They found me.

My Ether stirs—sluggish but awake. It reaches out on its own, following the threads back to wherever they lead. Pulling warmth and color back into me like I'm a cup that's been empty too long.

Someone's holding my hand. Calloused fingers, careful grip. There's a faint buzz where our skin touches.

Wes.

I know him by the hunger alone—the way it echoes the way I feel right now, the way his presence always feels safe even when it shouldn't.

Something shifts behind me. Weight and warmth. Familiar.

Stellan.

The air hums faintly. They're all close—sleeping maybe, or half-awake. Watching over me.

They came for me. All of them.

I try to move—just my fingers, just enough to squeeze Wes's hand—but I'm too tired. My body's not ready. But something is happening, because slowly the warmth starts replacing the cold.

For the first time since everything started, I don't feel like I'm falling apart.

I feel like maybe I can be put back together.

When I finally get my eyes open, the light hurts.

It's not harsh—soft, coming through silk curtains—but after the dark for so long, even this feels like too much. I blink hard, and slowly the room comes into focus.

Cream walls. A ceiling painted with stars. Furniture that looks expensive and unused.

This isn't the sanctuary.

My heart stutters. Where—

Movement next to me. I turn my head—slowly, everything hurts—and find Wes asleep beside me. His hand is still in mine, his face soft in sleep, dark curls falling across his forehead. I can't stop my mouth from turning up.

I look down and there's a glow where our hands touch. Silver mist curling between our fingers.

I watch it for a moment, the way the light pulses with his breathing. It doesn't look like it's hurting him. It just... glows. Like our connection made visible.

Gray's curled at the foot of the bed in wolf form, taking up way too much space. His ears twitch when I shift, but he doesn't wake.

Rhett's slumped in a chair by the door, head tilted back, arms crossed. Even asleep he looks tense—like he's ready to move at the first sign of trouble.

Theo sits near the window, eyes closed but his posture too straight to be real sleep. Probably watching from the inside.

Jace is sprawled on a couch in the corner, one arm over his eyes, blades on the floor next to him.

And Thane—

Thane's standing near the far wall. Silver eyes open. Watching me.

Our eyes meet, and something twists sharp in my chest.

He doesn't move. Doesn't say anything. Just watches with an expression I can't read—relief and guilt and something that might be fear.

I want to say something. Tell him I'm okay. That I'm here. That whatever happened doesn't matter now.

But my throat's too dry and the words won't come.

Before I can try again, I feel someone else. Watching.

I turn my head and realize—Stellan's still behind me. I can feel his presence at my back, steady and quiet.

"You stayed," I whisper. My voice comes out rough, barely there.

There's a pause.

"I stayed."

The memory surfaces—that night at the sanctuary when he came into my room. When I was breaking and he held me together even though it cost him. The way his control cracked just enough to let me feel safe.

This time, I reach for him.

I shift slowly—everything protests—and reach back, finding his wrist. Tug gently.

He goes still.

"Please," I manage.

For a second I think he'll say no. That he'll pull back like he always does, wrap himself in that distance he uses like armor.

But he doesn't.

He moves closer, and I take his arm and pull it around me, guiding his hand to rest over my ribs where I'm sure he can feel my heart beating too fast.

He goes completely still.

"Bree—"

"You did this for me once," I whisper. "Let me do it for you."

His breath catches. I feel the tension in his whole body, the war between what he wants and what he thinks he should do. But slowly—so slowly—he exhales, and I feel him relax.

The Ether responds.

Silver mist curls around us, warm and gentle, threading between us. It glows brighter where we touch, pulsing softly.

Stellan's forehead drops to my shoulder and I feel the shudder that runs through him—relief or exhaustion or something deeper. His hand tightens slightly over my ribs, holding on.

"You're alive," he murmurs against my hair. Not a question. A promise.

"I'm alive," I say quietly.

We just breathe together for a while. The Ether hums, wrapping us in light that doesn't hurt—just warms. Just holds.

I let my eyes drift closed. Exhaustion pulls at me again, but this time it doesn't feel like drowning.

It feels like I can finally rest.

Chapter 11
BREE

I'm so comfortable. The thought drifts through my mind slowly, lazy. I shift closer to the heat at my back, sighing as I settle deeper into it.

No cold. No screaming. No chains.

Just this. Just warmth and the slow rise and fall of breathing that isn't mine.

My body feels different. Not heavy. Not aching. For the first time in—god, I don't even know how long—I feel good. Really good. Like my skin fits again. Like my nerves remember how to feel something other than pain.

I open my eyes slowly, letting the soft morning light filter in through silk curtains I remember from the last time I woke up.

It's still not the sanctuary, but I'm still safe.

I turn my head and find Wes beside me, still asleep. His hand is loose around mine, dark lashes resting against his cheeks. There's a faint glow under his skin—like sunlight caught just beneath the surface.

My chest does something complicated looking at him.

Behind me, I feel Stellan. His arm is still around me, holding me tighter than before. His breath is warm against my shoulder, even and measured in sleep.

It's just the three of us.

The realization settles slowly. The others must have left at some point during the night—given us space, maybe, or gone to rest somewhere else. But Wes and Stellan stayed.

I don't want to move. Don't want to break whatever this moment is.

My body hums with energy I haven't felt in so long. The Ether pulses softly around me, threading between the three of us like silk. It doesn't feel desperate or wild or like it's tearing me apart. It feels full. Content.

Alive.

I take a slow breath, and even that feels good. My lungs expand without pain, my ribs don't ache, and for the first time since the Void, I feel like my body belongs to me again.

Wes stirs first, his fingers tightening slightly around mine. His eyes open slowly—dark and warm—and when he sees me looking at him, a slow smile curves his mouth.

"You're awake."

"I think so," I whisper. My voice is still rough, but it doesn't hurt to speak.

He shifts closer, just slightly, and brushes a strand of hair back from my face. The touch is gentle, deliberate, and it sparks something—warmth spreading where his fingers graze my cheek.

Something tightens in my chest. Hunger. But not the empty, desperate kind I've carried for what feels like forever. This is different. This is warm. This wants something I never thought I'd want again.

"How do you feel?" His thumb traces the line of my jaw, feather-light.

"Better." I swallow, my pulse picking up. "Better than I have in a long time."

Behind me, Stellan shifts. I feel the exact moment he wakes—the way his body tenses slightly, then relaxes when he realizes where he is. His arm flexes against my ribs, and I feel his breath catch when he registers how close we are.

I feel something else too—the hard length of him pressing against my lower back. Heat floods through me, pooling low in my belly.

I turn my head just enough to look at him over my shoulder. Gray eyes meet mine, unreadable and intense.

"You're both still here," I say quietly. My voice comes out breathier than I intended.

Stellan's voice is low, controlled. "Where else would we be?"

The Ether hums louder between us. I feel it pulling—reaching for connection.

Wes's hand slides from my jaw to the back of my neck, warm and grounding. "Bree."

I look back at him. His eyes are darker now, pupils wide. I can feel his hunger echoing mine—the same pull, the same ache.

I don't think. Don't second-guess.

It's soft at first, tentative, just a brush of lips against lips. But the moment we connect, the Ether flares, hot and bright, and Wes groans low in his throat. His hand tightens at my neck, pulling me closer, and the kiss deepens. His tongue parts my lips, sliding against mine with a hunger that makes my head spin. I moan into his mouth, my hands fisting in his shirt, pulling him as close as I can.

Behind me, Stellan goes completely still. I feel the tension in his body—the instinct to pull away, distance himself, retreat into that careful control he wraps around himself like armor. The bed shifts as he moves to leave, and panic flares in my chest.

"Stay." Wes's voice cuts through the haze, rough and commanding. He breaks the kiss, his dark eyes flicking past me to Stellan. "If you want him to."

I don't hesitate.

I shift in Wes's arms, turning toward Stellan, and reach for him. My hand finds his jaw, stubble rough under my palm. "Stay?" I whisper, my voice trembling.

Stellan pauses, his gray eyes searching mine for something—permission, certainty, maybe both. Then he crashes his mouth into mine.

This kiss isn't like Wes's. It's harder, desperate, like he's been holding back for so long that now he's letting go, he can't stop. His hand threads through my hair, gripping tight, and I press closer, moaning into his mouth. The Ether explodes around us, silver light flooding the room, wrapping around all three of us.

Wes's hand slides to my waist, fingers digging into my hip, and Stellan's other hand grips my thigh, tugging me closer. The combined touch is overwhelming—magic and need and heat tangled together until I can't think.

I pull back just enough to breathe, and Stellan's eyes have gone molten silver, his control cracking at the edges. "Bree," he says, and it sounds like a warning and a plea all at once.

"I want this," I gasp, my voice steadier than I feel. "I want both of you."

Wes sits up slightly, and there's something different in the way he moves now—confident, purposeful, like he's stepped fully into the power he's been growing into. "Then lie back," he commands, and the authority in his voice makes me shiver.

I do.

The sheets are cool against my skin, and I'm suddenly aware of how little I'm wearing—just a thin nightgown that clings to me, leaving nothing to the imagination.

Stellan shifts beside me, and I watch the way his gaze tracks to Wes. There's raw want in his eyes, his jaw clenched tight, his breathing controlled but shallow. Like he's barely holding himself together.

"We're going to take care of you," Wes says, his hand sliding up my thigh, slow and deliberate. The touch sends heat racing through me, and I bite my lip to stifle a moan. "But we're going to do this right."

"Wes—" I start, but his finger presses against my lips, silencing me.

"Trust me," he murmurs, his voice rough but steady. He looks at Stellan. "Help me."

Stellan's eyes flash silver. "Carefully."

"Always." Wes's hands find the hem of my nightgown, and he looks at me, waiting for permission. I nod, trembling, and he lifts the fabric slowly, revealing inch after inch of bare skin.

Stellan's hands join his, their fingers brushing as they peel the nightgown up and over my head. I'm left in nothing but my underwear and the silver light of the Ether wrapping around us.

I expect to feel exposed, vulnerable, but the way they're both looking at me—like I'm something precious and powerful—makes me feel anything but.

"Beautiful," Wes murmurs, his hand tracing up my ribs, fingertips dragging slow patterns across my skin. Stellan's hand mirrors the path on my other side, his touch more deliberate, like he's memorizing every inch of me.

When Stellan's thumb brushes the underside of my breast, I gasp, arching into his touch. "Careful," Wes says, but there's no reprimand in it—just a reminder. "Slow."

"I know," Stellan growls, his voice strained. His eyes find mine. "Tell me if it's too much."

It's not. God, it's not even close to enough.

Wes leans down, his mouth hot against my skin as he kisses a trail down my stomach. Every touch sends shivers through me, my breath coming in shallow gasps. Stellan's mouth finds my neck, teeth grazing that sensitive spot just below my ear, and the combination makes me arch off the bed.

"Easy," Wes murmurs against my skin, but his hands are tight on my hips, fingers digging in just enough to ground me. "We've got you."

Stellan's hand slides between my thighs, over my damp underwear, and the pressure makes me whimper. "Here?" he asks, his voice rough.

"Not yet." Wes's hand covers Stellan's, guiding it away. "She needs more first."

I watch Stellan's jaw clench, his whole body taut with restraint. He wants to touch me—badly—but he's holding back, letting Wes guide this. Like Wes sees something I don't yet—knows what I need before I do.

Wes's fingers hook into my underwear, dragging them down slowly. I lift my hips to help, and Stellan's hand moves to my stomach, holding me steady while Wes finishes pulling them off.

Wes shifts lower, settling between my thighs. His hands slide up the inside of my legs, gentle but firm, and then his mouth is on me—tongue sliding through my wet heat—and I cry out.

The pleasure is immediate, sharp, and overwhelming. His hands grip my thighs, holding me open, but he doesn't rush. He takes his time, learning what makes me shake, what makes me gasp.

Stellan's mouth finds mine, swallowing the sounds I make. His hand moves to my breast, thumb circling my nipple in time with Wes's tongue, and the layered sensations make my head spin.

I feel myself climbing fast—pressure building, coiling tight in my belly. "Please," I gasp against Stellan's mouth. "I'm so close—"

Wes pulls back, his breath ragged. "Not yet. I want to make this good for you."

Stellan groans, forehead dropping to my shoulder. "Wes—"

"I know." Wes's voice is rough now, his own control fraying. "Just a little longer."

"She's ready," Stellan growls, hunger lacing his words.

"Almost." Wes leans back down, and this time when his tongue moves, his fingers slide inside me too. The combination makes me arch, a sound escaping that I don't recognize.

Stellan's mouth moves to my breast, teeth scraping, and I'm climbing again—faster, higher.

"That's it," Wes says against me. "Let us feel it."

I'm right there—on the edge—my hands in Wes's hair, clutching at Stellan's shoulder.

Wes pulls back again, and I could cry. "Please," I beg. "Please, I need—"

"I know what you need." Wes moves up beside me, his hand gentle on my face. "One more time. I promise. Then we'll let you fall."

Stellan's hands find my wrists, pressing them into the mattress above my head. Not restraining—anchoring. His eyes are pure silver now, his control hanging by a thread. "Can you take more?"

I nod frantically, desperate for release.

"Good girl," Stellan murmurs, and the praise makes something in me clench.

"Hold her," Wes commands.

Stellan's grip tightens, and then Wes is there again—mouth and fingers working together with focused intensity. This time he doesn't stop. He drives me higher, my hips bucking against his face, begging now, words spilling out.

"That's it," Wes growls. "Come for us."

Stellan's mouth crashes down on mine, and I break.

The orgasm tears through me—white-hot and endless and so intense I can't breathe. The Ether explodes outward, silver light so bright it burns behind my closed eyelids. I feel the pleasure feeding back through the bonds, amplifying, multiplying between the three of us until I can't tell whose release is whose.

And then it surges outward.

Not just to Wes and Stellan. Through me. Through every bond connecting me to the others. I feel it racing toward them like lightning—Rhett's fire, Gray's earth, Theo's light, Jace's wind, Thane's cold, Seth's strange emptiness-turned-presence.

All of them. At once.

I feel them respond—shock, confusion, half-awake across the house. The connection flares bright and then settles, humming contentedly.

The feedback is overwhelming. Wes gasps, his hands tightening almost to the point of pain on my thighs. Stellan shudders against me, his control finally, completely breaking as his own release crashes through him untouched.

We collapse together in a tangle of limbs and ragged breathing. The light fades slowly, settling into a soft pulse around us.

For a long moment, no one moves. No one can.

My heartbeat slows enough that I can think again. My whole body feels loose, warm, complete.

Wes is the first to shift, pressing a kiss to my hip, then my stomach, then my ribs. "You okay?" he murmurs, his voice rough with concern.

I nod, not trusting my voice yet. My whole body is still trembling with aftershocks.

Stellan's forehead is still against my shoulder, his breath coming in harsh pants. His hands have loosened around my wrists but he hasn't let go entirely, like he needs the anchor point.

"What was that?" I finally manage, my voice wrecked.

"You fed from us," Stellan says quietly, and I can hear the awe in his voice. "Both of us. And then you sent it to all of them."

"What?! I didn't mean to—"

"You needed to." Wes moves up beside me, his hand gentle on my face, thumb brushing my cheekbone. "Your Ether knew what to do."

I close my eyes, feeling the bonds hum contentedly in my chest. They're all there—warm and bright and whole. Connected.

"They're going to know," I whisper. "They're going to know what we just—"

"Good," Wes says simply.

When I open my eyes, I catch the way Stellan is looking at Wes—something raw and unguarded in his expression that I've never seen before. And the way Wes holds his gaze, unflinching, a slow understanding passing between them.

Something shifts in the air. Unspoken but undeniable.

"We're really back," I whisper.

Stellan's hand finds mine, threading our fingers together. His voice is rough when he speaks.

"We're really back."

Chapter 12
THEO

The kitchen smells like butter and coffee. Jace is at the stove flipping pancakes, talking over his shoulder to Rhett who's nursing coffee at the table. Seth leans against the counter by the window, quiet like he's been since we got here.

The spatula clanks against the pan. Rhett mutters something about burnt butter. And then the vision hits me without warning—pleasure, feeding, connection. Her Ether surging outward. It's—

"Oh fuck."

Chapter 13
RHETT

The bond flares white-hot and I'm gripping the table, flames racing up my arms as her pleasure crashes through me like wildfire. The coffee in my mug boils over.

Chapter 14
JACE

My knees buckle and the spatula hits the floor. I'm clutching the counter, gasping, and all I can think is: I will never look at pancakes the same way again.

Chapter 15
SETH

The surge slams into me and I don't understand—I'm on my knees, overwhelmed, feeling her like she's right here even though she's not. What the hell just happened?

Chapter 16
GRAY

The pleasure crashes through me so suddenly I yelp—like some kicked puppy—and collapse onto the grass behind the house. My whole body shudders, paws scrabbling against the ground, and I feel her everywhere. Feel what she's doing. Feel who she's with.

Oh god.

I'm experiencing this as a wolf, and the mortification is almost worse than the pleasure.

Almost.

When it finally fades, I'm panting in the grass, ears flat against my head, and if anyone saw that I'm never coming out of the woods again.

Chapter 17
THANE

I'm standing just outside the kitchen door with Auren, discussing the wards around his estate, when I hear it.

"Oh fuck."

Theo's voice, followed immediately by crashes, a clatter of metal, Rhett's sharp exhale.

I turn toward the door. "What—"

Then it hits me.

The bond flares so bright I can't think, can't breathe, can't do anything except feel her. Pleasure crashes through me—hers, overwhelming and perfect—feeding through it, amplifying it until the sensation overloads. She's with Wes and Stellan. Both of them. And she just sent all of it to the rest of us.

My knees almost buckle. I brace one hand against the wall, teeth gritted, trying to maintain some shred of control as the sensation builds and builds and—

I lose it.

The release tears through me, unwanted and inevitable, and I feel the wet heat spreading across the front of my pants.

No.

The bond settles slowly, humming contentedly, and I'm left standing in the hallway with Auren, trying to catch my breath and pretend I have any dignity left.

I don't look at him.

"Well," Auren says, and I can hear the smile in his voice.

"Don't."

"Did your Source just—" He breaks off, and when I finally glance at him, he's staring at the wet spot on my pants with barely restrained glee.

"Don't say it."

"With two Incubi—" He's shaking now, trying not to laugh.

"Auren—"

The laughter bursts out—loud, delighted, uncontrollable. He's actually wheezing, one hand pressed to his stomach, tears forming at the corners of his eyes.

"I'm going to kill you," I say flatly.

"She just—" He can barely get the words out. "—broadcasted that to all of you—" More wheezing. "—and you—" He gestures helplessly at my pants.

"I hate you."

"No you don't." He's grinning so wide it has to hurt. "Oh my god, Thane. Your face. This is the best thing that's happened all year."

He takes a breath, trying to compose himself, but another laugh escapes. "You know this was because she was starving, right? Fed from two Incubi at once after being drained in the Void for god knows how long—the feedback loop had nowhere else to go. It's not going to happen every time she—"

"I'm leaving," I say flatly.

"—although if it does, you might want to invest in spare pants—"

"Auren."

He's still laughing.

I turn and walk away with as much dignity as I can manage, which is approximately none.

Behind me, Auren's laughter echoes down the hallway.

Somewhere upstairs, she's finally breathing easy—and the rest of us may never recover.

Chapter 18
BREE

I'm still catching my breath, tucked between them, when the giggle escapes.

I can't help it. The absurdity of it all—the intensity, the way my body still hums with pleasure, and the sudden thought that—

"I wonder if the guys actually felt that," I say, trying to sound casual and failing completely.

Wes looks down at the mess he made on my stomach, his expression somewhere between satisfied and mortified. "Oh god."

Stellan chuckles, low and warm against my back. "They definitely did."

My face heats. "All of them?"

"Every single one." Stellan's voice carries amusement and certainty. "The bond doesn't discriminate. They felt exactly what you felt."

"Fuck," Wes mutters, but he's grinning.

I should probably feel embarrassed. Instead, I feel... powerful. Like I just claimed something that was always mine.

"I need a shower," I announce, suddenly very aware of the state I'm in.

Wes shifts, starting to move. "I'll—"

"Stay," I say softly, pressing a kiss to his shoulder. "Both of you. Rest. I'll be back."

I slip out of bed, grabbing one of Wes's shirts from the floor—oversized and soft—and pull it on before padding toward the bathroom.

The bathroom is almost obscenely nice. All marble and gold fixtures, a shower big enough for ten people, towels so soft they feel like clouds. I turn on the water and don't wait for it to warm—I step under the spray immediately.

The heat hits my skin and I gasp.

A year. I haven't showered in a year.

The Void didn't have water. Didn't have soap or warmth or anything clean. Just endless darkness and Ethos's voice and the slow elimination of everything I was.

I stand there, letting the water pour over me, and something breaks open in my chest.

A sound escapes—half sob, half laugh. My knees buckle and I catch myself against the tile, water streaming over my face, into my mouth. I taste salt. Tears, I think, but I'm not sure. Everything is water now. Everything is warm.

I press my forehead against the cool tile and just breathe. Let the water run. Let myself feel it—all of it. The relief. The grief. The impossible truth that I'm here, I'm out, I'm still alive enough to break.

I wash my hair. Once. Twice. Three times. Watch the water run dark at first, then clearer. Scrub my skin until it's pink and raw and new. The soap smells like lavender and something green, and I use too much of it, not caring, just needing to feel clean.

My hands shake as I work the conditioner through my hair. A year of nothing, and now this. Hot water. Soap. The simple luxury of being able to wash away what touched me.

I stay under the spray long after I'm clean. Just stand there, feeling the heat soak into my bones, washing away months of cold and dark and hunger.

When I finally step out, wrapped in one of those impossible towels, I feel almost human again.

Almost.

There's an outfit laid out on the counter.

I stop, staring at it.

Pale leather pants and a fitted top, soft as butter. Leather straps designed to hold weapons at my thighs. And on the chest of the top, embroidered in silver thread that catches the light—

I stop breathing.

A daisy. Impossibly beautiful with radiating petals that look almost crystalline.

The same ones I planted by the oak tree in the backyard—from seeds I found scattered beneath that door in the attic. The same symbol that was carved into the doorframe itself. Back then, it was harder to see clearly, like my eyes kept sliding off it.

I don't know how I know this is the same, but I can feel it deep in my bones. And now? Now I can see every detail. Every petal, every line.

What does that mean?

My hands shake as I reach for it. The moment my fingers brush the embroidery, the petals flicker to life—silver light blooming outward like my Ether recognizes something it's been searching for.

This wasn't made for me.

The leather is worn in places, softened by time and use. The stitching is old but perfect. This is an heirloom. Something that's been waiting.

Brought for me.

How?

I touch the daisy again, watching the light pulse under my fingertips. It feels like coming home to something I didn't know I'd lost.

I never thought I'd have something like this. Something passed down, chosen, meant for me.

Not with my mother leaving when I was seven. Not with Kevin, who never saw me as a daughter—just another thing he owned, another object to use however he wanted.

But this was waiting anyway.

I dress slowly, feeling the weight of the clothes settle against my skin. They fit perfectly—like they were always meant to be mine. The leather is supple, the straps secure. Even without weapons, I feel... ready. Strong.

I look at myself in the mirror and barely recognize the woman looking back.

She looks like someone who could wear a crown.

I leave the bathroom to find the bedroom empty—Wes and Stellan must have gone downstairs already. The house is quiet except for the low murmur of voices somewhere below.

I follow the sound down the stairs and through a hallway until I reach what looks like a sitting room.

A man I don't recognize stands near a window, coffee cup in hand, talking quietly with Thane. He's older—maybe mid-forties—with dark hair threaded with silver and amber eyes that catch the morning light.

When I step into the doorway, conversation stops.

Every head turns.

Jace whistles—low and appreciative. "Well damn."

Thane's eyes track over the leather, the straps, the glowing daisy embroidered on my chest, and he chokes on whatever he was about to say. His hand goes to his throat like he's forgotten how to breathe.

Rhett's fire flares—actual flames rippling across his shoulders, smoke curling into the air. His eyes are molten gold when they meet mine.

Stellan crosses the room in three strides, moving with that elegant predator grace. He stops in front of me, silver-gray eyes taking in every detail.

"You take my breath away," he says quietly. Then, softer, with something almost like pride: "You're such a badass."

The stranger by the window chuckles, warm and genuine.

Stellan glances back at him, then at me. "Bree, this is Auren. He's... well, he's the reason we're all still breathing."

"And you," Auren says warmly, setting his cup down and crossing the room, "must be Bree." His amber eyes are kind, welcoming. "The Source everyone's been searching for." His gaze tracks to the daisy on my chest, and something like reverence crosses his face. "And wearing the sigil. It suits you."

"Thank you," I say, suddenly uncertain. "For... everything. The room, the clothes, letting us—"

"Don't." He waves a hand. "You're welcome here. All of you. For as long as you need."

He says it like he means it.

I glance past him and find the others scattered around the room. Theo sits at a small table near the window, a book open in front of him. Rhett leans against the wall, arms crossed, looking more rested than I've seen him in weeks. Jace is sprawled in a chair, playing with one of his knives.

I don't think. I just walk over to Theo and drop into his lap.

He freezes. Goes completely still except for the sharp intake of breath.

Jace snickers. "Smooth, Bree."

"Shut up," I mutter, but I'm smiling. Theo's arms come around me carefully, like he's afraid I'll disappear if he holds on too tight.

I lean closer, my lips near his ear. "I missed you," I whisper.

His arms tighten just slightly, and I feel him exhale against my hair.

"You okay?" he asks quietly, his voice close to my ear.

"Getting there."

Auren pours coffee from a carafe on the side table and brings it to me himself. "You look better. Less like you're about to shatter."

"I feel better." I take the cup gratefully. "What did I miss?"

His expression shifts—still warm, but serious now. "Quite a bit, actually."

He settles into a chair across from us, and Thane moves to stand behind him. The rest of the guys shift closer, sensing the change in tone.

"How long?" I ask, my voice quieter than I intended. "How long was I gone?"

Auren's amber eyes soften with something like sympathy. "For you? The Void distorts time. From what the others have told me, it felt like a year inside."

"But out here?" My chest tightens.

"Five years."

Chapter 19
BREE

Five years. Riley has had five years to become me.

"We knew time moved differently in the Void," Thane says, his voice low. "But we didn't realize..." He stops, jaw clenched. "We had no idea it had been this long out here."

"Five years," I whisper, looking at Auren. "You said five years?"

Auren nods carefully. "Time in the Void ran differently—what felt like months to you was half a decade here. For you and them, it felt like a year. Maybe less. But out here, the world kept moving."

Gray's massive white wolf form paces near the wall, silver eyes tracking every word. He hasn't shifted back yet—and I don't know why. His wolf's presence is both comforting and unsettling, a reminder of how much has changed.

"The magical world has changed," Auren continues. "Significantly, in that time."

My stomach drops. "What kind of changes?"

"Feeders are being hunted," he says simply. "The Council has spent almost five years systematically rounding them up."

I go still. "Why?"

"Reports started coming in about six months after you all disappeared," Auren says carefully. "Silver veins appearing on the Scarborne sanctuary grounds. Then they started spreading—through the stone, the surrounding forest, the entire property."

"The Council determined it was raw Ether," Auren continues, his voice hardening. "Powerful, concentrated magic just waiting to be harvested. And they decided someone needed to mine it." He pauses, then adds, "My sources have since confirmed the veins are coming from one of the mirrors in the Ashen Oath Chamber. One with large, curved horns."

Silence falls over the room.

"We saw them in the Void," Wes says quietly, and everyone turns to look at him. "The longer we were there, the more they grew. Thick silver threads running through everything, pulsing with light." His jaw clenches. "They were everywhere by the end."

"When we found you," Rhett says slowly, his voice hollow, "the veins started at your feet. Where you touched the ground—that's where they began."

The words hit like a fist to the stomach.

My breath catches. My hands go numb where they're gripping the coffee cup.

It can't be. It can't—

Seth's face goes pale. "When I found you, Ethos had already started. The veins weren't there yet, but the corruption was, the black within your Ether. He'd been feeding on you for a while by then."

The room tilts. I grip the edge of the table, knuckles going white. The coffee cup trembles in my other hand.

It's mine. All of it. He took it from me and it just—spread. Grew. Became something they could harvest.

Thane goes completely still. His silver eyes widen with something close to horror.

"The first time," he says, voice barely audible. "When we accidentally crossed into the Void together. That's when he—"

"Started feeding," Stellan finishes grimly. "Before any of us knew what was happening."

"Months," Rhett says, his voice shaking. "He'd been feeding on her for months before she was even trapped there."

Thane's hands curl into fists. "I was right there. I should have—" He stops, jaw clenched so tight I can see the muscle jump. "I should have known what he was doing to her."

Gray's wolf moves closer, a low whine escaping his throat. The sound carries weight—guilt, regret, things he can't say in this form.

Their voices blur together, guilt and self-recrimination building, but I can barely hear them over the roaring in my ears. Five years. He fed on me and it spread through the sanctuary like roots, like infection, and they've been mining it. Mining me.

"Stop." My voice cuts through their pity party. Everyone turns to look at me. "Knock it off. No one could have known what Ethos was doing." I meet Thane's eyes. "And besides, I brought us there. I did this to myself."

My vision tunnels until all I can see is the truth laid bare: Riley's been sitting on the Council for five years while enslaved Feeders mine my stolen power. Power that was ripped from me, thread by thread, while I was alone in the dark.

"The sanctuary Feeders," I whisper. "They're mining what he took from me."

Auren's expression shifts to horror. He didn't know. Couldn't have known where the veins truly originated.

"That's why they kept spreading," Stellan says, his voice tight. "The longer Bree was trapped, the more he drained from her, the more the veins grew."

"And Riley just—" Jace can't finish.

"Let them enslave people to harvest it," Stellan completes, disgust clear in his tone.

"Let them keep Bree captive to extract it," Wes says, his voice going cold in a way I've never heard before.

"Does that seem like a coincidence?" Theo asks quietly, but there's steel beneath the calm.

The implication slams into me. Riley wasn't just wearing my face—she was keeping me trapped. Feeding Ethos so he'd keep draining me so the veins would keep growing so the Council could keep harvesting.

I was livestock.

My Ether flares again, black threads pulsing through the silver like poison.

"And now?" My voice comes out flat. Dead. "What's happening to them now?"

Auren's expression darkens. "The Feeders are still being rounded up. Enslaved." He pauses, jaw tight. "The Council's been quiet about it, but my contacts—friends—they keep disappearing, even from hiding. The ones who've escaped, they all tell the same story. Forced labor, mining the veins. Besides, the Feeders can touch them without being burned," he says quietly. "Makes us useful."

"That means," my voice shakes, "the Feeders who came to me for help, Mairen, her family, they're..."

Auren's silence is answer enough.

"But why would—" I stop. "Riley. She's allowing this."

Auren nods slowly. "The woman claiming to be you has been... more than cooperative with the Council's plans. She didn't just authorize the expansion—she has a seat on the Council now—the fifth spot, repurposed."

My breath catches. "She what?"

"Took your place," Auren says carefully, looking at Thane. "Appeared publicly, played the role perfectly. And in exchange for her cooperation, they gave her everything. Council seat—the one stolen from the Feeders—access, authority."

Thane's jaw tightens. "She's exactly what they wanted. Compliant. Contained."

"That's bullshit," Rhett says, magic flaring.

"Yes. But it's effective bullshit." Auren takes a sip of his coffee. "Five years is a long time to build a system. The sanctuary isn't a refuge anymore—it's a labor camp. And the Feeders who escaped..." He gestures to himself. "We're underground now. Hidden networks. Safe houses. Moving people who can still run."

"It's disgusting it has to be that way," Wes says quietly.

"It is." Auren's expression darkens. "The Council actively hunts us. They have enforcers, trackers, entire squads dedicated to finding Feeders in hiding. Phil leads most of the operations."

I feel sick. Five years of this. Five years of Riley wearing my face, using my name, turning everything I built into a prison.

"And the Oath chamber?" I force myself to ask.

Thane's jaw clenches. "Locked down. A few of us discussed it this morning. The Council claimed it needed 'proper oversight' after Riley opened it. At first, access was restricted—Elementals, Seers, and Shifters with 'adequate control' only. Mentalists needed pre-approval."

"And Feeders?" I already know the answer.

"Banned completely." His voice is lethal. "Anyone who attempts to take the Oath faces binding. Magic stripped, feeding capabilities severed." He pauses. "Slow starvation. Death."

"But demand got so high," Stellan adds, his tone bitter, "they tightened restrictions even further. Now they rarely let anyone through who doesn't directly benefit the Council's interests."

"They turned your gift into a weapon," Auren says quietly. "Made it exclusive. Elite. Everything you never wanted it to be."

Wes shifts, his voice quiet but clear. "We all took the Oath. Before we went into the Void."

Auren's head snaps up. Then he laughs—actually laughs, sharp and genuine and slightly unhinged. "You're joking."

Rhett's mouth curves slightly. "We're not."

"Oh, that's beautiful." Auren's grin is sharp as broken glass. "The ones they're most afraid of—the ones they locked the chamber to keep out—already completed it." He looks at me, something wild in his eyes. "Do they know?"

"Not yet," Jace says, his smirk growing. "But they will."

My Ether flares—silver light edged with black, pulsing outward like a heartbeat. The temperature in the room drops.

"Five years," I whisper. "She's had five years to become me. To learn how to wear my face. To make them believe she's the Source they wanted."

I feel like I'm going to be sick. Riley took my place. Has been living as me.

"She switched with you after the Ashen Oath," Thane says quietly, and there's weight in his voice. "Stepped right into your life at the sanctuary."

"Some of the Feeders noticed something was off," Stellan adds. "The way she moved, spoke. Little things."

"Her Ether was inverted," Thane continues. "Black threaded with silver instead of silver threaded with black. Her scars were gone. She didn't hesitate, didn't flinch."

"We figured it out," Stellan says, his voice tight.

"Later," Auren cuts in gently but firmly. "First, we need to..."

"We need to stop her," I say. "Before she—"

"Before she what?" Auren's voice is gentle but firm. "Before she takes everything from you? Bree, she already has. She's been on the Council for five years. She's been living in your sanctuary. Sleeping in your bed."

I want to argue. Want to rage. But he's right.

"So what do we do?" Rhett asks, his voice rough.

"First, we need to figure out what Riley's endgame is," Thane says, stepping forward. "If she's been consolidating power for five years, she's not going to give it up easily. The longer she stays in Bree's place—"

"We should overthrow the Council," Rhett says, his voice hard and certain. "Take them down. All of them."

Gray's wolf form growls—a deep, rumbling sound of agreement that vibrates through the floorboards.

"No," Stellan says firmly. "Too dangerous. They'll—"

"What about the sanctuary?" Wes asks quietly. "The Feeders there—if we expose Riley, what happens to them?"

"They're already enslaved," Jace says, frustration sharp in his voice. "We can't just leave them—"

"We're not leaving anyone," Theo says, his voice calm but certain. "But we need a plan that doesn't get them killed in the crossfire."

Seth, who's been quiet this whole time, finally speaks. "What if she knows we're back?"

Everyone turns to look at him.

"She has Bree's memories," he continues. "She might feel the bonds. Know that something's changed. If she realizes the real Bree is free—"

"She'll move faster," Thane finishes grimly. "Consolidate her position before we can challenge her."

Their voices overlap, building on each other, planning around me instead of with me. Making decisions. Protecting me.

Like I'm not even here.

My chest tightens. The familiar sensation of walls closing in, of being pushed to the edges of my own life. They're doing it again. Talking over me, deciding for me, keeping things from me "for my own good."

They haven't changed.

How could I think they would? How could I believe a year in the Void searching for me would make any difference?

"—can't let her near the sanctuary," Jace is saying.

"We'll need to establish a perimeter," Rhett adds. "Make sure—"

Heat flares through the room—Rhett's magic responding to rising tension.

"Bree shouldn't go anywhere public until we know—" Rhett starts.

My hands curl into fists in my lap. The black threads in my Ether pulse, responding to the rising anger, the crushing disappointment.

Chairs scrape as people shift, voices building over each other.

"We could use the Feeders underground as—"

"Stop."

Theo's voice cuts through the chaos like a blade.

Everyone turns to look at him. He's staring at me, his dark eyes wide with something like horror.

I shift in his lap to face him fully, and his arms tighten around my waist—not holding me back, just... holding me.

"What are we doing?" His voice shakes. "We literally just got her back and we're doing this again?"

Silence crashes over the room.

"Doing what?" Rhett asks, confused.

"This." Theo gestures at all of them, then at me. "Talking over her. Deciding for her. Planning her life like she's not sitting right there." His jaw clenches. "Like we didn't lose her the first time because we kept secrets and made decisions she deserved to be part of."

The words make my breath catch.

I watch understanding dawn on their faces—Rhett's confusion shifting to guilt, Jace going very still. Even Gray's wolf form lowers its head, ears flattening against his skull.

"Bree—" Rhett starts.

"She deserves our trust," Theo says, his voice rough with emotion. "Our respect. Our complete and utter transparency. Not our protection at the cost of her agency." He looks at me, and there's something raw in his expression. "I'm sorry. We're sorry."

The apology sits in the air between us.

I don't know what to say. Part of me wants to accept it, to let it go because I'm so tired of fighting. But another part—the part that spent a year alone in the dark—knows that apologies without change mean nothing.

"I hear you," I say finally, my voice quiet but steady. "But I need more than sorry. I need you to actually stop doing it."

"We will," Wes says softly. "I swear we will."

"Show me." I meet each of their eyes in turn, including Gray's silver wolf gaze. "Don't tell me I'm part of this and then leave me out. Don't make decisions for me and call it protection."

They nod, various expressions of shame and determination crossing their faces. Gray's wolf form approaches slowly, pressing his massive head against my knee—an apology in the only way he can offer it right now.

Auren's eyes shift to Seth, and something careful enters his expression.

"You should know," he says quietly, "I've been tracking missing persons cases tied to the Void for decades. Helping families when I can." He pauses. "Your family reported you missing twenty-five years ago, Seth."

Seth goes very still. His face drains of color.

"Twenty-five..." He can't seem to finish the sentence. His hands start to shake.

"I'm sorry," Auren says gently.

Seth sinks slowly into the nearest chair, looking like he might be sick. "My parents. My sister. They've been—" His voice cracks. "Twenty-five years."

Nobody speaks. What can you say to that?

"You've only been gone a year for us," I say softly. "But twenty-five for them."

"They're gone," he whispers. "Aren't they? My parents, they'd be—" He stops, jaw clenching. "They thought I was dead this whole time."

Auren doesn't confirm it, but he doesn't deny it either. The silence is answer enough.

I watch Seth struggle with it—the weight of decades lost, of a family that mourned him, of an entire life that moved on without him. He looks so young, but he's lived through more time than any of us realized.

The room feels hollow, grief hanging in the air until Auren's voice cuts through it.

After a long moment, Auren clears his throat gently, and we all turn to look at him. There's something in his expression—understanding.

"There's something else," he says quietly. "Something that might help you understand why I knew you'd come here. Why I was waiting."

He stands, setting his cup down carefully.

He hesitates—as if deciding whether to ruin what's left of the night.

"First, you should know how I knew you'd come." He looks at me. "How I knew the real Bree would find her way to this house."

Something in his tone makes my chest tighten.

"Because this is where your mother came," he says quietly, "when she escaped the Void."

The world stops.

"What?"

The air shifts—colder, charged—as if the room itself knows what's about to happen.

Auren steps back, and a door I didn't notice before—set into the far wall—opens.

A woman steps through.

Dark hair. Green eyes. A face I've seen in every mirror, every photograph, every dream where I tried to remember what love felt like before it walked away.

My mother stands in the doorway, alive and real and looking at me like I'm the ghost.

My lungs forget how to work. No one moves.

"Hello, Bree."

Chapter 20
BREE

The silence stretches so long I forget how to breathe.

She's real. She's here. She left me.

All three truths exist at once, and I don't know which one to hold onto.

Claire's gaze sweeps the room—taking in Auren, the guys arranged protectively around me, Gray's massive white wolf form near the wall, the way I'm sitting on Theo's lap and still look like I might bolt at any second. Her expression shifts through a dozen micro-emotions too fast to name before settling on something that looks like understanding.

"Was it the fox or the snake that guided you here?" Her voice is softer than I remember, careful.

I blink, thrown by the question. "What?"

"The void creatures," she says, stepping fully into the room but not closer. "Your familiars. Which one led you to this house?"

My stomach drops. She knows about them. Of course she does.

I glance at Rhett, confused, and he answers before I can. "The fox." His voice is steady, protective. "He showed us the way."

Claire's mouth curves into a faint smile that doesn't reach her eyes. "He's always been the leader of the two."

"Three," Theo corrects quietly from beneath me, his voice rumbling through his chest where I'm pressed against him.

Gray's wolf form moves forward, ears pricking, a low questioning sound rumbling in his chest.

Her smile falters. "Three?"

"There's a raven too," I say, my voice coming out rougher than I intended.

Something shifts in Claire's expression—haunted, almost afraid. Her hand grips the doorframe like she needs the support.

"I never saw the raven," she murmurs, more to herself than to us. "Only the fox and the snake."

The words hang in the air, heavy with meaning I don't understand yet.

Claire's eyes find mine again, and I see her struggling with something—maybe the same thing I am. How to bridge years of absence with a single conversation. How to explain the inexplicable.

She glances around at everyone watching her with varying degrees of suspicion and hostility. Thane's silver eyes track her every movement like prey. Stellan's expression is carefully blank but his posture screams danger. Even Wes, usually so gentle, has gone completely still. Gray's wolf form is coiled tight, ready to spring.

"Bree," Claire says carefully, "maybe we should talk somewhere private."

The word "no" is out of my mouth before she finishes the sentence.

Everyone goes quiet.

Theo's arms tighten slightly around my waist—steadying me and I'm grateful for it.

"No," I repeat, quieter but no less firm. I look around at the guys, drawing strength from their presence. "There's nothing between us, right?"

I'm asking them, but I'm telling her.

Rhett nods first, jaw tight. Wes's is softer but just as certain. Theo's agreement comes as a gentle squeeze around my waist. Jace's smirk is more reassurance than humor. Thane doesn't move, but his silver eyes flash with approval. Gray's wolf form presses closer, a solid warm presence against Theo's leg where I'm sitting.

Seth just watches, steady and present.

Claire's expression flickers between guilt and something that might be acceptance. She exhales slowly, like she's been holding that breath for years, and moves to sit in the chair farthest from me. Not defensive—defeated.

"All right," she says quietly, folding her hands in her lap. They're shaking. "I'll tell you everything."

The room holds its breath.

"I met him a few months before I left," Claire says, and her voice cracks on the first word. "Ethos."

The name detonates like a bomb.

Thane goes completely rigid, his entire body coiling with barely restrained violence. Auren swears under his breath, sharp and vicious. Stellan's mask finally cracks, fury bleeding through. Gray's wolf form snarls, lips pulling back from teeth.

Theo's arms tighten protectively around me, and I feel his chest rise with a sharp breath.

My stomach twists so hard I think I might be sick.

"He was..." Claire struggles for words, staring at her hands. "Charming. Brilliant. Curious about everything. He sought me out because I carried the Scarborne bloodline, even if the magic was dormant." She looks up, meeting my eyes. "He told me he could help me find my potential. That I just needed the right guidance."

"But that wasn't what he wanted," Rhett says flatly.

"No." Claire's voice drops to barely a whisper. "The more we talked, the more questions he asked, the more they centered on you. Your birth. Your early years. Whether you showed any signs." She swallows hard. "I didn't understand at first. I thought he was just being thorough. But then..."

"Then you realized," Theo finishes, his voice careful but knowing. His breath stirs my hair.

Claire nods. "He thought your power was sleeping inside me. That I was the Etherbearer, and you were just... collateral. A normal child born to extraordinary lineage." Her hands clench in her lap. "But I didn't know. The magic had been dormant for generations—I had no way of knowing if it was me, or you, or neither of us." Her voice cracks. "All I knew was that he wanted one of us, and I couldn't let him have you. So I thought if I left—if I went with him—he'd lose interest in you. Whether you had the power or not, I thought I was keeping you safe."

My chest tightens. Each word lands heavier than the last.

"You left to protect me," I repeat, my voice hollow.

"Yes. I gambled everything on the chance that even if the power was yours, he'd follow me long enough for you to hide. To disappear. To have a chance." She finally meets my eyes. "I was wrong about so many things. But I wasn't wrong about needing to keep you away from him."

"You left me with him." I can barely get the words out past the tightness in my throat. "With Kevin. You knew what he was."

Claire flinches. "I knew Kevin wasn't... kind. I knew he drank, that he was rough around the edges." She won't meet my eyes. "But I thought that was survivable. I thought cold neglect was better than Ethos's attention. I thought—" Her voice cracks. "I thought I was choosing the lesser evil."

"You chose wrong," I say flatly.

"I know." The words are barely a whisper. "By the time I realized Ethos wasn't going to let me go, that he had me trapped—" Her voice breaks completely. "I couldn't check on you. Couldn't come back. Couldn't even send word. And I told myself you were safe because the alternative—" She stops, shaking. "What did he do to you?"

The question hangs in the air.

I don't answer. Can't. My throat closes around words I've never said out loud.

"He took my innocence before I even knew it was something to take," I say finally, my voice barely audible.

Gray's wolf form whines softly, the sound carrying grief. Theo's arms tighten around me, his chest rising with a sharp breath against my back.

Claire's face drains of color. Her hand goes to her mouth.

The anger that's been building in my chest suddenly deflates, leaving only exhaustion behind.

"You think that makes it better?" The words come out flat. Empty. "That you didn't know?"

"No." Claire shakes her head, tears spilling over. "But it's the truth. I took you to that apartment, outside magical territory, helped you vanish. No runes, no records, no Council oversight. A false life meant to hide your true lineage." Her voice shakes. "I thought if I disappeared, Ethos would follow me and leave you alone. I gambled that mundane cruelty was survivable. That it was better than what Ethos would do if he found you."

"But it didn't work," Stellan says, his tone lethal. "Did it?"

"No." The word is barely audible. "For generations, the Scarborne line hasn't produced an Etherbearer. The magic lay dormant—until you." She looks at me, and I see the weight of centuries in her expression. "The power skipped me entirely. It chose you."

"So it was never you," I whisper.

"No," Claire admits. "He thought it was. By the time he realized the truth, he already had me so far under his control that I couldn't fight him. Couldn't get away." Her voice shakes. "And by then, I couldn't warn you either."

Rhett shifts forward, his voice rough. "What did he do to you?"

Claire's expression goes distant, haunted. "He drained me. Tried to siphon Ether from a source that never existed." She touches her chest absently, like the phantom pain is still there. "He'd feed for weeks, years, searching for magic that wasn't there. And when he finally understood what I was—what I wasn't—it was too late for both of us."

The description makes my skin crawl. I know exactly what that feels like—the slow, inexorable pull of Ethos feeding, searching, taking. The way it leaves you hollow and desperate and willing to do anything to make it stop.

I lean back against Theo instinctively, needing the solid warmth of him. His arms adjust around me, holding me closer.

"How long?" I ask quietly.

"Years." Claire's voice breaks. "Until the void creatures found me. The fox and the snake—they led me through the dark, showed me a mirror I'd never seen before." She touches her chest absently. "They helped me escape. Led me through, and I came out here. In Auren's home."

She looks at Auren with something like gratitude before turning back to me.

"I arrived about four months ago."

The words hit me sideways. Four months. That would have been—

My chest tightens as the math clicks into place. Four months ago. Right when everything started at the sanctuary.

"You'd been in the Void the entire time?" My voice comes out hollow. "Since I was a child?"

Claire nods slowly. "I lost track of how long. But yes—from when I left you until I escaped, I was trapped." Her hands clench. "The creatures finally found me, showed me the way out. By the time I made it here, by the time I understood what was happening—" Her voice cracks. "Auren told me about the sanctuary awakening. About you. And then…"

She stops, swallows hard.

"Then you vanished. Just like I had."

The room goes quiet.

"I escaped the Void," she whispers, "only to lose you to it."

I stare at her—this woman who looks like me but isn't me, who made choices I can't comprehend, who loved me enough to leave and abandoned me in the process.

"You left me with lies," I say finally.

"I left you with a chance," Claire replies, and there's steel in her voice now. "If I'd stayed, he would have found you sooner. Would have known what you were before you had any chance to understand it yourself." Her voice cracks. "I tried to keep him from you by staying away, by keeping him focused on me instead. I failed."

The admission hangs between us—no justification, no defense. Just the raw truth of failure acknowledged.

My Ether stirs, silver mist curling around my fingers where they rest on Theo's arms. The air ripples faintly between us, responding to the emotion I can't quite contain.

The boys stay silent, but I feel them—solid presences at my back, ready to intervene if I need them but letting this be mine to navigate.

"When I was trapped," Claire says quietly, "the fox and the snake came for me four months ago—finally showed me the way out." She pauses, her expression distant. "By the time I arrived here, you were already gone."

The words make something crack in my chest.

"But the raven," I whisper. "Why didn't you see the raven?"

Claire's expression turns distant, almost prophetic. "I don't know. Maybe it hadn't found you yet. Or maybe..." She pauses, struggling with something. "Maybe it was waiting. For when you'd need it most."

I can't forgive her. Not yet. Maybe not ever.

But I can understand. Just a little.

"You should rest," I say finally, my voice flat with exhaustion.

Claire nods slowly, like she knows this is the best she's going to get. She stands, moving carefully, and turns toward the door.

At the threshold, she pauses and glances back at me.

"Be careful with the raven," she says softly. "It always sees the end before anyone else does."

Then she's gone, disappearing through the doorway.

Auren lingers, his amber eyes somber. "I'll show her to her room." He pauses, then adds quietly, "You have until dawn. Maybe less."

Everyone turns to look at him.

"I received word while you were talking," he continues, his voice tight. "Phil's forces are moving through the underground networks. They're systematically checking known Feeder safehouses, interrogating anyone they find." His jaw clenches. "They're getting closer. It's only a matter of time before they think to check here."

My stomach drops. "How long?"

"If we're lucky? Sunrise." Auren's expression darkens. "If we're not? They could be here in hours."

Thane's silver eyes flash. "Then we need to move. Now."

"No." Auren's voice is firm. "You need rest. All of you. Bree especially." He looks at me, and there's genuine concern in his expression. "You just escaped the Void. You're running on fumes and adrenaline. If you leave now, exhausted and unprepared, Phil will run you down before you make it a mile."

"So what do you suggest?" Stellan asks, his tone sharp.

"Get some rest while you can," Auren says. "Recover what strength you have. I'll keep watch, and I have wards that will alert us if anyone approaches." He pauses. "Tomorrow, at first light, we run. I know places they haven't found yet. People who can help."

The room falls into tense silence, everyone weighing the risk.

"He's right," Theo says quietly, his voice rumbling through his chest where I'm still pressed against him. "We're no good to anyone if we collapse from exhaustion."

Rhett looks like he wants to argue, but Gray's wolf moves and presses against his leg, and something in the gesture seems to settle him.

"Fine," Thane says finally. "But we leave at first light. No delays."

Auren nods. "Agreed." He glances at me one more time, then follows Claire's path down the hallway.

The silence he leaves behind feels heavier than his presence.

I sit there in Theo's lap, staring at the empty doorway, and think about birds that see the future and mothers who abandon their children to save them and the impossible weight of choices made with love and fear.

Theo's arms are still around me, solid and warm. After a moment, he shifts slightly, adjusting his hold.

"You okay?" he murmurs against my hair.

I don't answer right away. Don't know how to put into words the tangle of emotions in my chest.

Maybe that's why it found me first.

The raven, I mean.

Because unlike the fox and snake that guided her, the raven knows how stories end.

And mine isn't over yet.

Chapter 21
Gray

The others filter out slowly—Rhett's hand lingering on Bree's shoulder, Jace's backward glance as he closes the door behind him. Wes hesitates in the hallway. Even Stellan pauses, like he's considering saying something.

But they all leave.

All except her.

I feel Bree's eyes on me before I even move toward the door. That pull—the one that's been constant since I first shifted—tightens somewhere deep in my chest.

I don't look at her.

Can't.

If I do, I'll stay. And I can't stay.

Can't be there for her like this.

I move toward the door, my steps careful, measured. Controlled. Like if I just keep moving, I can outrun whatever the fuck is happening inside me.

But she follows.

Of course she does.

I make it to my room, the door closing behind me with a soft click. I move deeper into the space, toward the window, staring out at nothing.

You're fine. You're back. You're—

The door opens behind me.

I don't turn around.

"Gray."

Her voice is soft. Careful.

I huff out a breath—the only response I can give in this form—and keep staring out the window.

Footsteps. Closer.

"I'm not leaving."

I lower my head, ears flattening slightly. She should leave. Should rest. Should stop trying to fix what I don't think can be fixed.

"You don't have to turn back if you're not ready," she says quietly. "But I need you to hear me."

I turn my head slightly, just enough to see her in my peripheral vision.

She's standing a few feet away, arms wrapped around herself like she's holding something fragile together.

"I know you think this is easier," she says. "Staying like this. Keeping distance. But Gray..." Her voice cracks slightly. "I need you. Not just the wolf. You."

I close my eyes.

"When I was in the Void," she continues, and my ears perk forward despite myself. "When everything felt impossible, when I thought I'd never get out—do you know what kept me going?"

I don't move.

"It was you." Her voice is steady now, stronger. "The way you never backed down. Not once. Not when I pushed you away, not when I was at my worst, not when everyone else would have given up on me. You just... stayed. You were solid when I couldn't be. You were steady when everything else was falling apart."

Something tightens in my chest.

"That's who you are, Gray. That's what I need. Not the perfect version of you. Not the human or the wolf. Just... you. The one who doesn't give up. The one who stays."

I turn fully to face her now, and she meets my gaze without flinching.

"You being there for me has nothing to do with what shape you're in," she says. "It's who you are. And that doesn't change whether you're standing on two legs or four."

I shake my head, a low whine escaping my throat.

She doesn't understand.

I can't.

"So please," she whispers, stepping closer. "Come back. Not because you have to. But because I'm asking you to."

I back away slightly, and pain flashes across her face.

"Gray—"

I can't. I can't stay.

She takes another step forward, close enough now that I can feel the warmth radiating off her.

Her voice is a whisper.

"I love you."

My claws scrape the floorboards, the air thick with her scent—vanilla, fear, want.

The shift slams into me.

No warning. No choice.

One moment I'm standing on four legs, and the next I'm gasping, stumbling forward as my body tears itself back into human form.

It hurts—fuck, it hurts—but I can't stop it.

I collapse to my knees, hands bracing against the floor, my entire body shaking as the transformation rips through me.

"Gray!"

Bree drops beside me, her hands on my shoulders, steadying me as I struggle to breathe.

"I've got you," she murmurs. "I've got you."

I gasp, my vision blurring as I finally—finally—come back.

My hands.

Human hands.

I stare down at them, trembling, and something breaks inside me.

"I didn't think..." My voice is raw, barely recognizable. "I didn't think I could."

"But you did." Her hand cups my face, forcing me to look at her. "You came back."

I shake my head, tears burning at the corners of my eyes. "I don't know if I can stay."

"You don't have to hold it," she says firmly. "You just have to be here. Right now. That's all I'm asking."

I close my eyes, leaning into her touch.

"I thought if I couldn't stay like this, I couldn't be what you needed."

"You're wrong." She pulls me closer, her forehead pressing against mine. "What I need is you. All of you. The parts that are easy and the parts that are hard. The human and the wolf. All of it."

"Bree—"

"You were there for me in the Void," she says, her voice breaking. "You were there for me every single day before it. And you'll be there for me after. That's who you are, Gray. That's what I count on. Not your form. You."

Something inside me cracks wide open.

"I love you," I manage, my voice breaking on the words.

"I know." She smiles through her tears. "I love you too. Always."

Before I can second-guess myself, my mouth crashes into hers.

The kiss isn't gentle or careful.

It's desperate and raw and everything I've been holding back since the moment I came back from the Void.

She gasps against my lips, her hands sliding up my bare chest, pulling me closer. I roll us, caging her beneath me, one hand braced beside her head while the other slides into her hair.

"Gray—"

I kiss her again, swallowing whatever she was going to say. My body presses into hers, and the wolf inside me—the one that's been restless and unmoored for days—finally stops clawing at my ribs.

This.

This is what I needed.

Not control. Not distance.

Her.

She arches into me, her thigh sliding between mine, and I shift closer, pressing against the smooth inside of her thigh. I groan into her mouth—low and primal. My hand fists in her hair, not rough but possessive, angling her head so I can claim her mouth. My tongue slides against hers, tasting her.

"I need you," I growl against her lips, my voice thick with need. "Bree, I—"

"Then take me." Her words are breathless, shaky, but her green eyes are blazing up at me. "I'm here. I'm yours."

Something snaps inside me.

I kiss her again, harder this time, my hand sliding down her side to grip her hip. She's soft and warm beneath me. I can feel the wolf rising, demanding I claim her, mark her, make her mine. Her hands slide down my bare chest, tracing every slope of muscle like she's memorizing me. Her touch lights me up, and I shudder, my cock throbbing against her thigh.

"Your turn," I murmur, my fingers finding the hem of her leather top. She lifts her arms, letting me remove it, and when I see her—her skin pale and perfect, her chest rising and falling with every breath, her scars telling stories I know by heart—I have to close my eyes for a second.

"You're so fucking beautiful," I breathe, my voice raw.

Her laugh is soft, disbelieving. "Gray—"

"You are." I don't give her a chance to argue. I lean down, my lips brushing her collarbone before lowering to her breast. My mouth closes over her, and she arches into me. I groan at the taste of her.

I take my time, licking and teasing until she's writhing beneath me, her fingers tangled in my hair, tugging like she's desperate for more.

"Gray, please—"

"I know," I growl, kissing my way down her stomach, my hands sliding to her leather pants. "Let me taste you first."

Her breath catches. "You don't have to—"

"I want to." I look up at her, holding her gaze as my fingers hook under the fabric. "I need to. Please."

She nods, lifting her hips, and I strip her bare in one careful motion, tossing her clothes aside. And then she's there—bare and open and perfect, glistening for me.

I settle between her thighs, my hands gripping her hips as I lean in. The first taste of her makes me groan—she's sweet and I can't get enough.

My tongue slides through her folds, slow and deliberate, circling her clit before dipping lower. Her breath stutters, a broken sound that shoots straight through me, and her thighs tremble on either side of my head.

"Gray—oh god—"

I do it again, slower, savoring every sound she makes. When I close my lips around her clit and suck, her hips buck off the bed.

"Fuck," she gasps, her hands fisting in my hair. "Don't stop—please don't stop—"

I don't plan to.

I work her with my mouth and tongue, learning what makes her moan, what makes her shake. When I slide two fingers inside her, her body bows, a sound caught somewhere between plea and praise, her walls clenching around me.

"That's it, love," I murmur against her. "Let me feel you."

I pump my fingers slow and deep, curling them to hit that spot that makes her cry out while my tongue flicks her clit. She's close—I can feel it in the way her thighs shake, the way her breathing turns ragged.

"Gray—I'm—"

"Come for me, Bree," I growl against her. "I want to taste it."

She shatters.

Her orgasm crashes through her, and I hold her down as she thrashes, my mouth working her through it until she's gasping, oversensitive, pulling at my hair.

Only then do I pull back, pressing one last kiss to her inner thigh before crawling back up her body.

She looks wrecked. Beautiful. Mine.

"Holy shit," she breathes.

I grin, kissing her so she can taste herself on my lips. "We're not done."

Her eyes widen slightly, her gaze dropping between us. I'm already hard—have been since the moment I shifted back—and now there's nothing between us. Her hand slides down my stomach, wrapping around my cock, and I groan.

"Fuck, Bree—"

She strokes me once, twice, her thumb swiping over the head where pre-cum beads. "I want you inside me."

I nearly lose it right there.

"Tell me you want this," I manage, my voice rough as I settle between her thighs, the head of my cock brushing against her entrance. "Tell me you want me."

"I want you." Her hands slide up my back, pulling me closer. "I need you. Please."

I push inside slowly, and we both groan at the sensation.

She's so tight. So wet. So perfect.

I have to close my eyes, fighting for control as I sink deeper. When I'm fully seated, I pause, giving her time to adjust, her walls fluttering around me.

"Okay?" I manage, my voice rough.

"Yes." She rolls her hips, and I see stars. "Move. Please."

I pull back slowly, then thrust back in, deeper this time. She gasps, her nails digging into my shoulders.

"Like that?" I ask, doing it again.

"Yes—fuck, yes—"

I set a rhythm, slow and deep, watching her face as I take her. Every expression. Every moan. Every time her eyes flutter closed in pleasure.

But when she wraps her legs around my waist and pulls me even deeper, something shifts.

The control I've been clinging to fractures.

"I don't want to hurt you," I manage, my voice rough, every muscle locked tight.

"You won't." Her hands slide up to cup my face, forcing me to meet her eyes. "I want this. I want you. All of you."

My thrusts grow harder. Faster. Deeper.

She meets me stroke for stroke, her body arching into mine, taking everything I give her. There's a knock at the door, but I don't care. All I care about is her—the way she feels wrapped around me, the way she's saying my name.

"Gray—right there—oh god—"

I shift the angle slightly, hitting that spot inside her that makes her cry out, and her walls clench around me.

"Fuck," I grit out, my hand sliding between us to find her clit. "You feel so good, love. So perfect."

I circle her clit with my thumb as I move harder, and she falls apart.

Her orgasm slams into her, and she screams my name, her entire body shaking as she comes. The sight of her—lost in pleasure, trusting me completely—sends me over the edge.

I follow her with a growl, burying myself as deep as I can go, filling her with everything I have.

For a long moment, neither of us moves.

We just breathe.

Sweat cools between us. Her heartbeat steadies against mine.

Eventually, I pull out carefully, collapsing beside her and pulling her into my arms. She comes willingly, draping herself across my chest, both of us still trembling from the aftershocks.

"Holy shit," she whispers again.

I huff out a laugh, pressing a kiss to the top of her head. "Yeah."

"That was…" She trails off, lifting her head to look at me.

"Explosive?" I offer, the corner of my mouth twitching.

She laughs, the sound light and free. "That's one word for it."

I brush a strand of hair behind her ear, my thumb tracing the line of her jaw. "I meant what I said. About trying. About being here."

"I know." She leans into my touch. "And I meant what I said too. I love you, Gray. All of you."

"I love you too." The words come easier now, like saying them once opened something I didn't know was locked. "Always."

She smiles, pressing a kiss to my chest before settling back against me.

The wolf in me finally rests, quiet beneath her touch.

Content.

Because I'm exactly where I'm supposed to be.

Chapter 22
RHETT

I shouldn't be here.

That's the first thought that cuts through the haze when I hear her cry out—raw, desperate—and every instinct in me fires.

I push open Gray's door and see them.

Bree.

And someone over her.

My first instinct is to move—to protect, to intervene, to pull her away from whatever threat I'm sensing.

But I freeze in the doorway, Jace a half-step behind me, and for a moment, neither of us can move.

Because the threat isn't a threat—it's Gray.

Back in his body. Human. Whole.

The realization hits me like a punch to the chest, and beside me, Jace sucks in a sharp breath.

"Holy shit," Jace breathes. "He's—"

"Back," I finish, the word scraping out of me.

Gray's body moves over hers, deliberate and possessive, and Bree's wrapped around him like he's the only thing keeping her tethered to the earth. Her head is thrown back, her mouth open on a cry that's half his name, half something wordless and raw.

She's beautiful.

She's alive.

She's *here*.

And so is he.

And I can't look away.

It's not like before. Not like when Riley made me watch her with Jace, her eyes locked on mine the whole time, daring me to react, to break, to admit I wanted what wasn't mine.

This is different.

This is witnessing something holy—pleasure she chose, not something stolen.

This is Bree choosing. Gray giving. Both of them lost in something real.

And I want to see it.

I want to see her like this—safe and wanted and so fucking alive it makes my chest ache.

I want to see *him* like this—whole again, human again, after months trapped in fur and instinct.

Gray shifts, burying himself deep, and Bree cries out his name. I feel the heat rising in my palms, instinctive, protective, and I have to clench my fists to keep the fire from sparking.

Not now.

Not here.

Beside me, Jace's breathing has gone shallow. I glance at him, and his eyes are fixed on them both, his jaw tight, something broken and desperate flickering across his face.

He sees it too.

Gray follows her over the edge with a growl, as Bree comes apart beneath him, her entire body shaking. Something in my chest cracks wide open.

She's home.

She's safe.

She's *ours*.

For a long moment, the room is silent except for their ragged breathing. They don't move. Just breathe together, sweat cooling, heartbeats steadying.

Then Gray pulls out carefully, collapsing beside her and pulling her into his arms. She drapes herself across his chest, both of them still trembling.

"Holy shit," she whispers.

Gray huffs out a laugh, pressing a kiss to the top of her head. "Yeah."

"That was…" She trails off, lifting her head to look at him.

"Explosive?" Gray offers, the corner of his mouth twitching.

She laughs, the sound light and free, and something in me aches at the joy in it.

Gray brushes a strand of hair behind her ear. "I meant what I said. About trying. About being here."

"I know." She leans into his touch. "And I meant what I said too. I love you, Gray. All of you."

"I love you too." His voice is rough, broken open. "Always."

She smiles, pressing a kiss to his chest before settling back against him.

That's when Gray's head turns, his storm-gray eyes locking on us.

He doesn't move. Doesn't pull away from her.

Just watches.

Waiting.

I step forward, my voice rougher than I mean it to be. "We need to take care of her."

Gray's jaw tightens, and I see the wolf rise in his gaze—possessive, protective, ready to fight.

But Jace moves beside me, his voice quieter, steadier. "Please. Let us do this."

For a long moment, Gray doesn't move.

Then, slowly, he nods.

I cross the room, my footsteps quiet on the floor. Gray shifts, carefully disentangling himself from Bree, and I reach down, sliding one arm beneath her knees, the other behind her shoulders.

Bree's barely awake when I lift her.

She's warm and boneless in my arms—her skin still holding Gray's heat—and the scent of her wraps around me like a brand. Vanilla and sweat and *her*.

Her head lolls against my shoulder, trusting, and something in my chest cracks.

I carry her down the hall to her room, Jace ahead of me, Gray trailing behind like a shadow.

No one speaks.

Jace disappears into the bathroom, and I hear the water start—low and steady, filling the space with steam and warmth.

I lower Bree onto the edge of the bed, and she blinks up at me, her green eyes unfocused but trusting.

Gray lingers in the doorway, unreadable but unwilling to leave. Our eyes meet, understanding and gratitude passing between us. He nods once, then turns and disappears down the hall. "Rhett?" Her voice is soft, uncertain.

"I've got you," I tell her, brushing a strand of hair back from her face. "We've got you."

Jace reappears in the doorway, his expression tight. "Bath's ready."

I lift her again, carrying her into the bathroom, and the steam curls around us like a living thing. Jace strips down and climbs into the tub first, settling into the water. I lower Bree carefully into his waiting arms, then strip down myself before climbing in behind her.

He hands her back to me and immediately she leans back against my chest without hesitation, and something in me settles.

Jace moves closer to us, his green eyes locked on her face.

For a moment, no one speaks.

I reach for the soap, lathering it between my hands, and begin washing her shoulders, her arms, her back. Slow. Careful. Reverent.

Jace mirrors me, his hands gentle as he works through her hair, untangling the knots with infinite patience.

The water holds us, weightless, like it could dissolve everything we've done wrong if we just stay still long enough.

And I know—I *know*—we don't deserve this. Not after what we did.

"Bree." Jace's voice breaks the silence, raw and rough. "We need to tell you something."

She stills in my arms.

I close my eyes, my hands pausing on her shoulders.

Silence stretches.

"We didn't know," Jace says finally, his voice cracking. "We thought it was you. We—" He stops, swallowing hard. "We slept with Riley."

The words hang in the air like a blade laid on the table.

I force myself to keep going. "I didn't see it. Didn't feel it. I was so sure it was you, and I—" My voice breaks. "I'm never sure. About anything. But I was sure about that. And I was wrong."

Jace's hands have stilled in her hair, his eyes shining. "It was my first time with you. I thought—" His voice breaks. "I thought I was touching your soul. I thought some magic had taken your scars."

Bree's hand lifts, reaching for him, and Jace catches it like a lifeline.

"I'm sorry," he whispers. "I'm so fucking sorry."

"We both are," I add, my voice thick. "We failed you. We should have known. We should have—"

"Stop." Bree's voice cuts through the guilt, but not even her voice can make it go away.

I freeze.

She turns in my arms, her green eyes locking on mine, then shifting to Jace.

Silence again. The water ripples around us.

"You didn't fail me," she says quietly. "Riley did this. She manipulated all of us. She *wanted* this—for us to doubt each other, to tear each other apart." She swallows hard. "I don't blame you."

Jace's face crumples. "Bree—"

"I don't," she says firmly. "But I need to tell you something too."

My stomach drops.

She stares at the water until the ripples settle, as if waiting for it to tell her what to say.

"In the Void... I was with Ethos."

I can't breathe.

Jace goes still, his eyes wide.

"I didn't just—" She stops, her voice breaking. "He didn't have to trick me, or maybe he did. I wanted it. I wanted *him*." Her breath hitches. "That's the part I can't forgive."

Silence.

I stare at her, my chest tight, trying to process what she just said.

She wanted him.

She *chose* him.

And now she's sitting here, vulnerable and raw, admitting the thing that's been eating her alive.

Jace moves first, sliding forward and cupping her face in his hands. "Bree. Look at me."

She does, her eyes shining with unshed tears.

"You didn't know," he says softly. "You couldn't have known. And whatever you felt—whatever he made you feel—that doesn't change who you are. It doesn't change how we feel about you."

"He's right." My voice is rough, but steady. "You were manipulated. Just like we were. And if you can forgive us for not seeing through Riley, then we can damn well forgive you for not seeing through Ethos."

She shakes her head, tears spilling over. "But I *wanted* him—"

"And we wanted Riley," I interrupt. "We thought she was you, and we wanted her. Does that make it any less wrong? Any less painful?"

She stares at me, her breath hitching.

"We all fucked up," Jace says quietly. "We all got played. But we're here now. And we're not going anywhere."

Bree's face crumples, and she leans forward, burying her face in Jace's shoulder. He wraps his arms around her, holding her tight, and I press my forehead to the back of her neck, my hands steadying on her hips.

"We've got you," I murmur. "Always."

She cries.

We hold her.

And for the first time since she came back, it feels like maybe—*maybe*—we can put the pieces back together.

By the time the water starts to cool, Bree's breathing has evened out, her tears spent, and I feel her forgiveness in my bones.

Jace and I help her out of the tub, wrapping her in a towel, drying her carefully before carrying her back to the bed.

She's exhausted—physically, emotionally, completely wrung out.

I pull back the covers, and she slides in without protest. Jace tucks the blanket around her, his movements gentle, deliberate.

She looks up at us, her green eyes soft. "Stay?"

Jace climbs in beside her without hesitation, and I follow, flanking her on the other side.

She curls into Jace's chest, and I press my hand to her back, grounding her.

"We're not going anywhere," I promise.

She's asleep within minutes.

I watch her breathe—slow and steady and alive.

Forgiveness isn't erasure.

It's responsibility.

It's showing up, even when you've failed.

It's promising "never again" and meaning it with everything you have.

Jace meets my eyes over her head, his expression raw.

"We'll make it right," I tell him quietly.

He nods. "We will."

For the first time in days, I believe it.

But as I watch Bree sleep, something hardens in my chest. Riley. Ethos. They took everything from her—from all of us. They twisted love into weapon, trust into betrayal.

They're still out there.

And we're going to make sure they can't hurt anyone ever again.

Chapter 23
BREE

The pounding on the door jerks me awake; my heart tries to punch through my ribs.

For a split second, I'm disoriented—wrapped in warmth, Rhett's arm heavy across my waist, Jace's breath steady against my shoulder. The room still smells faintly of soap and steam from hours ago.

Then the door crashes open.

Auren stands in the doorway, chest heaving, eyes wild.

"Get up. We go now. Ten minutes before they're on us."

The words punch through the fog of sleep like ice water.

Rhett's already moving, rolling out of bed with the kind of speed that says his body was awake before his mind caught up. Jace swears under his breath, scrambling for his boots.

"What—" I start, but Auren's already gone, his footsteps thundering down the hall.

I throw back the covers and lunge for the leather outfit I wore earlier—pants, jacket, boots. My hands shake as I yank the zipper up, fumbling with the straps.

Gray appears in the doorway—human, solid—storm-gray eyes sharp. "Move. Now."

Theo's right behind him, already pulling on his coat, and Wes stumbles past with a pack slung over one shoulder.

Jace runs toward us from the kitchen when I make it to the hall, still shoving food into a bag—bread, apples, cheese, anything he could grab.

"Jace—"

"You'll thank me when we're starving," he mutters. "Priorities."

Rhett's hand closes around my wrist, steadying me. "We're getting out of here. Together."

I nod, my throat too tight to speak.

At the end of the corridor, Auren presses his palm to what looks like solid stone—but it isn't.

The wall slides open with a low grinding sound, revealing darkness beyond—narrow, damp, and ancient.

Tunnels.

"Go," Auren snaps, and we don't hesitate.

Rhett goes first, letting go of my wrist, but still holding his hand outstretched behind him for me. I take it, and the moment I step through the opening, my Ether flickers to life—curling around my wrists, lighting the edges of my vision with silver.

The air tastes metallic, like old wards waking up after years of sleep. It crawls along my skin.

Behind me, the others file in—Seth, Stellan and Thane bringing up the rear with Auren. The moment he crosses the threshold, the stone grinds shut, sealing the way.

"Wonderful," Thane mutters from behind me. "Darkness again."

I have to hold back a nervous laugh.

Too soon.

Torches flicker to life along the walls, casting long shadows that stretch and twist as we move. The tunnel is narrow—barely wide enough for two people side by side—and the ceiling is low enough that Rhett has to duck.

Our footsteps echo on damp stone, too loud, too real.

Everything we rebuilt tonight is already behind us.

I glance back once, catching Jace's eye. He's pale, his jaw tight, but he winks, and my body relaxes just a little.

We keep moving.

I realize halfway through that I haven't seen my mother.

The thought hits me so suddenly I almost stumble.

"Auren," I call softly, my voice bouncing off the walls. "Where's—"

"Safe," Auren says without turning around. "I moved her earlier."

The ache is quiet, settling somewhere under my ribs.

She wanted me safe. Maybe that's the only goodbye either of us knows how to give.

I keep walking.

The tunnel ends in a rough-cut arch, barely tall enough to stand upright. Beyond it, I can see the night—dark and cold and vast.

Auren stops at the threshold, turning to face us. His expression is grim, his eyes shadowed.

"Once you're through, it seals. No going back."

I look at each of them—Rhett, still holding my hand. Jace, clutching his bag of food like a lifeline. Theo, his dark eyes already distant, seeing something the rest of us can't.

And I nod.

Auren leans in close to Thane, his voice low but urgent. "Three days northwest. Town called Greymar. There's a pub—The Rusted Gear. Ask for Mo. He'll know what to do."

Thane nods once, sharp and certain.

Auren steps back, his gaze sweeping over all of us before landing on me. Something softens in his face—just for a breath.

"Good luck, Bree."

"Thank you," I manage. "For everything."

He inclines his head, then gestures toward the passage. "Go. I'll cover here."

"Let's go," Stellan says, seeing the determination in my eyes.

We step through.

The moment we emerge into the open air, my Ether hums—sharp and electric, like static before a storm.

Someone is coming.

I feel it in my bones.

Let them.

Chapter 24
BREE

We've been walking for three days.

The town that finally rises ahead of us—Greymar, Auren mentioned it—feels wrong.

It's not dangerous—not in the way the Void was dangerous, all teeth and shadow and silence that wanted to swallow you whole. This is different. Quieter. Like the air itself is holding its breath.

We move through narrow streets lined with weathered stone, the scent of earth and smoke curling through the damp night air. Lanterns flicker in windows, casting long shadows that stretch and twist. The sound of the water rolls in from somewhere beyond the buildings, rhythmic and relentless.

No one speaks.

Rhett walks slightly ahead, his hand never far from the blade at his hip. Jace flanks my left, eyes scanning every doorway, every alley. Gray moves like a shadow at my right—quiet, watchful, his wolf senses tracking every heartbeat in the dark.

Thane and Wes trail behind, close enough that I can feel their presence without turning around. Theo walks beside me, his silence heavier than the others'. I know that look—the one that says he's seeing more than what's in front of us.

Seth stays close to my other side, his presence grounding in a way I'm still learning to understand.

"Tell me this place isn't crawling with Council loyalists," Jace mutters, low enough that only we can hear.

"It's not," Thane says, voice clipped. "But it's not neutral either. This region's been unstable since—"

He doesn't finish. Since Riley. Since the world thought I was her.

I pull my hood lower, tucking hair out of sight. My Ether hums around me, quiet but restless. It knows we're not safe. None of us are.

"We need information," I say, keeping my voice steady even though exhaustion drags at every word.

"And sleep," Wes adds quietly. "Before someone collapses."

He doesn't look at me when he says it, but I feel the weight of his concern anyway. We're all still running on fumes—bodies pushed past breaking, held together by sheer stubborn will and whatever scraps of magic we have left.

"There," Rhett says, nodding toward a low stone building ahead. Warm light spills from its windows, and I catch the faint sound of music—something low and rhythmic, punctuated by laughter.

The sign above the door reads The Rusted Gear in elegant script, the letters worn but still legible.

"That's it," Thane says quietly. "The place Auren mentioned."

Gray tilts his head slightly, nostrils flaring. "Feeders. A lot of them."

My stomach twists.

Of course it's Feeders. Riley would have made this place hers—built networks, claimed loyalty, left her mark on everything she touched while wearing my face.

"We should keep moving," I say quietly.

"We're out of options," Stellan counters, already heading toward the door. "And if they're Feeders, they'll know something. Auren sent us here for a reason."

I hate that he's right.

Rhett pushes the door open first, stepping inside with the kind of casual confidence that dares anyone to challenge him. Jace follows, then Gray. Theo gives me a look—steady, grounding—before he slips in after them.

I hesitate.

Just for a heartbeat.

Then I step over the threshold.

The music stops.

Not fades—stops. Mid-beat. Like someone cut the strings.

Every head in the room turns toward me, and the shift in energy is immediate. Hostile. Bodies go rigid, hands moving toward weapons or curling into fists. Eyes narrow, assessing. Predatory.

I freeze.

The pub is packed—tables crammed with bodies, shadows shifting in the firelight. Feeders, every one of them. I can feel it in the air, the way the hunger hums just beneath the surface, controlled but barely. Waiting.

Someone stands. Then another. The scrape of chairs against stone sounds too loud in the sudden silence.

Rhett's hand drops to his blade. Jace shifts his weight, ready to move. Gray's eyes flash silver in the dim light.

Then one of them—a woman near the bar with sharp features and calculating eyes—tilts her head. Her nostrils flare slightly, and something shifts in her expression.

"Wait," she breathes.

The word ripples through the room like a stone dropped in still water.

Another Feeder steps closer, squinting at me in the firelight. His eyes widen. "That's not—"

"It's her," someone else whispers. "The real one."

My Ether pulses once, responding to the recognition even though I don't ask it to. Silver light bleeds through my skin for just a heartbeat—enough.

A glass shatters somewhere to my left.

And then—someone kneels.

The sharp-featured woman drops first, her knees hitting the floor hard enough that I hear the impact. Her hands press flat against the stone, head bowed.

Another follows. Then another.

The ripple spreads through the room like a wave—bodies dropping, some graceful, some stumbling, one man nearly falling into a table before he catches himself and sinks down. They move like they don't have a choice, like something deeper than thought is pulling them under.

My breath catches.

"Bree—" Rhett starts, stepping protectively in front of me.

But I can't move. Can't speak. Can only stare at the sea of bent heads, the weight of their recognition pressing down on me like a physical thing.

The silence stretches. Absolute. Suffocating.

And then—

"About time you showed up, bitch!"

The voice cracks through the room like a whip—sharp, delighted, impossible to ignore.

A collective gasp ripples through the Feeders still on their knees. Heads snap up, eyes wide with shock and something close to horror.

And then she appears.

Zira.

She moves through the crowd like she owns it, leather pants clinging to her legs, blood-red lipstick stark against dark skin. Her dark eyes lock onto mine, and the grin splitting her face is feral and warm all at once.

The Feeders part for her instantly, scrambling out of her way even while kneeling.

She reaches me in three long strides, throws her arms around me, and lifts me off my feet.

"Took you long enough to crawl out of the Void," she says, voice loud enough for everyone to hear. "You caused quite a scene, sweetheart."

I'm too stunned to move. Too stunned to do anything but let her squeeze the air out of my lungs while the entire room stares in frozen disbelief.

Zira sets me down, still grinning, and turns to face the kneeling crowd. Her expression sharpens, dangerous and amused all at once.

"Get up," she says, voice cracking like a whip. "Before you bruise your knees. She's not here to judge you."

Most of them obey immediately, scrambling to their feet with wide eyes and hushed murmurs. A few remain kneeling, whispering words I can barely make out—the Source returns, the Ether calls, she came back.

I force myself to breathe.

Thane steps closer, his silver eyes finding mine. There's something heavy in his gaze—confirmation, maybe. Or warning.

"They've been waiting for you," he says quietly.

"For who?" I ask, even though I already know the answer.

His jaw tightens. "Someone who isn't her."

Zira doesn't wait for questions. She jerks her head toward a narrow door at the back of the room, already moving. "Come on. We're not doing this out here."

The back room is small—cramped, really—with a single table shoved against one wall and chairs that don't match. A window overlooks the street, curtains pulled tight. The air smells like old wood and salt.

We file in and there's not enough space. Not even close. Bodies shift, trying to find room, and I end up pressed against Seth's chest, his hands coming up to steady me.

He doesn't step back.

Neither do I.

The air shifts—warmer, closer. My Ether hums faintly, aware of him in a way that makes my breath catch. I can feel his heartbeat through my palms where they've landed against him.

Seth looks down at me, and something flickers in his eyes. Heat. Recognition.

Across the room, Theo's watching us. His mouth curves—subtle, knowing—before he looks away.

Stellan lets out a low laugh, soft enough that only those closest hear it. When I glance over, he's looking between Seth and Theo like he just watched something click into place.

Zira closes the door, leans against it. Her grin disappears.

"First things first," she says, eyes flicking to me. "You're safe here. This place is owned by a Feeder named Mo—he's been running this station for years. Helps people get through when the Council decides they don't belong anymore."

"Station," Jace repeats, frowning.

"A network," Thane says quietly. "Safe houses, routes. Gets Feeders out when the Council is after them."

Zira nods. "And anyone else the Council wants gone. Mo's good people. Known him forever." She glances at Thane. "You probably know him too."

Thane's expression doesn't change, but recognition flickers in his eyes.

"We came here because we knew you'd be safe," Zira continues. "And because word's been spreading."

My stomach twists. "Word about what?"

"About you coming back." Her gaze locks onto mine, steady and unflinching. "The real you. Not the fake."

Riley.

The name sits heavy between us even though no one says it.

Zira pushes off the door, moving closer. "Bree, it's bad. It's real bad out there." Her voice drops, losing the edge of humor she usually carries. "The Council's cracking down harder than ever. Feeders are disappearing—some running, some getting caught. And the ones who stay? They're terrified."

I swallow hard, my hands curling into fists at my sides.

"They need help," Zira says. "Real help. Not just someone to hide them or smuggle them through. They need someone who can stand up and say enough."

"They need you," Theo says quietly.

I flinch. "I don't know if I—"

"Bree." Zira steps closer. "You've been running this whole time. I get it. You've had to. But this?" She gestures toward the door. "This isn't a story. This is your life. And theirs. And something needs to change."

"I haven't been running." The words come out sharper than I mean them to. "I was lured. Then held captive."

Zira blinks.

"We spent a year in the Void searching for her," Thane says, voice flat. "We've been back only a few days."

The room goes still.

Zira's eyes widen. "Wait, a year? In the—" She stops. Swallows. "Who had you?"

"Ethos," I say.

She gasps. Actually gasps, hand coming up to her mouth. "He's real? He can't be real."

I frown. "What are you talking about?"

"Bree." Zira's voice drops, all the humor gone. "Ethos rules the mirror realm. He wears whatever face you'll follow into the dark. He's death himself."

The words settle over the room and no one moves.

I swallow hard. "He had me for over a year."

Zira goes pale. "A year. With him."

"He..." I stop. Start again. "He made me think he was helping me. That he was the only one who understood. Who saw me." My voice cracks. "He fed on me. My Ether. Every day. I didn't realize at first. And then I let him because I thought—"

I can't finish.

Seth's hand finds mine. Squeezes once.

"He was beautiful," I say quietly. "Said things that made me feel safe. Made me believe the people I loved had abandoned me. That they'd moved on. That I was alone."

Zira's eyes glisten. "Bree..."

"But I wasn't." I look around the room at the guys. My guys. "They came for me. They fought through the Void to find me. And when they did—" My throat tightens. "When they did, I didn't know if I was worth saving anymore."

"You were," Gray says, voice rough. "You are."

Zira wipes at her eyes quickly. "Fuck. Okay." She takes a breath. "So Ethos had you. For a year. And you got out."

"Barely," Wes says quietly.

"But you're here now." Zira straightens, steel returning to her voice. "And that bastard doesn't get to keep you down. You hear me?"

I nod, throat too tight to speak.

"The Feeders out there?" She jerks her head toward the door. "They've been waiting for someone to stand up for them. Someone who understands what it's like to be hunted. Used. Thrown away." Her eyes lock on mine. "That's you, Bree. Not because you're perfect. Because you're the only one who can."

The weight of it presses down on me.

But this time, it doesn't feel like drowning.

"What do you need from me?" I ask.

Zira's mouth quirks. "First? Rest. You look like hell."

Jace snorts.

"After that?" Her expression hardens. "We take that imposter bitch down."

I glance around the room. Rhett's moved closer, protective instinct written in every line of his body. Seth's hand is still in mine, steady. And Thane—

Thane's watching me with something fierce in his eyes. Hunger, yes. But also pride.

"We'll figure it out," I say. "Together."

Zira grins. "Damn right."

She moves toward the door. "Get some rest. Mo's got rooms upstairs. We'll talk more in the morning."

"Zira," I say.

She glances back.

"Thank you."

Her grin softens. "Always, babe."

Then she's gone.

For a moment, no one speaks.

Wes exhales shakily. "That was a lot."

"Understatement," Jace mutters.

Theo moves to the window, pulls the curtain aside. His brow furrows.

"What?" I ask.

"Nothing," he says after a beat. "Just making sure we weren't followed."

But the way he says it makes my chest tighten.

"Theo."

He glances back. Something flickers in his eyes I can't quite read.

"We should rest," he says. "Like Zira said."

I want to push. Want to ask what he's not saying.

But I'm so tired. We all are.

As we file out and follow Zira's directions upstairs, Seth stays close. His presence is grounding in a way I don't entirely understand yet.

At the top of the stairs, Thane catches my arm gently. "You did well," he says quietly. "Telling her."

I meet his eyes. The hunger's still there, but so is something else.

Respect.

"Get some rest," he says. "We'll need you sharp tomorrow."

I nod, turning toward the room Zira pointed out. Then pause.

"Thane?"

"Yeah?"

"Stay with me?"

His eyes darken slightly. "Always."

As I step into the small room, Thane right behind me, I can't shake the feeling that whatever's coming, it's already closer than we think.

Chapter 25
THANE

The door closes behind us.

For a moment, neither of us moves. The room is small—stone walls, a narrow bed, moonlight cutting silver across the floor through the gap in the curtains.

Bree stands near the center, arms wrapped around herself. Not defensive. Just holding on.

I stay by the door because if I get closer right now, I'm not sure what happens.

My throat works against the hunger clawing up from my chest—sharp, relentless, alive with want that's not just hunger anymore. It's need, raw and undeniable, threading through every instinct I've spent centuries learning to control.

She's here. Real. Not Riley's polished edges and manufactured certainty, not the version that wore her face and tried to let me feed while my hunger turned sour in my mouth.

This is her.

The scent of her blood hums through the air between us—Ether-rich, electric, alive in a way that makes my fangs ache. Beneath it is her warmth, the faint trace of sweat and soap that makes heat coil low in my gut.

I lock my jaw. Force stillness into my hands even as my body tightens with need.

"You knew," she says quietly.

Not a question. A statement waiting for confirmation.

I don't pretend. "Yes."

"How?"

I let the silence stretch while I think through the answer, finding the shape of truth I can give her without admitting how much it cost to stay away.

"She wanted what you never offer," I say finally. "Control. Certainty. You don't beg."

Her eyes find mine across the small space. Something shifts in them—relief, maybe. Validation.

"She tried to let me feed. More than once." The admission costs me, but I give it anyway. "But my hunger refused every time she spoke because I could taste the difference before I ever got near her. It wasn't you."

Her breath catches. Just once.

"So you starved yourself," she whispers.

"I couldn't touch her." The words come out flat. Final. "Not when I knew."

She steps closer. One step, then another, closing the distance I've been maintaining like a lifeline.

The space between us shrinks and my control frays at the edges. I can see the pulse in her throat now, the way her chest rises and falls with each breath. The way her lips part slightly as she looks up at me.

"Thane."

My name in her mouth sounds like forgiveness. Like permission.

Her hand lifts, hesitates for just a heartbeat, then her palm cups my jaw. Her thumb brushes the corner of my mouth and the touch breaks something loose in my chest.

I don't move. Don't breathe. Just let her warmth sink into my skin, let the Ether humming beneath her pulse speak truths I can't afford to question.

Her other hand joins the first, framing my face while her eyes search mine. Looking for lies, maybe. Or giving me one last chance to pull away.

"I know you're starving," she says softly.

I can't deny it. Don't want to.

My hands lift before I can stop them. One settles at her waist, fingers spreading against the curve of her hip. The other cups the back of her neck, threading through her hair, and the feel of her—solid, warm, real—makes something primal surge through me.

"Bree—"

"Let me." Her voice is steady. Sure. "Please."

The please does something to me because it's not desperate—it's a choice she's making freely, without fear twisting through it. It's trust, offered like a gift I don't deserve but can't refuse.

"Are you sure?" My voice comes out rougher than I mean it to, hunger and want bleeding together until I can't tell where one ends and the other begins.

She nods. "I trust you."

Three words. Simple and devastating.

I lean in slowly—giving her time to change her mind, to pull away—but she doesn't. She tilts her head, baring her throat in a gesture that feels like both surrender and claiming. The sight of her pulse jumping beneath pale skin makes my fangs descend fully.

When I bite, it's careful. Reverent.

Her blood fills my mouth—warm, electric; Ether singing against my tongue like liquid light. I drink once. Twice. Feel the power of it chase away the hollowness I've been carrying, filling spaces inside me I'd forgotten existed.

She gasps softly, her fingers tightening in my hair, and the sound goes straight through me. Heat floods my body, sharp and insistent, a pulse I can't outrun, as her Ether mingles with my hunger and transforms it into something else entirely.

I pull her closer, the hand at her waist sliding around to splay across the small of her back, pressing her against me. She fits perfectly—curves to my angles, softness to my hard edges—and when she arches slightly into the bite, a low sound rumbles from my chest.

Her other hand grips my shoulder, nails digging in just slightly, and I force myself to stop drinking before I take too much. Pull back just enough to press my forehead against hers, both of us trembling in the space between heartbeats.

Blood—her blood—still coats my lips. Her pulse flutters wildly where my mouth had been, two small punctures already beginning to close as her Ether knits the wound.

"Thane," she breathes, and there's something in her voice that wasn't there before. Heat. Want.

I should step back. Give her space. Let the moment settle before I lose myself completely in what I've been starving for.

But she doesn't pull away. Instead, her hands slide from my hair to frame my face again, thumbs brushing across my cheekbones, and when her eyes meet mine they're dark with desire that mirrors my own.

"Stay," she whispers.

Not a question. A command wrapped in invitation.

My control, already threadbare, snaps.

I capture her mouth with mine, tasting her gasp as much as her lips. She opens for me immediately, no hesitation, and the kiss is hungry and deep and nothing like careful. Her tongue slides against mine and I can taste traces of her own blood mixed with the sweetness of her mouth, the combination intoxicating.

My hand tangles in her hair, angling her head so I can kiss her deeper, while the other slides down from her back to cup her ass and draw her flush against me. She makes a small sound—not quite a moan, not quite a whimper—and I swallow it greedily.

Her hands move to my chest, fingers curling into my shirt, and when she pulls me backward toward the bed, I go willingly. Every reason I had for staying away dissolving under the simple truth that she still wants this. Still wants me.

The backs of her knees hit the mattress and we tumble together, her falling back with me catching my weight on my forearms so I don't crush her. She's soft beneath me, all curves and warmth and racing pulse, and when she wraps one leg around my hip to pull me closer, grinding against the hardness pressing insistently against her, I groan into her mouth.

"Bree," I manage, pulling back just enough to look at her. To make sure. "Tell me to stop if—"

"Don't stop," she interrupts, her voice breathless but certain. "Don't you dare stop."

Her hands move to the hem of my shirt, tugging upward, and I help her pull it over my head before my mouth finds hers again. This time when I kiss her it's slower, deeper, letting myself taste and explore while my hands map the shape of her body through her clothes.

She arches into my touch, her own hands roaming across my bare chest and back, nails scraping lightly across my skin in a way that makes me shudder. When my mouth leaves hers to trail down her jaw to her throat—careful to avoid the healing bite—she tilts her head back and lets out a soft moan that makes my control fray even further.

I work my way down, pressing open-mouthed kisses along the column of her throat, across her collarbone, down to where her shirt prevents me from going further. My hands find the hem and I pause, looking up at her in silent question.

She nods, chest heaving, and lifts slightly so I can pull the fabric up and over her head.

The sight of her—flushed skin, rapid breathing, eyes dark with want—makes something possessive surge through me. *Mine.* The thought is primal and absolute, and when I lower my mouth to trace the curve of her breast through the thin fabric of her bra, she gasps my name like a prayer.

"Thane—"

My tongue finds her nipple through the fabric, circling and teasing until she's writhing beneath me, her leg tightening around my hip as she rocks against me in desperate need of friction.

I reach behind her, unhooking her bra with practiced ease and tossing it aside before lowering my mouth to bare skin. She tastes like salt and Ether and *her*, and when I close my lips around her nipple and suck, her back arches off the bed with a cry that goes straight to my cock.

My hand slides down her stomach, fingers finding the waistband of her pants, and I pause again. Waiting. Making sure.

"Yes," she breathes before I can ask. "Please, Thane. I need—"

She doesn't finish, but I understand. Can feel it in the way she trembles, in the desperate way she's grinding against me, in the pleading note in her voice.

I unfasten her pants and slide them down her legs, taking her underwear with them, and the sight of her—completely bare, spread beneath me, looking up at me with trust and hunger and something that might be love—steals whatever breath I have left.

"You're beautiful," I tell her, voice rough with need. "Perfect."

She reaches for me, fingers fumbling with my belt, and I help her, shedding the rest of my clothes until there's nothing between us but air and intention.

When I settle between her thighs, the heat of her against me makes us both groan. I want to take my time, worship her the way she deserves, but I don't know how long we have before the world intrudes again. Before we have to move, to run, to fight whatever's coming next.

She's slick and ready, and when I slide one finger through her wetness, testing, she bucks against my hand with a broken sound.

"Inside me," she demands, nails digging into my shoulders. "Now, Thane. Please."

I position myself at her entrance, the head of my cock pressing against her, and pause one last time. "Look at me."

Her eyes find mine, hazy with desire but clear enough that I can see the truth in them.

"I'm yours," she says simply. "Always have been."

The words hit like lightning. After everything—the distance I kept, the corruption I couldn't explain, the year she spent trapped while I searched—she's still mine. Still choosing me.

I push inside slowly, giving her body time to adjust, and the feel of her—tight and hot and perfect—makes stars burst behind my eyes. She gasps, then meets my gaze and nods, drawing me deeper with the leg still hooked around my hip.

"Move," she breathes. "Please."

I do. Starting slow, letting her body adjust, but she's having none of it.

A quiet laugh escapes me—the first time we did this, I led and she followed, uncertain but trusting. Now she knows exactly what she wants and isn't afraid to demand it.

She rocks against me, urging me faster, deeper; I follow her lead—driving into her with steady, powerful thrusts that make her cry out with each one.

Her hands roam, anchoring me until there's no space left between us. Our bodies move together, finding a rhythm that feels inevitable, like we've returned to something we'd only begun to discover.

I can feel her tightening around me, her breathing becoming more erratic, her moans pitched higher, and I reach between us to circle her clit with my thumb. The additional stimulation makes her keen, her entire body going rigid for a heartbeat before she shatters.

She comes with my name on her lips, her body clenching around me in waves that push me right over the edge with her. I bury my face in her neck, breathing in her scent as my own release crashes through me, leaving me trembling and emptied and more satisfied than I've been since the first time we were together.

The air tastes different—lighter, like the world's been reset.

We stay like that for a long moment—both of us breathing hard, bodies still joined, hearts racing in tandem.

Finally, I pull back just enough to look at her. Her eyes are soft, sated, and when she smiles up at me it's small and real and utterly devastating.

"Then we start from here," she whispers.

I nod, pressing my forehead to hers.

The quiet that follows isn't emptiness; it's the sound of everything we stopped running from.

Footsteps echo in the hallway outside—distant but deliberate enough to pull my attention toward the door. My instincts flare, protective and sharp even in the aftermath.

But I don't pull away from her. Don't move except to shift us both so I can tuck her against my side, her head on my chest, my arm wrapped securely around her.

The world can wait a little longer.

Chapter 26
SETH

The bar smells like coffee and burnt toast when I make it downstairs. Light cuts through the dusty blinds, catching on the bottles stacked behind the counter. It's quiet enough to hear the clock on the wall ticking.

Zira's behind the counter flipping something in a pan, humming under her breath. Steam rises from a pot of coffee that smells strong enough to wake the dead.

"Morning," I say, sliding onto one of the bar stools.

She glances over her shoulder, grinning. "Look who's alive. Sit. You look like you'd hurt yourself with a spatula."

"I resent that."

"Resent it sitting down." She slides a mug of coffee across the counter without asking. "Eggs? Bacon? Something that won't kill you?"

"All of the above."

The door to the back room opens and Theo appears, hair still damp from a shower, looking more awake than anyone has a right to be this early. He nods at me, then at Zira. "Smells good."

"Sit," she says again, pointing at the stool next to mine with her spatula. "I'm not running a cafeteria line."

Theo sits, accepting his own mug of coffee. We don't talk much—just the comfortable kind of quiet that comes from being too tired to fill silence with words.

Jace stumbles in a few minutes later, looking like he got maybe three hours of sleep. "Coffee," he mumbles.

"Magic word," Zira says without turning around.

"Now."

"Close enough." She pours him a mug and he takes it like a lifeline.

"Where's everyone else?" Theo asks.

"Rhett's doing perimeter check," Zira says. "Gray's with him. Wes is still asleep. Thane and Bree are—" She pauses, smirking slightly. "Resting."

Jace snorts into his coffee.

We eat in relative peace—bacon, eggs, toast that's only slightly burnt. It's the first normal meal we've had in days, and I let myself sink into the ordinariness of it. The clink of forks on plates. The smell of grease and coffee. The easy rhythm of people who've survived something together and made it to the other side.

Theo finishes first, pushing his plate away. "I'm going to check on the others. Make sure everyone's actually awake."

"Good luck with that," Jace mutters.

Theo leaves. Jace drains his coffee and stands, stretching. "I'm gonna grab a shower before all the hot water's gone."

And then it's just me and Zira.

She hums while she scrapes the grill clean, then disappears into the back room muttering something about needing more eggs.

I'm alone.

Zira's humming fades down the hallway, the only sound left the slow drip of coffee behind the bar.

The bell over the front door jingles.

The sound cuts through the quiet—not urgent, just unexpected.

I turn toward the door as it swings open, and a woman steps inside.

She moves like she owns the place. She wears a leather jacket and dark pants, boots that don't make a sound on the wooden floor. Her hair is black—crow-black, with a faint iridescence when the light catches it just right. Sharp features, eyes like polished obsidian, and a smile that knows too much.

She looks at me once—quick, deliberate, assessing—and the smile widens slightly.

"Morning," she says, voice smooth. "Didn't expect anyone that pretty to be conscious at this hour."

I blink. "Bar's closed."

"Good thing I'm not here for the food." She leans against the counter, one elbow propped casually like she's settling in for a conversation.

Something about her sets my instincts on edge; I can't put my finger on why. She doesn't feel dangerous exactly—more like the kind of person who could be dangerous if they wanted to be.

"Can I help you?" I ask, keeping my tone neutral.

"Maybe." Her eyes flick over me again, slower this time. "You're new."

"To what?"

"To all of this." She gestures vaguely at the room, the world beyond it. "You've got that look. Like you're still figuring out which way is up."

I don't answer. Don't know how to.

She tilts her head slightly, studying me. "What's your name?"

"Seth."

"Seth." She repeats it like she's tasting the word. "I like it. Simple. Strong."

Before I can respond, the door to the back hallway opens.

Stellan appears in the doorway and freezes.

His entire demeanor shifts in a heartbeat—from casual to lethal, every line of his body going tense. His eyes lock onto the woman at the counter and his expression hardens into something cold and dangerous.

"Get the fuck away from him," he says. His voice is calm, controlled, but there's a razor's edge underneath it.

The woman raises her hands slowly, smile never fading. "Easy, Stellan. I'm not here to start anything."

"Then leave."

"Can't." She straightens, pulling something from inside her jacket with slow, deliberate movements—a small silver coin that catches the light as she sets it on the counter between us.

It hums once. A sound I feel in my teeth more than hear.

"Tell your queen I'm here to talk," she says, eyes still on Stellan. Then her gaze flicks back to me, just for a heartbeat, and her smile turns sharp. "Preferably before the others find out I came alone."

The coin continues humming, faint but insistent, vibrating against the wood.

Stellan doesn't move. Doesn't speak.

The silence stretches until Zira reappears from the back room, arms full of supplies. She stops dead when she sees the woman, her expression shifting from surprise to something darker.

"Nyx," she says flatly.

The woman—Nyx—inclines her head slightly. "Zira. Still playing chef, I see."

"Still playing games?" Zira sets the supplies down hard enough to rattle the counter. "What do you want?"

Nyx's smile doesn't waver. "Like I said. To talk."

The coin hums again, louder this time.

The smell of coffee still hangs in the air, but the peace is gone.

Whatever we'd managed to find this morning just shattered.

Chapter 27
STELLAN

The room smells like cooled coffee and nerves.

No one says it, but we're all waiting for the same sound—footsteps on the stairs.

Seth sits at the counter, fingers drumming once against the wood before going still. Jace perches on a stool nearby, spinning a knife between his fingers in that restless way he does when tension sits too heavy. Zira leans against the wall, arms crossed, eyes fixed on nothing. Theo's silent by the window, Gray stands near him with his arms crossed, and Rhett stands near the door with his jaw set tight.

The breakfast plates are still scattered across the bar. The coffee's gone cold.

We're all bracing.

Then I hear it—her laughter, bright and unguarded, filtering down from upstairs. The sound fills the space like sunlight breaking through storm clouds, and for a heartbeat, the tension in the room eases.

Thane's voice follows, low and softened in a way it never is around the rest of us. I can't make out the words, but the tone is unmistakable—intimate, easy, the kind of closeness that doesn't need an audience.

Bree appears at the top of the stairs, still laughing over her shoulder at something he said. Her hair's loose, feet bare, and she's wearing one of Thane's shirts—sleeves rolled up, hanging past her thighs. For a moment, she's just a girl in love.

I let myself believe it could stay that way.

She hits the last step and turns toward us, smile still bright. "Morning."

Then she sees our faces.

The joy drains in a breath. Her smile falters, her eyes moving from one person to the next, reading the weight we're all carrying.

"What happened?" she asks quietly.

The silence greets her first. Then the weight of what we have to tell her.

I'd give anything to keep that light on her face. But some truths won't wait.

I clear my throat. The sound is louder than I mean it to be.

The others look at me—unspoken consensus that I'll be the one to tell her.

"Nyx was here," I say, keeping my voice even. "This morning. She came alone."

Bree blinks. "Nyx?"

She repeats the name like tasting a memory she hoped was gone.

"Yes," I continue. "She left a coin. Said she came with a peace offering. That she wants to talk." I pause. "To you."

Her expression shifts—confusion bleeding into disbelief, then settling into something calmer. Focused.

Thane appears behind her on the stairs, his hand settling at her lower back. She leans into the touch without looking away from us.

"A peace offering," Bree says slowly, like she's testing the words for traps. "From Nyx."

"That's what she claimed," Zira mutters from her spot against the wall, arms still crossed. "I wouldn't trust it."

"Peace offering, huh?" Jace spins his knife once more, then catches it. "Maybe it's poison. Or coupons."

Bree's mouth quirks—half a smile that doesn't reach her eyes. But the humor lands, cutting through the tension just enough to let everyone breathe.

She steps fully into the room, moving toward Jace first. Her hand settles on his shoulder, squeezing once. "Thank you for making me smile when I probably shouldn't."

Then she turns to Theo, her fingers brushing his arm briefly. A grounding touch that pulls them all back together.

She steadies us without trying to. That's what she does—pulls chaos into orbit.

She exhales slowly, then her expression shifts—softening into something more focused. Strategic.

"Zira," she says, turning to face her. "I need intel on how to get back into the sanctuary and what it looks like now. Anything you know."

Zira nods once, sharp. "I'll tell you everything."

Bree's gaze moves to Jace. "Find out what provisions we can take from Mo. And how we can work off payment."

"On it," Jace says, already moving toward the back.

"Theo." She looks at him steadily. "See if you can get a vision of what it looks like inside the sanctuary. Anything that might help us."

He nods, eyes already distant with the weight of what she's asking.

"Gray." Her voice gentles slightly. "Can you shift and check the perimeter? Try to follow Nyx's scent. Get an idea of where she went and make sure it's safe."

Gray's jaw tightens, but he nods.

"Rhett, go with him," she continues. "Show Seth how it's done."

Rhett glances at Seth, then back at Bree. "Got it."

Her gaze finds Wes next. "See how many Feeders in town are willing to make the journey to the sanctuary with us."

Wes straightens, surprise flickering across his face before he nods.

Finally, she looks at Thane, then at me.

"Thane and Stellan, you're with me."

Her gaze sweeps the room again, landing on each of us in turn. Seth. Theo. Gray. Rhett. Wes. Me.

Then she squares her shoulders.

"We meet back here. We face it together," she says, voice quiet but carrying weight. "No running. No hiding."

I thought the crown would make her dangerous. I was wrong. It made her certain.

Rhett nods once, sharp and final. Gray shifts closer to her side without seeming to decide to. Wes exhales shakily but doesn't look away.

Bree glances toward the counter where the coin still sits, humming faintly against the wood.

She exhales slowly, then looks back at us.

"All right then, back here in an hour," she says. "Then we'll see what the bitch has to say."

The room breaks into motion.

Zira pushes off the wall, heading out of the room, phone in hand. Rhett straightens, shoulders squared. Theo moves toward the coin with a frown, studying it like it might reveal something if he stares long enough. Jace smirks like the world just got interesting again as he disappears in his search for Mo. Seth crosses to the window and closes the blinds.

We move like a single thing. Not perfect, not polished — but together.

Whatever waits outside won't find her alone.

The coin hums louder for a moment, then goes silent.

The air holds still, charged and waiting.

For the first time in a long time, I'm not afraid of the storm.

We are the storm.

Chapter 28
WES

The bar's cooler than it should be when I step back inside, dust on my boots and adrenaline still buzzing in my veins. Half grinning, half disbelieving she actually sent me—*me*—to rally half the town.

The others are already here. Jace is sorting through crates near the corner, Theo's nursing what has to be his fourth coffee, and Zira's checking the edge of a blade like she's contemplating which neck it'll find first.

And Bree's at the center of it all.

Calm. Focused. In command.

She turns when I walk in, and every smartass comment I had lined up burns off like morning fog.

"Half the damn town," I say, steadier than I feel. "Every Feeder who's not half-feral or scared out of their mind wants in. They're ready to move the second you give the word."

Her eyes widen slightly in pride and validation.

It lands in my chest like sunlight through rain clouds.

"You did that," she says softly.

I shrug, fighting the grin that wants to break free. "You asked."

Jace snorts from across the room. "Look at him. Practically preening."

"Damn right I am," I shoot back, but I'm still looking at Bree.

Zira steps forward, all business. "Getting back in won't be easy, but it's not impossible. There are old tunnels under the eastern edge of the sanctuary. Feeders have been clearing them for months. We can use those."

Theo shifts, his coffee cup still halfway to his mouth. His eyes are unfocused, fixed on something the rest of us can't see.

"Riley's slipping," he says quietly. "She puts on a show in public, but behind the mask... she's unraveling."

The room goes still.

"And Ethos is there with her."

The silence that follows is heavy enough to crush.

Gray breaks it, his voice low and deliberate. "We found her. Nyx. About five miles outside town, camped near the treeline."

"Camping," Jace mutters. "Pretty sure her idea of roughing it is a hotel without room service."

A few snickers ripple through the room—quiet, but enough to cut the edge off the tension.

Rhett crosses his arms, heat flickering faintly at his fingertips. "She's alone for now."

Seth finishes quietly, "Means we get to choose how this plays out."

Bree nods once, absorbing it all. I watch her process each detail, each advantage. Her shoulders straighten. Leadership settles into her like breath.

Jace stands with a grin and a box under one arm. "Good news and better news. We've got more food than we can eat, and Mo says payment's 'on the house.'" He smirks. "Apparently, Bree's reputation pays in full."

Laughter breaks out through the room for a few seconds, before the weight of everything settles back over us.

Thane and Stellan step forward together, their combined presence shifts the air.

"Transport's ready," Stellan says. "Enough for us and whoever's coming. There's another safehouse near the border Mo told me about last night. We can regroup there after."

Bree's jaw tightens, her gaze sweeping over all of us. "Well, let's go find her. Then we get on the road."

No hesitation. No question.

Everyone moves at once—grabbing gear, weapons, whatever they need. The bar transforms from a safehouse into a staging ground in seconds.

Bree heads for the door first, and one by one, we follow.

I catch her eye as we step outside into the fading light.

She gives me a quick smile—grateful, warm—and it hits like the first warm day after rain.

For the first time since the crown, I don't feel hungry.

I feel *useful*.

Whatever's waiting for us out there, she's not walking into it alone.

We're done waiting.

This time, the Ether moves with us.

Chapter 29
BREE

The clearing appears through the trees just as the sun dips below the horizon, washing orange and violet across the sky. Nyx is there, slumped against a fallen tree, one hand still loosely curled around a dagger.

I signal the others to hold back. Gray and Rhett left, Jace and Wes right, Theo and Seth behind. Thane and Stellan stay close, watching.

I let my Ether slip forward, silver threads drifting through the air. They curl around Nyx's sleeping form—not binding, not threatening. Just holding.

Her eyes snap open.

She jerks upright, dagger flashing into her hand as her gaze darts wildly around the clearing. She sees us—all of us—surrounding her, and panic flares across her face.

"Don't—" she starts, voice sharp with fear and fury.

The Ether tightens slightly. Not painful. Just... immovable.

She tries to lunge forward and can't. Tries to shift left. Nothing. The realization hits, and her breathing goes shallow and fast.

"Let me go," she hisses, eyes blazing.

"Not yet." I keep my voice calm, steady. "You were looking for me. Here I am."

She freezes. Her gaze snaps to mine, searching.

"So let's talk," I say.

For a long moment, she just stares at me. Then her shoulders drop, just slightly, and the fight bleeds out of her posture.

"Fine." She lowers the dagger but doesn't sheath it. "The Ashen Oath. It's not working."

I blink. "What do you mean it's not working?"

"I mean exactly that." Her voice is flat now, resigned. "I've watched hundreds go through successfully. But every time I try, it rejects me. The mirrors won't take me. The bond won't form. I've tried everything—every preparation, every ritual. Nothing changes."

Behind me, Wes murmurs, "That shouldn't be possible."

"Unless something's blocking it," Theo adds quietly.

Thane's voice is sharp. "Or she's already fractured."

Nyx's eyes flash. "I'm not fractured. I'm *stuck*. And I need to know how to fix it."

I study her, trying to piece it together. The Oath is supposed to work for anyone who approaches it with intent. If it's not...

"I don't know," I admit.

Her expression hardens. "You're the Source. You're supposed to—"

"I know what I'm supposed to be," I cut in. "But I don't have all the answers. Not yet."

The Ether hums around us, restless, like it's searching for something too. And then the air shifts.

A hum threads through the clearing—old, deep, familiar. The space between us thickens, growing dark, and I feel it before I see it.

The raven.

It slips through from the Void like water through a crack, black feathers shimmering violet in the fading light. It lands on my shoulder, solid and real. The Ether brightens; the air smells like rain before a storm.

Nyx's dagger hits the ground.

"No." Her voice breaks completely. She drops to her knees. "No, that's—"

She reaches toward it, hands shaking, eyes wide and desperate. "I don't— I don't understand. Why do I—" She chokes on the words. "Please. *Please.*"

The raven tilts its head—calm, unbothered.

Nyx is unraveling in front of me, gasping like she can't breathe. "I need it. I don't know why but I *need it.*"

Every instinct in me wants to step forward. But I stay still. The Ether curls tighter, holding her without touching.

I take a slow breath. "Help us get into the sanctuary," I say quietly. "Do that, and when this is over, we'll help you finish the Oath. Whatever it takes."

Her head lifts. Her eyes are wide, glassy with unshed tears. "You'd do that?"

"Yes."

She studies me for a long moment, searching for the lie. She doesn't find one.

Finally, she nods. "You'll have your way in."

The raven lets out a low, echoing croak. The sound settles into the clearing like a vow.

Nyx rises slowly, not meeting my eyes. She picks up her dagger and sheaths it, then steps closer to the edge of the Ether's light.

"There are tunnels," she says, voice steadier now. "Old ones, under the eastern wall."

"I know," I say. "We already learned of those."

Her jaw tightens. For a second I think she's going to argue, but then she exhales. "There's another way. Older. Goes deeper, comes up inside the sanctuary—not just the outer grounds. The Feeders don't know about it because it's sealed from their side. You just need to know where to look."

I study her. "And you know where to look."

"I do."

"Good," I say.

She glances at the raven one more time, something raw and broken flickering across her face. "Look for the patch of glowing daisies. That's your way in." Then she turns toward the trees. "After that, we're even."

"After that," I answer, "we'll see."

The forest exhales around us. The others move in closer, forming up behind me as we follow Nyx into the darkness.

For the first time, she doesn't look like an enemy.

Just another ghost trying to find her way home.

Chapter 30
JACE

The pub appears just as the last daylight bleeds out of the sky, and I can already tell something's different.

There are people everywhere.

Not just a few stragglers hanging around the entrance. I'm talking dozens—maybe more—crowding the street, leaning against buildings, sitting on crates. Feeders, all of them. Some I recognize from earlier, but most are new faces. They're armed, geared up, waiting.

"Holy shit," I mutter, slowing my stride.

Wes catches up beside me, eyes wide. "I didn't— I mean, I knew there were more, but..."

"Half the town, huh?" I grin at him. "Undersold it, sweetheart."

He doesn't even have a comeback. Just stares.

Then he laughs—loud and bright—and before I can process it, he's kissing me. Right on the mouth. Quick, warm, utterly fearless.

He pulls back, still laughing, and I'm frozen.

Bree's laugh cuts through the air behind us, and when I glance over, she's grinning wide at us, eyes bright.

Wes just shrugs, still grinning. "You called me sweetheart."

I blink. Open my mouth. Close it.

The bastard just grins.

"...Fair."

Bree steps up on my other side, and the moment she does, the crowd shifts. Heads turn. Conversations drop off. It's not fear—it's *recognition*. They see her, and something settles.

She doesn't say anything. Just meets their eyes, one by one, and nods.

That's all it takes.

The door to the pub swings open, and Mo steps out—arms crossed, half-grin in place, cigarette tucked behind his ear like punctuation.

"Well," he says, voice carrying across the street. "Looks like we're throwing a party after all."

I laugh. Can't help it. "You got a guest list, or are we just winging it?"

"Winging it's more fun." He jerks his chin toward the crowd. "You coordinate this mess, or did it just happen?"

"Little bit of both." I step forward, scanning the faces. "How many vehicles you got?"

"Not enough." He pulls a battered phone from his pocket and starts scrolling. "But I know people. Give me ten minutes."

"Ten?"

"Five if you stop talking."

I grin wider. "I like you."

"Everyone does." He's already dialing, phone pressed to his ear as he walks back inside. "Yeah, it's me. I need every truck, van, and beater you've got that still runs. No, I don't care if it's registered. We're moving an army."

It takes closer to fifteen minutes, but Mo wasn't kidding.

Vehicles start rolling in from every direction—pickup trucks with rusted beds, vans with peeling paint, a couple of sedans that look like they've seen better decades. One guy shows up on a motorcycle with a sidecar, and I'm pretty sure that's not going to fit anyone, but the effort's appreciated.

The Feeders don't wait for instructions. They just start loading up—gear in the back, bodies piling in wherever there's space. It's chaotic, but it works. Somehow, it works.

I'm helping tie down a stack of supply crates when Zira appears at my elbow, eyebrow raised.

"This your doing?"

"Wes's, actually." I nod toward where he's standing with Bree, looking somewhere between proud and terrified. "He's got a gift."

"Apparently." She glances around, assessing. "Think we'll all fit?"

"If we get creative."

"Creative's one word for it."

Mo reappears, wiping grease off his hands with a rag. "All right, listen up!" His voice cuts through the noise, and everyone stops. "We're heading out in five. Stay together, don't do anything stupid, and if you see trouble, you radio ahead. Got it?"

A murmur of agreement ripples through the crowd.

It took longer than expected to get everyone ready—loading the vans, securing supplies, arguing over routes. By the time the last engine started, the city lights had dimmed to a low glow against the clouds. We'd already lost a couple of hours to chaos.

He turns to me. "You riding with the Source, or you want shotgun in the lead truck?"

I glance back at Bree. She's talking quietly with Thane and Stellan, the raven still perched on her shoulder like it belongs there. Gray's nearby, arms crossed, scanning the street like he's already expecting threats.

"Lead truck," I say. "Someone's gotta make sure we don't drive off a cliff."

"Smart man."

The convoy forms up quickly after that—vehicles lined up in a ragged procession that looks more like a junkyard parade than an invasion force. But there's something about it that feels *right*. Like we're not just moving—we're *claiming* something.

I climb into the passenger seat of Mo's truck, and he cranks the engine. It groans, sputters, then roars to life.

"Think they'll follow?" I ask, nodding toward the line of vehicles behind us.

"They came this far, didn't they?" He shifts into gear. "Besides, they're not following *us*."

He's right. Through the side mirror, I can see Bree in the third vehicle back, framed by the window. Even from here, the Ether around her is visible—soft silver light threading through the air.

They're following *her*.

Mo pulls out onto the road, and one by one, the rest fall in line. Headlights flicker on, engines rumble, and the whole mess of us starts moving.

I lean back in my seat, watching the mismatched convoy stretch out behind us in the mirror.

"Guess we're really doing this," I mutter.

Mo glances over, grin still in place. "Hell of a party."

Yeah. Hell of a party.

Chapter 31
BREE

The convoy rolls out of the city like a parade that forgot to ask permission.

I'm in the third vehicle with Thane and Stellan, the raven still perched on my shoulder like it's claimed permanent residence. Through the windshield, I can see the line of headlights stretching ahead—trucks, vans, sedans, some that look like they're held together with hope and duct tape.

Behind us, even more lights.

The energy is intoxicating. Windows down, voices carrying over the rumble of engines, laughter cutting through the night air. For the first time in what feels like forever, it doesn't feel like we're running.

It feels like we're *moving*.

My Ether hums quietly, threading through the space between us and the vehicle ahead. I let myself sink into it—the warmth, the connection, the sense that something impossible is finally happening.

Then we pass the last streetlight.

The road opens up into countryside—dark fields stretching out on either side, the faint scent of water on the air from somewhere in the distance. The city lights fade behind us, and suddenly all I can see is us.

Headlights for miles.

A chain of mismatched vehicles, loud and obvious and impossible to miss.

My stomach drops.

"Stellan," I say quietly.

He glances over. "What's wrong?"

"We're too visible."

"We look like a festival caravan," Thane nods from the backseat, voice dry. "Or a very poorly planned invasion."

I twist in my seat, looking back through the rear window. The line of vehicles behind us curves around a bend in the road, lights blazing like stars falling in formation.

"Every person with a phone is about to record this," Stellan says calmly. "We'll be trending before we hit the freeway."

My chest tightens. "We can't— we need to stop."

Stellan doesn't argue. He just reaches for the radio clipped to the dash and clicks it on. "Lead vehicle, pull over. Now."

Mo's voice crackles back immediately. "Copy. You got a reason, or we just taking a scenic break?"

"Bree's call," Stellan says, glancing at me.

I lean forward. "Pull over, Mo. Everyone."

One by one, the vehicles slow and stop along the shoulder of the road. Headlights cut through the darkness, illuminating cornfields and open grass. The lake is faintly visible in the distance, a dark line against the horizon.

I step out before the truck fully stops, boots hitting gravel. The night air is cooler here, sharp and clean. Engines tick as they cool, and voices rise in confusion.

"What's going on?"

"We stopping already?"

"Is something wrong?"

I pace once, hands in my hair, trying to think. The raven shifts on my shoulder, wings rustling softly.

Then I turn and face them.

Mo's already walking over, Jace right behind him. Thane and Stellan flank me without being asked. Gray, Rhett, Wes, and Theo emerge from the vehicles nearby, forming a loose circle.

"We can't take this many people on the highway," I say, voice steady even though my pulse isn't. "Someone's going to notice. There'll be drones, checkpoints, news coverage—we'll be front page by sunrise."

Mo crosses his arms, considering. "You're not wrong. But you're also not turning back."

"No." I shake my head. "We split up."

Silence. Then murmurs ripple through the crowd.

"Groups of five or six," I continue, louder now. "Take different routes. Avoid main roads. Meet at—" I pause, looking at Thane.

He steps forward. "The boundary markers. Stone pillars with old Scarborne sigils—about an hour out. That's the sanctuary border." He checks his phone, scrolling before reading off coordinates. "Forty-three point two-one north, eighty-eight point four-seven west. Follow those, you'll find them."

Stellan nods. "Five, maybe six hours if the road stays clear. Gives us time to regroup before we move in."

"Do **not** cross the border," I add. "Pull over and wait near the treeline until everyone's accounted for. No lights once you leave the main road. No magic use unless absolutely necessary. If anyone's stopped or questioned, you're running charity supplies or doing a delivery route. Nothing more."

Wes steps forward. "And if someone doesn't make it?"

"Then we go without them," I say quietly. "But we don't wait. We can't."

The weight of that settles over the group like fog.

Jace breaks it with a half-grin. "So much for the party."

I almost smile. "The party's still on. We're just not giving the world an invitation."

A few quiet laughs. Nods. The tension eases, just slightly.

Mo claps his hands once. "All right, you heard her. Group up, pick your routes, stay smart. Move out in five."

The crowd scatters, voices rising again as people divide into smaller clusters. Engines start back up one by one, headlights flickering as vehicles peel away in different directions.

I watch the first group disappear into the darkness, taillights swallowed by the night.

Then the second. The third.

The road feels quieter now. Heavier.

Thane steps up beside me, hands in his pockets. "You're learning what leadership costs."

I don't look at him. "Feels like I'm just learning how to breathe with it."

He nods. "Good. Because this is only the beginning."

I look toward the horizon where the sanctuary lies hidden in the distance, and I whisper, "Then let's finish it."

I climb back into the truck. Stellan starts the engine, and we pull back onto the road.

The convoy is fragmented now—invisible, scattered, impossible to track.

But we're still moving.

And we're not stopping.

Chapter 32
GRAY

We're the second vehicle to arrive.

I step out of the truck, boots hitting gravel, and the first thing I notice is how quiet it is. No birds. No rustling. Just the low hum of idling engines and the sound of doors opening behind me.

The others are getting out too—voices low, cautious. Nobody crosses the road yet.

I scan the treeline, and something tugs at the back of my mind. Familiar, but I can't place it yet.

Stone pillars rise out of the undergrowth ahead, half-buried in moss and vines. The boundary markers Thane mentioned. I walk closer, and the moment my hand touches the rough surface, recognition hits.

"We've been here before," I say quietly.

Rhett stops beside me. "What?"

"This exact spot." I look back toward the road, then at the forest. "This is where we parked the first time. When Bree found the well."

Understanding ripples through the group. Jace's eyes widen. "Oh shit. You're right."

Seth moves closer to the markers. "Same place?"

"Yeah." I nod toward the trees. "The well's about fifty yards in that direction."

Jace laughs—sudden and bright. "Remember when we all ran back to the cars like idiots?"

Rhett grins despite himself. "You nearly took me out."

"Because Gray cut in front of me without warning—"

"Because Theo was spiraling about foxes—"

"There *was* a fox," Theo mutters.

Wes shakes his head, almost smiling. "And Bree just... walked into the forest like it was the most natural thing in the world."

"While we panicked over leaving the engines running," Jace finishes, still grinning.

The laughter spreads—quiet, warm, human. For a second, the tension breaks. We're just a bunch of guys remembering the first time everything changed.

Then the moment fades.

Because this isn't the same.

I turn back toward the markers, and the warmth drains out of me.

The Ether around them is brighter than it should be. Thicker. Vibrating against something I can't see.

"You feel that?" Rhett asks, his grin gone.

"Yeah." I step closer to the treeline. "Something's off."

"Different from last time?" Seth asks quietly.

"Way different." I crouch, press my palm to the earth. The ground hums with old magic. "The Ether wasn't this active before. It's like something woke it up."

And then I see it.

Silver threads run the forest floor like veins—faint, frayed, pulsing weakly. They aren't creeping in; they're pulling out, all of them drawn in the same direction. They stop hard at the boundary markers, like they've hit glass.

"Those are hers," I say. "Bree's."

Stellan studies the line where the threads hit the ward. "The border's holding. For now."

Rhett's jaw works. "How much did he take?"

Bree doesn't answer. She's staring at the pale threads with that steady, dangerous calm. "Enough."

I stand. "Then we cut the line at the source."

The hair at the base of my neck bristles. My wolf stirs, uneasy.

Bree appears at my shoulder, voice low. "What is it?"

"Not sure yet." I stand, brushing dirt off my hand. "But something's been here. Recently."

She doesn't flinch at the charge in the air; she never does anymore.

Her jaw tightens. "Riley?"

"Maybe." I scan the treeline. "Or someone else."

Thane's voice cuts in from behind us. "Nyx was watching us the first time we were here. At the well."

The memory hits me—that damn crow perched in the trees, eyes too intelligent, tracking Bree's every move.

"She knows we're here," I say quietly.

The last few vehicles trickle in over the next half hour. By the time everyone's accounted for, there are maybe one hundred and forty people scattered along the roadside—Feeders, mostly, with a handful of others who followed because they believed in something they didn't have words for yet.

Bree stands near the center, flanked by Thane and Stellan. She's giving quiet instructions, coordinating the approach. Stellan says something low, and she laughs—soft, unexpected.

I catch the moment Stellan's hand lingers at her waist before he steps back.

Something shifts in my chest. Not jealousy. Just... awareness.

She's not just ours anymore. She's becoming herself in ways none of us can fully claim.

And that's how it should be.

Her eyes find mine across the space between us. She smiles—warm, certain—and nods slightly. An invitation.

I move closer without thinking, drawn by that quiet pull that's always been there.

When I reach her, she doesn't say anything. Just lets her shoulder rest against mine for a breath, solid and real.

It's enough for both of us.

Bree looks past the markers, toward the sanctuary hidden somewhere in the darkness. "Nyx said to look for the glowing daisies. That's our way in."

I nod. "Then we move careful. Stay tight."

She glances back at the group, then at me. "You think it's a trap?"

"I think we're about to find out."

We cross the boundary together—Bree first, the rest of us close behind.

The moment we pass the pillars, the air shifts. Warmer. Heavier. The Ether coils tighter around us like mist, silver threads weaving through the trees.

Bree looks toward the forest, eyes unfocused for a moment. Then she turns, voice quiet but certain. "This way."

I glance at the others. No one questions it.

She starts walking, and we follow—deeper into the trees, away from where we entered last time.

The Ether shifts around us as we move, silver weaving through the darkness. I stay close, watching the way the light flickers against the undergrowth.

Wrong. Like something disturbed it before we arrived.

Like something's been using this path.

"Gray?" Bree's voice pulls me back.

I meet her eyes. "Stay close. Whatever's waiting for us in there already knows we're coming."

Chapter 33
SETH

I've never been here before.

That's the first thing that hits me as we move deeper into the trees—this place is older than anything I've seen in the Void. Older, and somehow more alive.

The air hums. Not with sound, but with presence. Like the forest itself is breathing.

Bree walks ahead, leading us without hesitation. The others follow close—Thane and Stellan flanking her, Gray and Rhett just behind. I stay near the back with Wes and Jace, watching.

That's when I notice the veins.

As Bree passes over the silver threads that run through the earth beneath our feet, they lift—thin ribbons of vapor rising like steam, drawn toward her.

I stop, watching one thread curl upward and dissolve against her ankle before disappearing entirely.

"You seeing this?" I ask quietly.

Wes glances down, then at Bree. His eyes narrow. "Her Ether's—different."

I look closer. He's right. The silver still swirls around her, but the black that's been threaded through it is thinner now.

The land is giving it back. Whatever was taken from her, the sanctuary is trying to return it.

"There's a fox."

Theo's voice cuts through the quiet, and everyone stops.

He's staring into the trees, eyes bright. "There's a fox."

And then I see it.

The fox steps out from between the trees—sleek, silver-eyed, its edges shimmering like it's made of mist and starlight.

"Isn't that the one from the Void?" Jace asks.

Wes nods slowly. "Yeah. What's it doing here?"

Gray's voice is rougher than usual. "No idea. But it saved us. All of us."

We all nod in agreement, watching as the fox circles Theo's boots once—almost playful—then trots straight to Bree.

She kneels, and the fox presses its head against her knee.

Her Ether shifts, almost welcoming the creature, while the raven on her shoulder ruffles its feathers, leaning forward slightly.

Rhett's voice is quiet. "We never got to say thank you."

The fox looks up, ears twitching. A pulse of light moves through its fur—silver, soft, warm.

"You just did," Bree whispers.

The trees open into a clearing, and the well appears.

It's smaller than I expected—stone rim worn smooth by time, veined with light that pulses faintly like a heartbeat. Daisies bloom thick around the base, their petals shimmering with silver and black threads woven through the white.

The air smells like rain and ozone. Like magic held in suspension.

Everyone goes silent.

Even the Ether hum quiets, as if the forest is holding its breath.

Bree walks forward slowly, the fox padding beside her, the raven still perched on her shoulder. She stops at the edge of the well, staring down into the darkness.

I move closer, careful not to disturb whatever's happening here.

"It's beautiful," I say quietly.

She doesn't look at me. "It's alive."

A hiss breaks the quiet.

The snake glides from the grass, crossing my boots before I can react. I freeze, every instinct screaming don't move, but it doesn't stop. Just continues forward, climbing Bree's wrist in one fluid motion.

The moment it settles, something changes.

All three familiars are touching her now—the raven on her shoulder, the fox pressed against her leg, the snake coiled on her wrist.

The last of the black begins to move—slow at first, then faster. The darkness unspools, drawn through all three of them until it fades into nothing.

In a blink, she's radiant. Pure silver light.

The air shifts and the whole forest exhales.

No one moves.

Bree looks lighter. Not brighter, not stronger—just free.

She doesn't claim the magic.

The magic claims her.

Bree reaches out, fingers brushing the daisies' glow. Her voice trembles, reverent. "It's been so long since I saw something so beautiful."

From the shadows, a voice answers—quiet, strained.

"I knew you'd be back."

Everyone freezes.

A figure steps forward into the light—black, unsteady, magic flickering weakly around her.

My brain stutters.

Wait.

There are two of them.

Same face. Same build. Same dark hair.

But the one in the shadows looks wrong—hollowed out, exhausted. Her green eyes are dim, her shoulders tight with stress.

Riley.

Gray's growl rumbles low. "What the hell—"

"Is that—" Jace cuts himself off. "What the fuck?"

Bree doesn't move back.

Doesn't look afraid.

Just meets Riley's gaze and waits.

Riley's eyes track the familiars, the daisies, the way the Ether pools around Bree's feet.

For a heartbeat, it's like the forest itself can't tell which one of them is real.

Chapter 34
BREE

Riley steps out of the shadows across the clearing—and her knees buckle.

I move. Around the well's stone rim, through the glowing daisies.

"Bree, don't!"

"It's a trap!"

"Stay back!"

Voices behind me. I don't stop.

My arms wrap around her waist before she falls.

The Ether between us flares—silver meeting black. Then settles.

No attack. No trick. Just grief.

I brace her weight, adjusting my stance. The ground gives beneath us. The well rises behind me now, stone veined with faint light.

The air tastes of the Void—thin and wrong.

Up close, I see the details I couldn't from across the clearing. Shoulders curved inward. Hands trembling. Silver threads barely flickering through black Ether that clings like ash.

My own Ether rises, steady and bright.

She looks hollow, waiting to break.

My Ether reaches toward her—slow and careful. Recognition like a scar I know the shape of.

"I'm sorry," she whispers, and her voice cracks. "I'm so sorry."

Behind me, the guys close in. Rhett's flames dim to embers. Thane's face is carved from stone. Theo's eyes go unfocused. Wes shakes his head. Seth stays at the edge, silent.

Riley's staring at me like I'm the last light in existence.

"I thought it was my idea." Her voice breaks, knees threatening to give out again. I adjust, lowering us both until we're kneeling. "Ethos just... whispered. Said he believed in me. Said I could fix what you were too afraid to touch."

My chest tightens.

"He told me power was the same as love." A sob tears free. "That if I took your place, people would adore me. That I'd be the one they chose."

Her fingers curl into my shirt. "People suffer because of me. All those people—enslaved, starving—because I wanted to be... enough."

Enough.

The word breaks something in my chest.

I know that word. I know that weight.

"You were always enough," I say quietly.

She shakes her head, frantic. "No. I wasn't. That's why I did it. Why I let him convince me that switching places would—" Her voice catches. "I thought I was using him. I thought having one of the most powerful beings in existence bonded to me meant I had control."

Behind us, Thane's voice cuts in, low and dangerous. "Ethos is bonded to you?"

Riley's eyes squeeze shut. "He told me it was different. That our bond was special. That with me, we could reshape everything."

"And you believed him?" Gray's wolf ripples beneath his skin.

"Yes," Her voice drops to barely a whisper. "I wanted to believe someone saw me as more than just a reflection. More than just... her shadow."

The Ether pulses between us—recognition, understanding, shared pain.

I've spent my whole life being told I was too much or not enough.

She spent hers being told she was only an echo.

"Riley." I wait until she meets my eyes. "What did he do to you?"

Her breath hitches. "After you escaped, he came back. Angrier than I'd ever seen him. Said you weren't worthy of him. That he needed to feed to regain what you'd taken." She swallows hard. "Every time I tried to pull back, he'd whisper that I owed him. That this was the cost of becoming you."

Ice slides down my spine.

The guys exchange looks, tension crackling in the air between them.

"How long?" Stellan's voice is colder than I've ever heard it.

Riley's laugh is bitter and broken. "I lost track. Time doesn't work right when someone's feeding from your soul."

Wes moves closer, his hunger carefully controlled. "Is he still feeding?"

She shakes her head slowly. "He stopped. Two days ago, maybe three. Just vanished." Her voice drops. "I think he's done with me. Used me up."

The forest goes silent.

Even the daisies seem to dim.

Riley's fingers tighten on my shirt.

"We could still be whole."

Everyone stiffens.

"What?" I breathe.

Riley lifts her head, and for the first time since she appeared, there's something other than despair in her eyes.

Hope.

Desperate, fragile hope.

"Your Ether," she whispers. "It can do it. Even without the mirrors. I can feel it. You could... we could..."

"No." Thane's voice cuts through the moment like a blade.

Riley flinches but doesn't look away from me. "Please. I don't want to be alone in the dark anymore."

The Ether between us swirls—two threads reaching for each other. Mine hesitates first, because it remembers what happens when I don't.

"Bree, don't." Rhett's hand lands on my shoulder. "We don't know what she's carrying."

"That's exactly how Ethos baited her," Thane adds, moving closer. "Promises of wholeness. Of being enough."

Theo staggers forward, eyes whitening with vision, breath caught mid-word. "If you merge with her, you merge with him."

Gray's voice is rough, half-growl. "She's still tethered. I can smell it on her."

"She's the conduit," Stellan says, his expression carefully blank but something sharp beneath it. "If you fuse, you finish his work."

Riley's breath hitches. "No. It's not like that. I just—I don't want to disappear. Please, Bree. You're the only one who can—"

"Stop." My voice cracks.

Everyone freezes.

I look down at Riley—at my own face hollowed out by betrayal and hunger and regret—and feel the Ether inside me reaching toward her.

It wants to heal. To make her whole.

That's what it does. What it's always done.

But it also taught me something in that chamber of ash and mirrors.

Creation through choice. Not compulsion.

"I can't," I whisper.

Riley's face crumbles. "Why not?"

"Because I don't know where you end and he begins." The words tear out of me. "And I won't risk losing myself to find out."

The Ether lashes once—like something wounded—before sinking back into my skin.

Her sob echoes through the clearing.

Something between us finally shatters—not with light or sound, but with understanding.

The guys move closer—a protective ring around us both, magic and weapons ready, Ether bristling.

But Riley doesn't attack. Doesn't fight back.

She just slumps in my arms, every bit of fight draining out of her as consciousness starts to slip.

"Without the mirrors," she murmurs, voice fading. "It's still you and me. We could be whole."

Then her eyes close, and she goes limp.

The daisies' glow dims. The forest holds its breath.

I lower her carefully to the ground beside the well, my hands shaking.

The guys close in, forming a tighter circle.

"What do we do with her?" Jace asks quietly.

"We can't kill what's left of her," Thane says, though he doesn't sound happy about it. "But if Bree listens to her, Ethos wins."

Rhett plants his palms on the ground, fire flickering under his skin, the heat steady—anchoring all of us. "Then we don't leave her side."

I stare down at Riley's unconscious form—at the silver threads still woven through her Ether, at the exhaustion carved into her features.

"She's not wrong," I say quietly.

Everyone looks at me.

"If we could rejoin—maybe I could close him off. Cut the connection. Make her whole without..." I trail off, unable to finish the thought.

The clearing seems to darken, as if the Void itself is leaning closer to hear my choice.

"Bree." Theo's voice is gentle. "You don't have to save everyone."

"I know." My throat tightens. "But what if I can?"

Thane crouches beside me, silver eyes meeting mine. "And what if trying costs you everything?"

I don't answer.

Because I don't know.

The daisies pulse with silver light, and somewhere in the distance, I swear I hear Ethos laughing.

"If wholeness means losing myself," I whisper, "what does that make me now?"

Chapter 35
BREE

The silence stretches.

Riley lies unconscious between us, her breathing shallow. The daisies' light pulses in time with her heartbeat—faint, struggling.

"We need to move her," Gray says, breaking the quiet. "Get her somewhere we can protect."

"Protect her from what?" Jace asks. "Us or him?"

"Both, maybe." Wes shifts his weight, eyes on Riley's face. "If Ethos can reach her through that bond—"

"Then we sever it," Thane says flatly. "Cut the connection before he tries again."

"You mean kill her." Stellan's voice is cold.

"I mean end what he started."

"That's the same thing."

The air crackles with tension.

"She doesn't deserve to die for this," Rhett says, fire flickering under his palms. "Ethos manipulated her. Used her."

"And she let him," Thane counters. "She chose to switch places. Chose to wear Bree's face. Chose to—"

"She was alone." My voice cuts through. "Told her whole life she was nothing but a reflection. An echo. Then someone powerful tells her she could be more—that she could be chosen, loved, worthy—and you think that's a real choice?"

Thane's jaw tightens but he doesn't look away.

"I'm not saying what she did was right," I continue. "But I understand why she did it."

"Understanding doesn't make it safe," Gray says quietly. "The tether's still there. I can smell it on her. Ethos could come back through that bond anytime he wants."

"Then we find a way to break it."

"How?" Jace asks. "We don't even know what we're dealing with."

"She could be a weapon he's planted," Thane adds. "Waiting to go off the moment we trust her."

The words land heavy.

For a moment, no one speaks.

Then Theo's voice cuts through, calm and certain. "This isn't our choice to make."

Everyone goes still.

"It's hers," he continues, eyes clear now. "It's always been hers."

The words hang in the air.

One by one, the guys turn to look at me.

Rhett's the first to speak, his voice gentler than I've heard it in days. "What feels right, Bree?"

I stare down at Riley's unconscious form. At the silver threads trying to flicker through the black. At my own face worn hollow by betrayal and hunger.

"I don't know," I whisper.

"You don't have to know," Wes says softly. "You just have to feel."

"What do you want to do?" Gray asks.

My throat tightens. "I want to help her. But I don't know if I can without losing myself."

Seth moves closer, crouching at the edge of our circle. "Then don't do it alone."

"Whatever you choose," Stellan says, "we'll stand with you."

"Even if it's dangerous?" I ask.

"Especially then," Jace says, and there's no humor in his voice now. Just certainty.

Thane's silver eyes meet mine. "I still think it's a risk. But it's your risk to take. And we'll face whatever comes after together."

Something in my chest cracks open.

They're not trying to protect me from the choice. They're promising to stand in it with me.

"I want to try," I say finally. "To heal her without merging. To make her whole while keeping us separate."

"Is that possible?" Rhett asks.

"I don't know." I look down at my hands. "But the Ether wants to heal."

I kneel beside Riley, placing one hand flat against the earth and the other on her chest—over her heart where the corrupted bond must anchor.

The moment my palm touches the ground, I feel it.

The sanctuary responding. The land itself humming with Ether that's been spreading here for who knows how long, fed by my presence, my power, my choices.

It rises through me like a tide.

Silver light floods up through my arm, into my chest, spreading like warmth before flowing down through my other hand into Riley.

She gasps, back arching off the ground.

The black Ether wrapped around her begins to move—not retreating, but balancing. The corruption doesn't disappear. It clarifies. Black and silver weaving together until they're equal—half shadow, half light. Not corrupted anymore. Just... different.

Mirror-born.

Healed but not erased.

And yet, whole.

The bond to Ethos shivers, straining against the flood of pure Ether—then snaps.

The sound breaks the clearing open.

Riley's eyes fly open, glowing pure silver for one impossible breath before fading back to green.

She stares up at me, gasping for air.

"You didn't—" Her voice cracks. "We're not—"

"No," I say quietly, pulling my hands back. The Ether settles, sinking back into the earth. "You're still you. I'm still me."

Her eyes fill with tears. "Why?"

Riley sits up slowly, staring down at her own hands. The Ether threaded through her fingers is steady now—black and silver weaving together until they're equal. Half shadow, half light. Not corrupted anymore. Just... different.

Mirror-born.

"I can't feel him anymore," she whispers. "The bond—it's gone."

"Good," Thane says flatly.

Riley's eyes find his, then move to each of the others. Lingering on their faces like she's seeing them for the first time. "I'm sorry. For all of it. For what I did, what I let happen, what I—"

"Later," Gray cuts in, not unkindly. "Right now we need to move."

Riley looks back at me, tears threatening to spill. "Why did you save me? After everything?"

I pull my hands back, the Ether settling. "Because you don't have to be whole to be worthy of being seen."

The words hang in the air.

I look up and find Theo watching me, his eyes soft with recognition. He smiles—small and certain.

I smile back.

He nods, just once. Understanding passing between us without needing words.

Riley's breath catches, something breaking open in her expression. She nods too, slower, like she's testing the weight of those words and finding them true.

"Thank you," she whispers.

For a moment, the clearing holds its breath. The daisies pulse once, bright and steady, like the land itself is acknowledging what just happened.

"He's right," Stellan adds, already scanning the forest. "That bond breaking made noise. Ethos felt it. And if he felt it—"

"Others did too," Thane finishes grimly.

The air shifts. Colder.

"The sanctuary," I say, pushing to my feet. My legs shake but hold. "We need to get to the sanctuary."

Riley struggles to stand, swaying. Her knees give out.

I catch her before she falls, sliding my arm around her waist. She stiffens, then leans into me.

"You're with us now," I say quietly, meeting her eyes. "We've got you."

Her breath hitches. For a moment she just stares at me—at the face that's not quite hers anymore, at the power she tried to steal and the mercy she doesn't deserve.

Then she nods.

Stellan steps forward, his fingers going to his lips. The whistle that cuts through the forest is sharp and clear—three short bursts, then one long.

A signal.

In the distance, I hear movement. Voices. The sound of over a hundred people stirring to life in the darkness.

The Feeders we came with now headed our way.

"They'll follow," Stellan says, lowering his hand. "We move now, we move together."

Rhett's flames flare brighter, lighting our path. Gray shifts half-way, senses sharpening. Jace's knives catch the silver light. Wes moves to my other side, steady and quiet. Theo's already three steps ahead, eyes distant with vision. Seth takes up the rear, silent as always.

Thane looks at me once—silver eyes unreadable—then turns toward the sanctuary.

"Let's go."

We move as one.

Riley stumbles but I keep her upright, and Wes shifts closer to help bear her weight. The forest parts around us, the daisies lighting our way like breadcrumbs leading home.

Behind us, the caravan follows.

And ahead—somewhere in the dark—the sanctuary waits.

Chapter 36
BREE

We move through the forest in silence, the daisies lighting our path like stars fallen to earth. Riley stumbles between Wes and me, her weight shared, her breathing steadier now. Behind us, the caravan follows—all those footsteps moving as one.

Thane leads, silver eyes cutting through the dark. Gray ranges ahead in half-shift, senses sharp. Rhett's flames pulse steady, anchoring the center of our formation. Jace and Stellan flank the sides. Seth brings up the rear, silent as always.

The forest feels different now. Lighter, like it's been holding its breath and finally let go.

Another set of footsteps behind us—quick but unhurried.

I glance back. Silver-rimmed eyes catch the light.

Zira.

"Sources say the sanctuary's empty," she calls, falling into step beside Thane.

I slow, turning. "Empty?"

She nods, then spots Riley and stops short—double-take, eyes wide. "Oh."

"She's with us," I say quietly.

Zira's gaze flicks to me, then back to Riley. "Looks that way." Another beat. "Phil and the Counsel are already moving. They're calling it theirs now. The sanctuary. Determined to keep what they've 'reclaimed.' Should be here in a few days."

Thane mutters a curse under his breath. Stellan's jaw tightens.

"That gives us a few days. Then we'll show them what reclaimed really means," I say.

The words come out steadier than I feel. But they're true.

The group keeps moving, faster now. Riley leans heavier on Wes, exhaustion catching up. I ease back, letting them move ahead.

Theo's a few steps behind, eyes distant but aware. Always aware.

I fall into step beside him.

He glances at me, the corner of his mouth lifting. "You okay?"

"Yeah." I look ahead at the others, at Riley's silhouette between Wes and Gray now. "I think so."

"You did good back there."

"I did what felt right."

"That's the same thing," he says quietly.

We walk in silence for a moment, the forest breathing around us. The daisies glow brighter where our feet touch the earth, like the land itself is welcoming us home.

"You said that to me once," I say, the words slipping out before I can stop them. "That thing about being seen."

Theo's steps slow, just slightly. "I remember."

"Back when none of us knew what we were doing."

His mouth twitches. "Still not sure we do."

I laugh—soft, unexpected. "Maybe not. But it's still true. What you said."

He looks at me then, really looks at me, and something in his expression shifts. Softens.

"You don't have to be whole to be worthy of being seen," I whisper, echoing the words I just gave Riley. The words he gave me first.

The Ether hums low in my chest, answering the truth of it.

Theo stops walking.

I stop too, turning to face him.

The forest holds its breath around us. The caravan moves ahead, giving us space without seeming to notice. Or maybe they notice and just... let us have this moment.

"Bree—" he starts, but I don't let him finish.

I step forward and kiss him.

It's not tentative. Not questioning. Just... real.

For half a heartbeat, he goes still—surprised.

Then he moves.

His hand comes up to cup my face, thumb brushing my cheek as he tilts my head back and takes the kiss deeper. Bold. Certain. This is Theo I've never seen before—Theo who knows what he wants and isn't afraid to claim it.

His other arm slides around my waist, pulling me closer, and I feel the steady thrum of his heartbeat against my chest. The Ether rises between us, warm, present, right.

When we finally pull apart, I'm breathless.

He's smiling—really smiling—and it transforms his whole face.

"I've wanted to do that for years," he says quietly.

"Why didn't you?"

"Because you weren't ready." His thumb traces my jaw. "And I would've waited forever if that's what you needed."

My throat tightens. "I'm still not whole, Theo. I'm still—"

"I know." He leans his forehead against mine. "And I don't care. You're exactly who you're supposed to be."

The words break something open in my chest—something that's been locked tight for so long I forgot it was there.

I kiss him again, softer this time. A promise instead of a question.

When we pull back, the forest has gone quiet. The caravan's moved ahead, giving us space, but I can see Rhett's flames in the distance, waiting.

"And somehow you still manage to surprise me," he says running his fingers down my arm. He takes my hand, lacing our fingers together.

"Come on," he says gently. "Let's go home."

We catch up to the others, and no one says anything. But I feel the shift—the way Gray's shoulders relax slightly, the way Jace's grin widens just a fraction. The way Rhett glances back and nods once, approval clear in his eyes.

Ahead, the forest begins to thin.

The first outline of the sanctuary appears through the trees—stone and light, waiting.

"Home," I whisper.

And for the first time in my life, the word feels true.

Chapter 37
THANE

We crest the hill just as the first light breaks through the trees.

Bree reaches the top first—and stops so abruptly I nearly walk into her.

"Thane," she breathes.

I step beside her and look down.

The sanctuary spreads below us—stone and garden, walls and pathways. It should be empty. Zira said it was empty.

It's not.

The courtyard is alive with movement. Dozens of figures working the grounds—tilling, hauling, building. But the rhythm is wrong. Too uniform. Too quiet.

Then I see the collars—silver bands around every throat, glowing faintly with suppression runes. The kind the Counsel uses to dampen Feeder magic. To keep us compliant.

My stomach drops.

"They're bound," Bree whispers beside me.

"They're enslaved," I correct, voice flat. The word tastes like ash. "We used to call it protection."

Two guards stand at the gate, relaxed and bored. They're not expecting trouble. Why would they? The Ether's doing Riley's work for her—keeping everyone docile, obedient.

Bree's hands curl into fists. Her Ether rises, silver threads flickering at her fingertips. "I can feel them. Their magic—it's crying out."

"I know." My throat tightens. "I can too."

Because that's what we do. What Feeders do. We feel the emotional weight of everyone around us, and right now it's crushing.

Despair. Exhaustion. Resignation.

The others catch up behind us. Riley stumbles between Wes and Zira, her face pale.

"I'm sorry," Riley whispers, voice breaking. "I'm so sorry."

No one answers her.

Gray moves to my other side, taking in the scene below. His jaw works, but he doesn't speak.

Rhett's flames flicker out completely.

Theo's eyes go distant, seeing futures I don't want to know about.

Bree's breathing hard beside me, her whole body trembling. Not with fear. With rage.

"I can't stand here and watch this," she says quietly.

I look at her. Really look at her. The woman who's been broken and rebuilt more times than anyone should have to endure. The woman who just healed her own mirror self instead of destroying her. The woman who keeps choosing compassion when the world gives her every reason not to.

She's looking at me now, waiting. Asking without words: *What do we do?*

And I realize this is the moment. The choice I've been avoiding for centuries.

Stand with the Counsel's order, or stand with her truth.

"Then don't," I say.

Her eyes widen slightly.

"We go down there," I continue, voice steady now. "Together."

She nods once, certain.

I turn to the others. "Stay back. All of you. If this goes wrong—"

"It won't," Bree says.

Gray steps forward. "Bree—"

"Please." She meets his eyes, then each of the others in turn. "Trust me."

Rhett's the first to nod. Then Theo. One by one, they step back.

Riley's still whispering apologies, tears streaming down her face. Zira puts a hand on her shoulder, steadying her.

Bree and I start down the slope.

The Ether responds to her immediately—daisies blooming in our footsteps, the air warming despite the morning chill. The land recognizes her. Welcomes her.

The guards at the gate finally notice us approaching. One straightens, reaching for his weapon.

Bree doesn't break stride.

The air shifts. The daisies at the gate shimmer, and a soft pulse of silver light rolls outward like a wave.

Both guards sway, then collapse—breathing slow and even. Asleep.

"You didn't kill them," I say quietly.

"They're not the enemy," Bree replies. "Not yet."

We reach the stone wall together. It's higher than it looked from above, rough stone that's stood for centuries.

Bree climbs first. I move beside her, steadying her hand when she slips on a loose stone. Our eyes meet for a breath—silent understanding passing between us.

We're in this together now. Whatever comes next.

We pull ourselves up and over, dropping down into the courtyard on the other side.

The moment we land, heads turn.

Feeders stop working, tools falling from numb hands. They stare at us—at Bree's silver Ether, at my face they probably recognize from Counsel meetings.

One woman meets my eyes and flinches.

And I feel it run through me.

They fear me. They see me as the enforcer. As the one who kept this system running.

And they're right.

Then Bree goes rigid beside me.

"Mairen," she breathes.

I follow her gaze across the courtyard. A woman kneels in the garden, hands in the dirt, collar glowing at her throat. Her face is lined with exhaustion, but I recognize her—the one who cooked for us, for everyone, who came to the sanctuary months ago with her family.

Beside her, a man works silently. Torn. Her husband.

And further back, near the stone wall—their son, Kellan. Barely sixteen, shoulders hunched under the weight of a collar that shouldn't exist.

Bree's hand finds mine, squeezing so hard it hurts.

"They came here for safety," she whispers, voice breaking. "I promised them safety."

More faces turn toward us now. The collars flare, then flicker—fighting her Ether and losing.

Mairen looks up. Her eyes widen—recognition, then hope, then fear all crossing her face in the span of a heartbeat.

My voice cracks when I finally find it.

"Stop."

The entire courtyard goes still.

Chapter 38
RHETT

By the time we reach the gate, the guards are out cold—laid down gentle by Bree's Ether, not a mark on them.

Thane and Bree stand inside the courtyard, every eye fixed on them. Every collar still glows faintly in the morning light. Every breath feels wrong.

I step through the arch and stop.

She's shaking.

Not from fear—from everything she's holding back. Her Ether rises around her, bright enough to paint the air itself silver. The sun climbs over the wall behind her, turning the mist into light.

The Feeders stare like they don't believe what they're seeing.

Maybe they don't.

Hell, maybe I don't.

Gray moves up beside me, tension coiled in every line of his body. Theo's eyes are distant, seeing futures I don't want to know about. Jace's usual grin is gone, replaced by something harder. Zira next to Riley, who's almost standing on her own.

The courtyard is too quiet. The kind of quiet that comes from people who've forgotten what hope sounds like.

It's deafening.

The collars hum—faint and constant, like insects in summer heat. But underneath that, I feel something worse. The pressure of despair radiating off the crowd, thick enough to choke on.

My fire senses it like temperature. Pain has weight. Grief has heat.

And there's so much of it here I can barely breathe.

Bree lifts her hands.

The Ether swirls around her—not wild, not chaotic. Deliberate. Controlled. Like sunlight turning solid.

I instinctively move forward, ready to shield her if this goes wrong. But Gray catches my arm, shaking his head once.

She's in control.

The Ether surges outward in a single, rolling wave.

The Feeders flinch back. Some drop to the ground, arms raised to protect themselves. Others brace, eyes squeezed shut, waiting for pain that's always followed power like this.

It crashes over the courtyard like dawn breaking—silver light wrapping around every collar, every throat, every bound soul standing in the dirt.

The collars flare bright.

Then crack.

The sound hits like shattering glass in a thunderstorm—hundreds of silver chimes fracturing at once. Pieces fall to the ground, ringing against stone, disappearing into dust.

Gasps tear through the crowd. Someone sobs. Another laughs—broken and disbelieving.

People fall to their knees, hands flying to their throats, touching skin that hasn't been free in months. Maybe years.

The air smells like ozone and burned metal, but there's no pain. Just release.

I feel it through the bond—her determination, her compassion, her exhaustion threatening to pull her under.

But she doesn't fall.

She stands in the center of it all, glowing like the dawn itself, and when she speaks, her voice carries.

Not loud. Just impossible to ignore.

"You did not deserve this."

The Ether flares brighter with the words, and every freed Feeder looks up.

"No one does. You have a right to freedom. To peace. To your magic—just like everyone else."

Her hands shake, but her voice doesn't.

"This sanctuary will be safe again."

A woman near the front touches her throat, tears streaming down her face.

"You will not mine another bit of Ether for anyone."

The Ether pulses with each vow, alive and answering.

"The oath is here for you. Take it if you choose—or not. The choice is always yours."

Silence stretches, heavy and alive.

"I understand if you want to leave. But if you stay, we rebuild this place the way it was meant to be."

Bree's breath catches, just slightly. I see it in the rise of her shoulders, the way her fingers curl.

"I didn't run. I was captured. I didn't leave you. I couldn't escape."

Her voice cracks on the last word—but she pushes through.

"But I will fight for you. For this sanctuary. For everything it stands for."

She meets their eyes—one by one, steady and certain.

"The freedom to choose."

The words hang in the air like lightning about to strike.

No one moves.

No one breathes.

Then Mairen—the cook who came here with her family, who Bree promised safety—touches the broken collar at her throat and sinks to her knees.

Not in worship.

In release.

Her husband drops beside her, pulling their son close. The boy's shoulders shake with sobs.

One by one, the rest follow.

Heads bowed. Not to Bree's power, but to what she just gave them back.

Choice.

The Ether settles, still shimmering faintly in the morning air. The courtyard glows with it—silver threads weaving through stone and soil, through the people kneeling in the dirt.

It's beautiful.

It's devastating.

Bree sways.

I'm moving before Thane can, before anyone can. My arm slides around her waist, catching her before she falls.

She leans against me, breath shaking, eyes wet.

"You did it," I say quietly.

"We did," she whispers back.

Her weight settles against my side, and I hold her steady while freed Feeders begin to rise, touching their throats, touching each other, confirming the collars are really gone.

I've seen fire burn cities to ash.

I never knew it could heal.

Thane steps forward, his expression unreadable—something between pride and grief and determination. Stellan's already scanning the horizon, calculating retaliation from the Counsel.

In the distance, ravens call from the treeline.

A warning or a witness, I can't tell.

Bree straightens slowly, exhausted but unbroken. She looks at the crowd of newly freed Feeders—at faces that are starting to remember what hope looks like.

"We begin again," she says quietly.

Almost to herself.

But I hear it.

We all do.

The sun clears the wall completely now, flooding the courtyard with full morning light. The daisies at the gate bloom brighter, spreading through cracks in the stone.

And for the first time in longer than I can remember, I think maybe we're not just surviving the fire.

Maybe we're becoming it.

Chapter 39
BREE

The courtyard settles into quiet murmurs as we approach the sanctuary doors.

Scarred, blackened at the edges—like something tried to burn through from the inside.

The doors swing open before we reach them.

Three Feeders step out—exhausted, wary, but unarmed. They glance at me, then at the freed crowd still touching their throats, still testing their freedom.

One bows his head. The others follow.

"Thank you," I say quietly. "For staying."

The oldest one—gray-haired, face lined with years I can't count—meets my eyes. "What would you like us to do... the ones who are staying?"

I smile, though it feels fragile. "Whatever you want. Rest. Eat. Take the Oath, if you wish."

I hesitate, the next words harder to say. "Please pass along that we believe the Counsel will be here in a few days. I understand if some choose to leave before then."

His eyes flicker—gratitude mixed with relief. He nods once, then turns back toward the courtyard to relay the message.

I watch him go, the weight of leadership settling over my shoulders again. But softer this time.

They're not following orders.

They're choosing.

Rhett's hand finds the small of my back, steadying. "Ready?"

I nod, even though I'm not sure.

We move toward the open doors—all of us together. Riley hangs back with Zira, still uncertain of her place.

The moment I step inside, I stop.

The hall is wrong.

Obsidian walls stretch before us, black and polished like glass. Silver flame flickers in sconces that weren't there before, casting shadows that move wrong. The floor is smooth stone—dark, endless, reflecting nothing.

Just like the Void.

Just like his chamber.

My chest locks. I can't breathe.

The air is thick with the residue of Ethos and Riley's power—corrupted, clinging, reshaping the sanctuary into something that looks like the place I was kept.

Every surface pulses faintly, like a heartbeat that's forgotten its rhythm.

This was supposed to be *home*.

The Ether inside me surges before I can stop it—silver mist rippling outward, brushing across corrupted stone.

The sanctuary responds.

Too fast. Too much.

My knees buckle.

Rhett is there instantly, heat at my back, an arm at my waist. "I've got you."

But the Ether doesn't stop.

It spreads like water finding cracks—soft, deliberate, unstoppable. Silver light flows over every surface they twisted.

The black crystal melts back into living stone.

Light floods through windows that had been dark.

Vines turn green along the arches, curling upward like they're waking from a long sleep.

The air warms, filling with the scent of clean earth and daisy pollen.

I can barely breathe through the exhaustion pulling at my edges, but I feel it—the sanctuary remembering what it was meant to be.

Behind us, gasps rise from the courtyard—the silver already climbing the outer walls.

Rhett's grip tightens as I sway again. "You need to sit down."

"I'm fine."

"You're not."

He's right. I'm not.

My legs are shaking, my hands trembling, and the Ether is still pulsing faintly around me like it's not done yet.

Footsteps approach from the side hall.

I look up.

Mairen.

Her apron is still damp, tears shining on her cheeks, but she's smiling—really smiling—as she crosses the restored hall toward us.

"Bless you, sweetheart," she says, voice thick with emotion. "Come, sit. You all look half-starved."

She doesn't wait for an answer, just takes my hand and starts leading us deeper into the sanctuary. Rhett keeps his arm around my waist, supporting most of my weight as we follow.

The kitchen appears ahead—warm light spilling through windows that weren't there before. Or maybe they were, and I just couldn't see them under all the corruption.

The room smells like home. Like bread and herbs and the clean bite of morning.

Mairen pulls out a chair, guiding me into it with gentle insistence. "Sit. All of you. I'll make something."

Gray and Rhett move to the stove without being asked, carrying in wood from the stack by the door. Wes starts clearing space on the counter. Jace raids the cupboard with practiced mischief, pulling down mugs and jars like he's done a hundred times before.

Thane lingers in the doorway, watching the sunlight spill across the kitchen floor like he doesn't quite trust it yet.

Mairen presses a mug into my hands—something steaming and sweet that smells like honey and warmth.

"You did right by us, child," she says quietly, brushing hair back from my face. "That's enough for today."

My throat tightens. "Not enough. But it's a start."

She smiles, soft and knowing. "Starts are all we get. The rest comes after."

I take a sip, letting the warmth spread through my chest, chasing back some of the exhaustion.

Footsteps in the hall.

Riley and Zira appear in the doorway, hesitant.

Mairen gasps, the mug in her hand trembling. Her eyes lock on Riley—on the face that wore mine, that gave the orders, that put collars on her family.

"It's okay," I say quickly, standing despite the exhaustion. I cross to Mairen, taking her hand. "She... she was being used. Just like I was."

Mairen's breath shakes, but she nods slowly. Her gaze shifts between Riley and me, seeing the differences now—the black and silver Ether threaded through Riley's fingers, the exhaustion in her eyes that mirrors my own.

"I'm sorry," Riley whispers from the doorway. "For everything."

Mairen doesn't answer, but she doesn't look away either.

The moment stretches, taut and fragile.

Then Mairen turns back to the stove, her shoulders still tight but her voice steady. "Well. I suppose we'll all need feeding then."

Riley's breath catches—relief and gratitude tangled together.

She and Zira move into the kitchen carefully, taking seats at the far end of the table where they can see everyone but aren't in the way.

Mairen busies herself with pots and spoons, then pauses, glancing back at me. "Oh—your band of misfits arrived while you were... occupied. They're already getting settled in the back of the sanctuary."

My chest warms. "They made it."

"All of them," she confirms. "Loud bunch, but good-hearted."

Around me, the guys settle into the kitchen like they belong here. Rhett leans against the counter beside me, close enough to catch me if I fall again.

Gray stands near the window, watching the courtyard. Theo pulls out a chair across from me, eyes clearer than they've been in days.

Wes sits beside me, quiet but present. Jace perches on the edge of the counter, swinging his legs. Seth stays near the door, silent as always. Stellan examines the restored stonework with something like approval.

Even Thane eventually moves from the doorway, taking a seat at the far end of the table where he can see everyone.

The kitchen fills with the sounds of life returning—mugs clinking, quiet conversation, Mairen humming under her breath as she works.

I look toward the doorway where sunlight spills across the floor, proof that the sanctuary has begun to heal.

Outside, through the window, I catch a glimpse of the garden—daisies blooming wider, vines climbing the walls, color returning to earth that had been gray.

The heart of the sanctuary beats again.

And somewhere beyond these walls, the Counsel is coming.

But for now—just for now—we're home.

Chapter 40
JACE

The kitchen settles into comfortable chaos—Mairen cooking, the guys finding their places, Riley and Zira keeping to the edges. Bree's still at the table, mug in hand.

But I'm watching her.

She's fading.

Her head keeps dipping forward, then jerking back up like she's fighting sleep and losing. The mug in her hands trembles slightly, and she's barely touched whatever Mairen put in it.

I catch Rhett's eye across the room. He sees it too.

"Come on," I say quietly, pushing off the counter and moving to her side. "You need to sleep."

She blinks up at me, confusion flickering across her face. "I'm fine."

"You're exhausted." I hold out my hand. "Let me walk you to your room."

For a second, I think she'll argue. But then she just nods, setting the mug down and taking my hand.

Her fingers are ice-cold.

Gray starts to stand, but I shake my head once. He understands. She needs rest, not a crowd.

I help her up, and she sways immediately. My arm goes around her waist, steadying her.

"Easy," I say.

She leans into me, most of her weight pressing against my side. "Thank you."

We move through the restored hallway slowly. The sanctuary hums around us—soft and alive again, vines curling along the arches, daisies blooming in cracks that shouldn't hold life.

It's beautiful.

I wish I felt it.

"Place *looks* alive again," I say, aiming for lightness and missing by miles.

Bree hums in agreement, eyes half-closed.

Every step closer to her room, my chest gets tighter.

The last time I crossed that threshold, it wasn't her.

I didn't know. Couldn't have known. But I should've felt the difference, shouldn't I? Should've sensed that something was wrong, that the woman in that bed wasn't the one I'd been waiting for.

We reach her door. It's half-open, gauzy curtains shifting in a breeze that smells like rain and daisies.

I stop.

Can't move forward. Can't breathe.

The scent hits me like a fist—same as before. Same as when Riley wore her face and let me—and I can't even finish the thought.

"Jace?"

Bree's voice pulls me back. She's looking at me, concern cutting through the exhaustion.

I force a smile. "Yeah. Just... remembering."

She doesn't push. Just leans harder against me, trusting me to hold her up.

We step inside.

The room responds immediately. The sheets ripple, Ether re-threading itself across the bed, cleansing what Riley left behind. The walls brighten. The vines at the window turn greener.

It's like the room itself is exhaling.

I help her to the bed, and she sits on the edge, swaying slightly.

"Boots," I say, kneeling in front of her.

She doesn't argue, just lifts one foot, then the other. My hands shake as I pull them off, setting them aside carefully.

"Thank you," she murmurs, already lying back against the pillows.

I should leave. Let her sleep. Find somewhere else to stand watch.

But before I can move, her hand catches mine.

"I want you here, Jace," she whispers. "Please."

My throat closes.

"Bree—"

"Please, Jace." Her eyes are barely open, but there's something raw in her voice. "I don't want to be alone."

I can't say no to her. I never could.

"Okay," I say quietly.

She shifts over, making room, and tugs me gently onto the bed beside her.

I lie down stiffly, every muscle locked. This is fine. This is just comfort. She needs someone, and I can be that person.

Even if it's killing me.

Bree curls into my side immediately, her head resting on my chest, one arm draping across my ribs. She sighs—relief and exhaustion tangled together.

"I love you," she breathes—barely a whisper, half dream.

And then she's gone, sleep pulling her under.

I freeze.

The words hang in the air between us, and I don't know if she even meant to say them. Don't know if she'll remember saying them.

But they're mine now.

I wrap my arm around her shoulders, holding her close while my mind spirals through every reason I don't deserve to hear those words from her.

And I lie there in the dark, staring at the ceiling, feeling her warmth against me.

This bed.

This room.

The same walls that heard a lie I didn't stop.

Riley was here. In this exact spot. And I didn't know.

I thought it was Bree. Thought she'd finally let me close, finally trusted me enough to—

My chest aches.

I remember the way Riley looked at me—confident, certain, nothing like Bree's careful vulnerability. I remember her hands, her voice, the way she moved.

All wrong.

But I didn't see it. Didn't feel it.

What kind of person does that make me?

Bree shifts slightly, pressing closer, and I force myself to breathe through the guilt threatening to choke me.

She trusts me. Right now, in this moment, she's choosing to be here with *me*. Seeking comfort. Offering it.

And all I can think about is how the last time I was in this bed, it wasn't her.

"I'm sorry," I whisper into the dark, knowing she can't hear me. "I didn't know it wasn't you. But I should've."

The Ether stirs faintly around us, warm and alive.

On the windowsill, a single daisy blooms.

I hold Bree closer, feeling her heartbeat against my ribs, steady and real.

The sanctuary quiets around us. Voices fade down the hall. The world narrows to this room, this bed, this woman sleeping peacefully in my arms.

If she's the heart of this place, then the least I can do is stand guard while it learns to beat again.

I press my face into her hair and breathe her in.

"I love you too," I whisper.

Chapter 41
Jace

I wake to warmth—not the cold ache of guilt that's lived in my chest for months, but real, human warmth.

Bree's body pressed against mine, her head still on my chest, one arm draped across my ribs. The morning light filters through the gauzy curtains, turning everything soft and gold.

For a moment, I just breathe.

The sanctuary hums quietly around us—alive again, the Ether threading through the walls in gentle pulses. Outside, I hear faint voices, the rustle of people moving through the courtyard. The world keeps turning.

But in here, it's just us.

Bree shifts slightly, and I freeze, not wanting to wake her. Not wanting this moment to end.

Because the second she wakes up, I'm going to have to face it again.

The fact that I was in this bed before. With Riley. Thinking it was her.

My stomach twists.

I should've known.

I stare at the ceiling, counting the cracks in the stone, trying to breathe through the weight pressing down on my chest.

She deserves better than this. Better than *me*.

Bree stirs, this time lifting her head slightly. Her eyes flutter open, still heavy with sleep, and for a second she just looks at me—like she's checking to make sure I'm real.

"Morning," she murmurs, voice rough and low.

"Morning."

She blinks slowly, then smiles—small and soft, like she's surprised to find me still here.

"You stayed."

"You asked me to."

Her smile widens just a fraction, and she settles back against my chest, fingers tracing idle patterns on my shirt. The touch is light, absent-minded, but it sends sparks through my skin.

I should say something. Apologize. Explain. But my throat's too tight.

Instead, I just hold her.

The silence stretches, comfortable but fragile.

Then she says, so quietly I almost miss it, "I meant it. What I said last night."

My heart stops.

"Bree—"

"I love you, Jace." She lifts her head again, meeting my eyes. No hesitation. No doubt.

Just truth.

And it destroys me.

Because I don't deserve those words. Not after what I did. Not after—

"Hey." Her hand cups my jaw, thumb brushing over my cheek. "Where'd you go?"

I can't look away from her. Can't breathe.

"I was in this bed before," I whisper. "With Riley. And I didn't know it wasn't you."

Her expression doesn't change. Doesn't harden or pull away.

She just nods. "I know."

"I should've known, Bree. Should've *felt* the difference. Should've—"

"Jace." Her voice is firm now, cutting through my spiral. "It wasn't your fault."

"But—"

"No." She shifts, sitting up slightly, forcing me to meet her eyes. "Riley had my memories. My face. My voice. She was designed to fool you. And she did. That's on *her*, not you."

The words hit me, but they don't stick. Can't stick.

"I should've known," I repeat, voice breaking.

Bree watches me for a long moment, her hand still cradling my face. Then she leans forward, pressing her forehead to mine.

"Then let's make something that's ours," she says softly. "Right now. Just us. No ghosts. No lies. Just this."

My breath catches.

"Bree—"

But she's already kissing me.

Soft at first. Tentative. Like she's asking permission.

And I answer.

My hands move to her waist, pulling her closer. The kiss deepens, and the guilt twists harder in my chest—but so does the need.

The need to prove that *this* is real. That *she's* real. That I can tell the difference.

When she pulls back, we're both breathing hard.

"I want this," she whispers, her lips brushing mine. "With you. Here. Now."

Her hand slides down my chest, fingers curling in the fabric of my shirt.

"Let's make a memory that's just ours."

My throat's too tight to answer, so I just nod.

And kiss her again.

This time, I don't hold back.

My hands slide under her shirt pushing it up slowly. She lifts her arms, helping me pull it over her head, and the fabric falls away.

She's bare underneath.

And I freeze.

Silver lines trace across her ribs. Her hip. The underside of her breast. Some are thin and faded, barely visible in the morning light. Others are raised, pink and angry, like what Kevin did to her can never fully heal.

They map her entire body like a language I'm only just learning to read.

And they're *hers*.

"Jace," she whispers, and there's uncertainty in her voice now. Her arms start to cross over her chest, covering herself.

I catch her wrists gently, stopping her.

"Don't," I say, voice rough. "Don't hide from me."

She meets my eyes, and I see it—the fear still there under all the healing she's done. That I'll be repulsed. That I'll see damage instead of survival.

So I show her.

I lean down and press my mouth to the scar that runs along her collarbone. Then the one on her ribs. The one on her hip.

She gasps, hands unclenching.

"I'm going to memorize every single one," I murmur against her skin. "Every mark. Every line. So I always remember everything we've been through to get here."

Her breath hitches. "Jace—"

"You didn't deserve these," I say, tracing a particularly deep scar along her ribcage with my tongue. She shudders beneath me. "You're the strongest person I've ever met."

A soft sound escapes her—half sob, half relief—and her hands find my hair, holding me to her.

"I see you," I whisper. "All of you. And you're so fucking beautiful it hurts to look at you."

She pulls me up into a kiss—desperate and grateful and real.

Her hands move to my shirt, tugging it up. I help her pull it off, tossing it aside, and then we're skin to skin.

The contact sends a jolt through me—heat and need and something deeper.

She presses closer, her breasts soft against my chest, and I groan into her mouth.

"Bree—"

"Don't stop," she whispers. "Please don't stop."

I won't.

I can't.

My hands slide lower, tracing the curve of her hips, the line of her thigh. She's still wearing the loose sleep pants, and I hook my fingers in the waistband, pausing.

Asking.

She nods, lifting her hips, and I pull them down slowly—taking my time, watching the way her body reacts to every touch.

When she's bare beneath me, I pause.

More scars. Along her thighs. The curve of her hip. One that runs from her navel down.

I trace each one with my fingertips, committing them to memory. Getting flashes of moments that aren't mine.

"Jace," she says, and there's heat in her voice now. Need.

I lean down, pressing my mouth to her hip bone. Then lower. The inside of her thigh.

She gasps, hands fisting in the sheets.

The air stirs.

Not just in the room—*around* her.

My magic responds to the spike in my pulse, the way my hands shake as I touch her. But this time I don't let it scatter aimlessly through the room.

I focus it.

A cool breath of air ghosts across her skin—down her sternum, circling her breast, teasing her nipple until it peaks.

Bree's back arches off the bed. "Oh—"

I do it again. This time letting the current trace lower, down her stomach, swirling around her navel.

"Jace," she breathes, and I can hear the wonder in her voice. "What are you—"

"Shh," I murmur against her thigh. "Let me."

I kiss my way higher, and with every press of my lips I send another current of air ahead of me—cool and teasing, building anticipation.

By the time I reach the apex of her thighs, she's trembling.

I blow a soft, deliberate breath directly against her center, and she cries out—hips bucking.

"Please," she gasps.

I don't make her wait.

I press my mouth to her, tasting her fully, and at the same time I let my magic work—gentle currents of air swirling around her clit, alternating pressure and temperature while my tongue moves inside her.

She shatters almost immediately—crying out, one hand flying to my hair and gripping hard enough to hurt.

I don't stop.

I work her through it, tongue and magic and hands all coordinating until she's gasping my name, thighs trembling on either side of my head.

When I finally pull back, she's boneless—chest heaving, eyes glassy.

"Holy shit," she whispers.

I grin against her thigh. "We're just getting started."

I kiss my way back up her body, taking my time. Her skin is flushed, warm under my lips, and the Ether hums around her—silver threads weaving through the air.

When I reach her mouth, she kisses me hungrily—tasting herself on my tongue.

Her hands move between us, fumbling with the waistband of my pants.

"Off," she demands.

I laugh—breathless and desperate—and help her shove them down. They tangle around my ankles and I kick them away, finally bare.

Bree's eyes drag down my body, lingering, and when she reaches for me I have to catch her wrist.

"Wait," I grit out. "If you touch me right now, this is going to be over way too fast."

She smirks—just a little. "That bad?"

"Worse."

But she doesn't listen. Her hand wraps around me, stroking slowly, and I nearly come undone right there.

"Bree—*fuck*—"

She leans up, kissing me while her hand moves, and I'm lost.

I reach between us, sliding two fingers inside her, and she gasps into my mouth—hips rolling forward to meet my hand.

We move together like that for a while, learning each other's rhythm. Her hand on me. Mine inside her. Breath and heat and magic tangling between us.

The Ether flares brighter, reacting to the building pleasure. My air magic spirals through it, and I feel it—the way our powers thread together, weaving something new.

"Jace," she whispers against my mouth. "I need you. Now."

I pull my hand away, positioning myself between her thighs, and she guides me to her entrance.

The first press inside makes us both groan.

She's so tight, so warm, and I have to force myself to go slow—to let her adjust.

But she doesn't want slow.

Her legs wrap around my hips, pulling me deeper, and I sink into her fully—buried to the hilt.

We both freeze.

Just breathing. Just feeling.

Then she rolls her hips, and I'm lost.

I set a rhythm—slow and deep at first, watching her face for every reaction.

Her eyes flutter closed. Her mouth falls open. Her nails dig into my shoulders.

Every thrust sends a ripple of Ether through the room, silver light pulsing beneath her skin.

I lean down, capturing her mouth in a kiss, and she moans into it—the sound vibrating through me.

"More," she whispers. "Jace, *please*—"

I give it to her.

I move faster, harder, angling my hips until I find the spot that makes her cry out.

And then I add my magic.

A focused current of air, cool and deliberate, swirling around where we're joined—brushing against her clit with every thrust.

Bree's entire body arches off the bed, a shocked gasp tearing from her throat.

"Oh god—Jace—*what*—"

"Feel good?" I manage, barely holding on.

"Yes—don't stop—don't you *dare* stop—"

I don't.

I keep the rhythm steady, the pressure constant, and I watch her climb—teetering on the edge of something bigger than either of us.

The air in the room moves with us now, warm currents spiraling around our bodies. The Ether flares brighter with every thrust, and I feel it threading through me—binding us together.

"Come for me," I whisper against her ear. "Let me feel it."

And she does.

She shatters beneath me, crying out my name, her body clenching around me so hard I nearly follow her over.

But I hold on.

I need to see it. Need to feel it. Need to memorize the way she looks when she falls apart.

When she finally stills, breathing hard, I press my forehead to hers.

"I love you," I whisper. "I love you so much."

She smiles—soft and sated and real.

"I know."

I'm about to move again—to chase my own release—when the door opens.

We both freeze.

Firelight spills into the room—low and warm—and I know before I even turn my head.

Rhett.

He stops in the doorway, eyes locking on us.

For half a second, shame crashes back—hot and suffocating.

Not again.

Chapter 42
RHETT

I shouldn't be here, but my feet keep moving down the hallway—drawn by something. A pull. A need.

The sanctuary hums around me, alive again. Vines curl along the archways, daisies blooming in cracks that shouldn't hold life. The Ether threads through everything—silver and warm and *hers*.

I've been wandering for a while now. Restless. Unable to settle.

Gray went to check the perimeter and the Feeders who stayed. Theo's holed up in his room with constant visions. Wes is somewhere with Stellan, Seth's smirk when I asked told me everything I needed to know. Thane's avoiding everyone.

And Bree—

Bree is resting.

With Jace.

I told myself it was fine. That she needed sleep. That Jace needed to be with her, to work through whatever guilt's been eating him alive since we learned about Riley.

But I can't stop thinking about it.

About *her*.

About the way she looked at me in the kitchen yesterday—tired but whole, choosing to be here, choosing to stay.

About the way her Ether reached for me even when she was exhausted.

About the fact that I walked in on her with Gray. Stood there and watched. And realized I *wanted* to stay. To see them together.

The sun's still low, light slanting through the windows in pale gold bars.

I stop outside her door.

It's half-open. Gauzy curtains shift in a breeze that smells like rain and daisies.

I should leave.

I should walk away and give them privacy and not—

A sound drifts through the doorway. Soft. Breathy.

My entire body goes still.

That's not sleep.

My hand moves before I can stop it, pushing the door open just enough to see inside.

And I freeze.

Jace. Bree.

Tangled together on the bed, her body arched beneath his, silver mist curling around them like a living thing.

For half a second, my brain doesn't process it.

Then it does. It hits me—it's not Riley at all. It's Bree.

And every muscle in my body locks.

Not again.

The memory crashes into me—sharp and suffocating.

Riley's voice. *"You're going to watch."*

The way she moved. The way she looked at me while she touched Jace, daring me to react.

The hollow, sick feeling of being forced to witness something that should've been private. Sacred.

My hands curl into fists, heat sparking along my veins.

I should leave.

I need to leave.

But I can't move.

Because—

Because something's different.

Jace shifts, and I catch a glimpse of her face.

Her eyes are closed, lips parted, one hand fisted in Jace's hair. Her body moves with his—fluid and desperate and real.

And then I see them.

The scars.

Silver lines tracing across her ribs. Her hip. The curve of her breast.

Riley didn't have those.

Riley's skin was smooth. Perfect. Wrong.

But Bree—

God, Bree is covered in them.

Evidence of everything she's survived. Every wound she's carried. Every battle she's fought just to be here.

They're beautiful.

She's beautiful.

My chest tightens, and the heat in my hands flares hotter.

This isn't Riley.

This is *Bree*.

And I'm not being forced to watch.

I'm choosing to stay.

Jace's magic stirs in the room—cool currents of air swirling around them, teasing her skin in ways that make her gasp.

I see the moment he focuses it. The way her entire body arches off the bed, a shocked cry tearing from her throat.

"Oh god—Jace—*what*—"

My breath catches.

The fire inside me pulses in response—answering the spike of need, the heat building between them.

I should leave.

But I don't.

I step forward instead.

One step. Then another.

The floorboards creak under my weight, and they both freeze.

Jace's head snaps toward me, eyes wide.

For half a second, I see it—the shame crashing over him. The memory of Riley.

Not again.

But I'm not here to hurt him.

I'm not here to take anything.

Not this time.

I'm here because I *choose* to be.

Bree shifts, reaching for the sheet and drawing it loosely over her chest as Jace moves. The movement is careful. Bashful.

Nothing like Riley.

She stands slowly, the sheet draping around her like a cloak, and crosses the room toward me.

I can't move. Can't breathe.

She stops just in front of me, one hand holding the fabric in place, the other reaching for my wrist.

Her touch is warm. Solid. Alive.

"I know you were there," she says quietly. "When I was with Gray."

My throat closes.

She *knows*.

Of course she knows.

Bree's voice drops lower, and I see the faint blush creeping up her neck.

"I didn't mind." She hesitates, then adds, softer, "I think I liked it."

The words hit me right where it counts, and my body reacts before I can stop it.

She's not angry. Not hurt.

She's *inviting* me.

My eyes flick to Jace, still frozen on the bed, and then back to her.

"Bree—"

"I want you here," she says. "If you want to be."

I stand there, hand curling into a fist at my side, fighting the war raging inside me.

The memory of being forced. Of Riley's cruelty.

Against the invitation in Bree's eyes. The choice she's offering.

This isn't the same.

She's not the same.

I step forward.

Bree exhales—relief and something deeper—and leads me back toward the bed.

But instead of sitting on the edge, she turns to face me fully.

"Sit," she says, voice soft but certain. "Against the headboard."

I blink. "Bree—"

"Please, Rhett." Her hand tightens on my wrist. "I want you here. Really here."

Jace shifts on the bed, making room, his eyes flicking between us.

I move slowly, sitting on the bed and leaning back against the headboard. The wood is cool against my shoulders, solid.

Bree climbs onto the bed and settles between my legs, her back to my chest. The sheet has fallen away entirely, and I can see everything—every scar, every curve, every mark that proves she's *hers*.

She leans back against me, and I feel her warmth through my shirt.

"Better?" she asks, glancing up at me.

I can't speak. Can only nod.

She reaches for Jace, pulling him closer, and he settles between her thighs—his hands on her hips.

"This is ours," she says. "No more ghosts."

Jace's gaze meets mine over her shoulder.

And I see it—the fear that I'll hate him for this. That I'll leave. That I'll see Riley instead of Bree.

But I don't.

I see forgiveness.

The heat radiates off me in waves, and I feel Bree shiver against my chest—not from cold, but from anticipation.

My arms move without thinking, wrapping around her waist, holding her steady.

Jace kisses her, and she arches forward into it, her body moving against mine.

I see everything from this angle. The way Jace's hands trace her scars. The way her breath catches. The way the Ether curls around them both—silver and alive.

"She's beautiful," I say, voice rough.

Jace glances up at me, and I see the gratitude in his eyes.

"Yeah," he agrees. "She is."

Bree turns her head slightly, pressing a kiss to my jaw. "So are you," she whispers.

The words hit me harder than they should.

My hands move to her hips, steadying her as Jace settles between her thighs.

I watch as he pushes inside her, and she gasps—the sound vibrating through her body and into mine.

And this time, it doesn't hurt.

It doesn't feel like violation or cruelty or control.

It feels like *belonging*.

The Ether pulses—brighter now, reacting to all three of us.

My fire stirs in response, low flames flickering along my forearms. The heat rolls through the room in waves, mixing with the cool drift of Jace's air magic.

Bree's hands find mine where they rest on her hips, threading our fingers together.

"You're both here," she whispers, and there's wonder in her voice. Relief.

I lean forward, pressing a kiss to her shoulder. "We're here."

The magic responds—silver and gold and the faint shimmer of blue, weaving together in the space between us.

I feel Jace's magic against my skin, cool and deliberate. Feel the way Bree's Ether threads through everything, binding us together.

And I let myself *feel* it.

Let myself be part of this.

Jace sets a rhythm—slow and deep—and I feel every movement through Bree's body pressed against mine.

Her head falls back against my shoulder, eyes fluttering closed.

One of my hands moves from her hip to her stomach, then higher. I cup her breast, thumb brushing over her nipple, and she gasps.

I feel Jace stutter inside her, barely holding on.

"Fuck," he breathes.

I meet his eyes, and I see it—the question. The permission.

I nod once.

My hand slides lower, finding the place where they're joined.

Bree cries out—head falling back against my shoulder.

"Rhett—"

"I've got you," I murmur against her ear. "We both do."

My fingers press against her clit, circling in time with Jace's thrusts, and I feel it—the way her body clenches, the way she trembles between us.

Jace adds his magic back into the mix—cool currents of air swirling around where my fingers work.

Bree's entire body goes taut, a strangled sound tearing from her throat.

The magic flares—gold and silver and blue, pulsing so bright it fills the room.

My fire surges in response.

I feel her climbing. Feel the tension coiling tighter and tighter.

"Let go," I whisper against her ear. "Let us see you come apart."

And she does.

She shatters between us, crying out both our names, her body arching as Ether explodes outward in a wave of light.

Jace follows immediately, burying himself inside her one last time, gasping her name.

And I hold them both.

Grounding them. Anchoring them.

My fire pulses in time with her heartbeat, and I feel it—the bond flaring bright between all three of us.

When it's over, we're all breathing hard, tangled together in the aftermath.

The light settles. The magic quiets.

And we're just... here.

Jace pulls out slowly, and Bree winces. He brushes a kiss to her temple, murmuring something I can't hear.

I help her lie back, and she curls between us—one hand on Jace's chest, the other reaching for mine.

I take it, threading my fingers through hers.

For a long moment, none of us speak.

Then Bree says, voice soft and drowsy, "No more ghosts."

I look down at her—at the woman who chose us, who forgave us, who's still choosing us even after everything.

"No more ghosts," I echo.

Jace presses his face into her hair, and I see the way his shoulders finally relax.

The sanctuary hums softly around us, alive and whole.

And for the first time since Riley, I don't feel like I'm watching from the outside.

I feel like I *belong*.

This isn't forced. Isn't cruel.

This is *ours*.

And I'll protect it with everything I have.

Chapter 43
BREE

For a long moment, none of us move.

We're tangled together—warm and sated and quiet. The Ether hums softly around us, silver threads weaving through the air, calm and content.

Rhett's arm is still draped over my waist, his chest pressed against my back. Jace is on my other side, propped up on one elbow, watching me with those green-gold eyes.

Nobody speaks.

We just... breathe.

Eventually, Jace breaks the silence.

"We should probably get up," he says quietly.

"Probably," Rhett agrees from behind me—but his arm tightens slightly, like he's not quite ready to let go.

I smile despite myself. "The sanctuary's not going to run itself."

"It's been doing fine without us for the last hour," Jace points out.

"Two hours," Rhett corrects.

I blush, and Jace grins—crooked and unrepentant.

But he's right. We can't stay here forever, no matter how much I want to.

I slip out from between them—reluctantly—and start looking for clothes. Rhett's shirt is on the floor, and I pull it on without thinking. It hangs to mid-thigh, warm and smelling like fire and safety.

When I turn around, both of them are watching me.

"What?" I ask.

Jace's grin widens. "Nothing. You just look good in his clothes."

Rhett makes a low sound of agreement, and I feel heat creep up my neck.

I'm halfway to the door when Jace speaks again.

"No panties?"

I freeze.

And I—

I giggle.

Actually *giggle*, and it feels good.

For a few moments, I feel lighter and I want to stay like that forever.

Rhett chokes on a laugh behind me, muffled and low, and for once the sound isn't edged with worry.

I giggle again—really giggle—and it feels foreign and perfect, like remembering how to breathe after holding it too long.

"Nope," I say, popping the 'p' and heading for the door.

Behind me, I hear Jace mutter something that sounds like "I'm a dead man," and Rhett's low rumble of amusement.

"Come on," I call over my shoulder, trying to sound normal and failing completely. "I smell pancakes."

The kitchen is alive with warmth when we walk in.

Mairen stands at the stove, humming under her breath, flipping pancakes like it was only yesterday we were here, like this. The air smells like cinnamon and butter and something sweet that smells like home.

Theo sits at the table with a book, Gray leans against the counter with his arms crossed, and Wes—

Wes takes one look at the three of us and smirks.

"Well, well," he drawls. "Look who finally decided to join us."

I freeze.

Jace doesn't miss a beat. "We were busy."

"I'll bet you were."

Rhett just grunts, crossing to the coffee pot like nothing happened.

But Wes isn't done. His eyes flick between the three of us—taking in my borrowed shirt, bare legs, Jace's rumpled hair, the way Rhett's hand brushes my lower back as he passes.

"Busy doing what, exactly?" Wes asks innocently.

"Wes," Theo says without looking up from his book. "Don't."

"I'm just curious."

"You're nosy," Gray mutters.

Wes grins wider. "That too."

The laughter bounces off stone and sunlight, and something in my chest loosens for the first time in over a year.

For a second the whole kitchen feels light—sun on skin, laughter without consequence. I catch myself smiling and don't fight it.

I feel my face burning, but before I can respond, Jace crosses to Wes and leans in close.

He whispers something—too quiet for me to hear—and Wes's eyes go wide before snapping to me.

His smirk turns wicked.

Whatever he said, it changes everything about how Wes is looking at me.

"That's cruel," Wes says.

Jace's mouth quirks. "You're welcome."

Wes mutters something under his breath that sounds like a curse, but his eyes are still on me.

It's not the time to unpack whatever that was—but the air feels charged when he walks away.

Jace just grins and turns away, crossing to Mairen at the stove.

And Wes is still looking at me like he knows something I don't want him to know.

"Teach me how you do it, please," Jace says.

Mairen laughs—bright and surprised. "You already know how."

"Yours are better," he admits, reluctantly. "What's the secret?"

I smile as I watch them, surprised Jace isn't already driving her crazy.

"Coffee," Mairen calls over her shoulder to the rest of us. "Is fresh and on the counter. Help yourselves."

She grabs her phone, listing off her favorite ingredients to add to pancakes. "Last time I added cinnamon..."

Jace listens intently, his usual humor muted by genuine focus.

It's... sweet.

I pour myself coffee and settle at the table, still watching them.

I glance over as Wes slides into the seat next to Theo, and I see him lean over—whispering something.

Theo's eyes flick to me.

And he *smiles*.

Slow. Knowing.

His gaze drags down, then back up, and he licks his lips—deliberate and unhurried.

Oh god.

My face burns hotter, and I have to look away before I combust.

Rhett moves to the counter, pours his own mug, and leans against it—watching me.

His gaze is steady. Calm.

No regret. No hesitation.

I smile at him, and he smiles back—small but real.

Gray takes the seat next to Theo. His eyes find me immediately, and Theo—

Theo leans over and whispers something to Gray.

What the hell?

Gray's entire body goes still. His silver-gray eyes lock on me, and I watch his nostrils flare slightly.

Oh.

Oh.

His jaw tightens, and the look he gives me is so heated I have to look away.

My face is on fire.

I should have worn pants. Dammit.

When I risk glancing back up, Theo's still watching me—slower, more deliberate than before. Like he's taking his time cataloging every reaction.

I grab my coffee mug just to have something to do with my hands.

Wes immediately steals a pancake straight off the plate and earns a swat from Mairen.

"Patience," she scolds.

"I'm starving," Wes protests, mouth full.

"You're always starving," Theo mutters, but there's no heat in it.

Stellan appears in the doorway, Seth beside him. Gray catches Stellan's eye and tilts his head toward me—some silent communication passing between them.

Stellan's gaze shifts to me, travels down, then back up.

One elegant eyebrow arches.

Seth smirks outright.

I want to sink through the floor.

The kitchen fills with noise—teasing, laughter, the clatter of plates being passed around. It feels normal. Safe.

Like we're just people having breakfast.

Not survivors preparing for war.

Jace flips a pancake—and it sticks to the ceiling.

Everyone freezes.

Then Mairen bursts out laughing, and the rest of us follow—loud and helpless and real.

Jace stares up at the pancake, then at the spatula in his hand.

"I have no idea how that happened."

"Magic," Gray deadpans.

"The distracting kind," Jace mutters, but he's grinning.

I laugh so hard my ribs ache, and it feels like the first real breath I've taken in days.

The sound mixes with everyone else's until it's impossible to tell who started it.

For a blink, I forget the Council, the scars, everything but this: the smell of butter, the heat of the stove, people I love around a table.

So this is what it could be like. Someday.

Zira appears in the doorway a few minutes later, elegant even in exhaustion.

"I thought I smelled food," she says.

"There's plenty," I tell her, gesturing to the table.

She slides into the seat across from me, and Theo hands her a mug of coffee without asking. She takes it with a grateful nod.

For a moment, she just drinks, letting the warmth settle into her.

Then she speaks.

"Riley's staying with me for now. She's resting. Not well enough to travel yet, but safe."

I feel a pang at her name, and Zira's eyes flick to mine—sharp but understanding.

"She burned most of her power in the switch," Zira says quietly. "What's left is weak. Barely there."

I nod slowly. "Is she okay?"

Zira pauses, considering. "Physically? She'll recover. Everything else..." She shakes her head. "She just looks... lost."

Rhett mutters something under his breath that sounds like, "Lost is better than dangerous."

Zira's mouth twitches, but I don't smile.

Riley isn't dangerous. She never really was.

She was just another one of his victims.

The conversation shifts after that—small talk, plans for the day, things that need fixing around the sanctuary.

It's... normal.

And for a little while, I let myself believe it can stay that way.

The knock comes sharp and sudden, cutting through the laughter like a blade.

Everyone goes still.

The Ether stirs, silver threads shifting in the air—reacting to the shift in tension.

My heart thuds once, hard, and I feel it—something urgent pressing against the edges of the sanctuary's calm.

Mairen wipes her hands on her apron, but Rhett moves first.

"Stay," he says. "I've got it."

He crosses to the door and pulls it open.

A young Feeder stands on the threshold. He's breathless, dust on his boots, sweat beading at his temples.

"They've been spotted," he says.

Rhett's voice drops. "Who?"

"Four Council members. And a man traveling with them." He pauses, eyes flicking to me. "Phil."

The name lands like a stone in my chest.

Wes's voice is flat, dangerous. "I'm going to kill him."

"Wait," Thane says from the archway, stepping forward. "Four?"

The scout nods. "They're about eighteen hours out."

Silence.

"Someone's missing," I say, looking at Thane.

"Nyx," he confirms, silver eyes narrowing.

I turn back to the scout. "A woman—dark hair, sharp features?"

The young Feeder shakes his head. "No one in the group matches that description."

Thane's jaw tightens, and I see the calculation happening behind his eyes.

The room tightens—every expression hardening in the space of a heartbeat.

"Fuck," Jace mutters.

Theo's eyes flash silver, and I know he's seeing something—fragments of what's coming.

Gray's jaw tightens, his body going still in that way that means the wolf is close to the surface.

Seth looks between us, confusion flickering across his face. "What's—"

Stellan pushes off the wall. "Let's go for a walk," he says, meeting Seth's eyes. "I'll catch you up on everything."

He glances at me, waiting.

I nod once.

Seth follows him out, still looking lost, and the door closes behind them.

The Ether pulses around me like a heartbeat.

I look around the kitchen—at the half-eaten pancakes, the warmth fading under the weight of what's coming, the faces of people I love staring back at me.

We finally felt like we could breathe.

And now the world is coming again.

I meet Jace's eyes. He nods—calm but ready.

I exhale slowly.

"Then we have eight hours," I say. "And we need to get every Feeder that's still here through the Oath before the Council arrives."

Thane's voice is low and certain. "To get ready."

He's still there in the archway—arms crossed, silver eyes unreadable.

He's been listening.
Of course he has.
I nod once.
"Then we start now."
The laughter dies completely.
Outside, the wind shifts.
The world feels closer again.
The Ether stirs—waiting.

Chapter 44
WES

An hour's passed since breakfast, and I'm still nursing coffee gone cold.

The others have dispersed—planning, preparing, doing whatever needs doing before the Council arrives. But I'm distracted. Something has been shifting since Bree walked out, subtle but wrong. Like the air pressure dropping before a storm. But it feels like a warning.

I'm about to convince myself I'm imagining it.

Then she's there.

Bree passes through the kitchen dressed and focused, her magic wrapped tight around her now—armoring herself. I notice before I mean to. Can't help it. That humming pull under my skin, the way her emotions taste before she even speaks.

My hunger flickers. Not the kind that asks to take. The kind that demands I keep her safe.

Gray's near the doorway, leaning wolf-casual but watching the courtyard with that feral alertness he gets since the Void.

Bree walks past us, intent.

"Where are you going?" I call out.

She pauses. Turns. "Oath Chamber. Checking on the Feeders going through."

Gray straightens immediately, body language sharp.

I set my mug down, already moving. "Not to be overprotective, but one—or both—of us is coming with you."

She starts to protest.

Gray cuts in. "This isn't about stopping you. It's about not letting you walk into something alone."

Bree meets both our eyes. Something shifts in her expression—not surrender, just acceptance.

"Fine."

We fall into step beside her.

Morning light filters through the garden, dew still clinging to the grass. The Ether feels heavier here, like fog before a storm. Bree's emotions pulse steady but distant, as if she's already somewhere else.

Gray walks slightly ahead, every movement watchful.

A few Feeders pause their work as we pass—rebuilding something near the gate, tending the gardens. I catch faint flickers of what they're feeling. Worry. Reverence. Curiosity. None of it reaches Bree. She's single-minded right now.

Gray breaks the silence first, voice lazy but amused. "So. Pants."

Bree's stride doesn't falter. "What about them?"

"You found some," I say. "After breakfast."

Her mouth quirks. "I did."

"Impressive turnaround time," Gray adds. "Considering."

She shoots him a look. "Considering what?"

"Considering you didn't seem too concerned about them an hour ago."

Bree's cheeks flush but she doesn't slow. "I was concerned about pancakes."

"And that's all?" I can't help the grin. "Just pancakes?"

She doesn't answer.

Gray's smirk deepens. "What exactly did you, Rhett, and Jace get up to before you came down?"

"Wouldn't you like to know."

"Actually, yes," I say. "We would."

Bree glances between us, something flickering in her expression—part amusement, part heat, part deflection. "Maybe I'll tell you later. If you're good."

"If we're good," Gray repeats, voice dropping low.

Before she can respond, he catches her wrist and pulls her in. His hand slides up to cup the back of her neck, fingers threading into her hair. The kiss is slow at first—testing, tasting—then deeper. His other hand settles at her waist, thumb pressing against her hip bone through the fabric. She makes a soft sound in the back of her throat and Gray's grip tightens slightly, like he's anchoring himself.

When he pulls back, her lips are swollen, her breathing uneven.

I step in before she can recover.

My hand cups her jaw, tilting her face up. Her pulse hammers against my palm. I kiss her slower than Gray did, savoring the warmth still there from him, the way her mouth opens under mine without hesitation. My other hand finds the small of her back, pulling her closer. She tastes like morning and heat and something sweeter underneath—maple syrup, maybe, or just her.

Her fingers curl into my shirt.

When I finally pull back, she stays there for a moment, eyes half-closed, chest rising and falling.

Then she opens her eyes and looks between us. Waiting.

Gray and I exchange a glance.

"What?" I ask.

"Your turn," she says simply.

Gray blinks. "Our—"

But I'm already moving.

I catch his jaw with one hand, rough enough that his eyes flash—surprise first, then something darker. I don't give him time to think. Just lean in and kiss him.

He freezes for half a second.

Then his hand comes up to grip my shoulder, fingers digging in hard enough to bruise. His mouth is different than Bree's—more demanding, less yielding. There's stubble against my palm, the taste of coffee still on his tongue. He kisses like he fights—controlled but barely, like he's holding himself back from something.

My other hand fists in his shirt and he makes a low sound in his chest. Not quite a growl. Close.

When we break apart, we're both breathing harder.

Bree's watching us with that look—pupils blown wide, lips parted, the Ether curling around her like visible heat.

"Yep," she says, voice slightly breathless.

Then she turns and keeps walking.

Gray and I stand there for a beat, both trying to remember how to think. Then we follow.

The teasing energy fades as we draw closer to the Chamber. Nodding to a few Feeders as we pass them. The air shifts, heavier now. The veins of Ether at our feet becoming thicker the closer we get.

Gray murmurs, "It's strange, isn't it? Ethos wasn't with the others."

Bree freezes slightly at that name.

My senses sharpen feeling her heartbeat spike, her magic tremor. Her fear tastes like static and metal, but she's holding it down hard. The same way she did that first night in the Sanctuary. She always does. I just didn't know that's what it was then.

Gray and I exchange glances. Something about Ethos's absence doesn't sit right.

"If Nyx is missing, and Ethos isn't here…" Gray says. "That's not coincidence."

Bree doesn't respond. Just keeps walking.

The trees thicken. The air changes.

The entrance appears—a stone stairway half-swallowed by roots and mist. The Ether gathers here, silver-bright and waiting, like it knows what's coming.

I feel it against my skin. Pressure. Anticipation. Fear.

Bree slows, shoulders squaring, eyes fixed ahead.

Gray glances at me. Silent communication: *Stay close. Don't let her out of reach.*

The moment we step off the stairs and into the chamber, the air stills.

The mist curls inward, gathering like breath being held.

Then—a voice. Smooth, feminine, threaded with shadow.

"Hello, Bree."

Bree freezes.

My magic surges, instinctive and predatory. Gray moves closer, a low growl building in his throat.

And just like that, the light from the kitchen is gone.

Only the storm remains.

Chapter 45
BREE

"Hello, Bree."

I stop mid-step.

The voice comes from everywhere and nowhere—smooth, laced with shadow. My pulse kicks hard against my ribs.

Wes and Gray close in immediately, flanking me without a word.

The Oath Chamber spreads before us, alive with motion. Dozens of Feeders move through the space, their footsteps quiet against stone traced with glowing Ether veins. The air hums with layered voices—oaths spoken low, power acknowledged, bonds forming one after another.

The mist rises around them like breath made visible.

But near the back wall, away from the flow, someone waits.

Nyx.

She's paler than I remember. Frayed at the edges. Her shadows hang thin and weak around her shoulders.

I force myself forward. The crowd seems to part without meaning to, magic sensing the tension coiling between us.

"You didn't hold up your end of the bargain," I say.

Her mouth curves—not quite a smile. "Didn't need to. You found your way in without me."

Her tone is casual, but her eyes are tired. Haunted.

I stop a few feet away. Close enough to see the exhaustion carved into her face. "Then why are you here?"

Her gaze flicks past me, toward the veins of Ether winding across the floor, toward the Feeders stepping up to take their Oaths one by one.

"You think this will protect them?" she asks quietly.

"It already is."

She shakes her head. "Not from him."

Wes bristles beside me. "Him?"

Nyx's attention shifts back to me, something sharp and knowing flickering in her expression. "Ethos."

My breath catches. "What are you saying?"

Her voice drops, softer now. "He's coming—and thanks to you, it seems he's learned to feed on other types of magic. On them."

Gray's growl rumbles low in his chest. "You brought him here?"

"He doesn't need to be brought." Nyx's smile is thin, bitter. "He follows the Source."

The words settle like stones in my stomach.

"You came to warn me," I say.

"I came because I don't want to die when he arrives."

Silence stretches between us. The mist curls tighter around my ankles, mirroring the tension crawling up my spine.

I study her—the way she holds herself, the exhaustion in her posture, the desperation she's trying to hide.

"You still want the Oath," I say.

"It's the only thing keeping me alive."

I glance at Wes, then Gray. Neither speaks, but I feel their silent question: *Are you sure?*

I'm not.

But I gesture toward a quiet corner anyway, away from the main flow of Feeders. Wes and Gray follow as I lead Nyx to the edge of the chamber where the light dims.

The Ether rises without me calling it, wrapping both of us in silver-white.

I speak the words—the invocation I'll say dozens of times today. My voice is steady, certain.

Nyx repeats them, her tone trembling but clear.

For an instant, the circle holds. Light flares between us, bright and sharp.

Then it snaps.

The connection fractures into static sparks that fade as quickly as they appeared.

I stagger. Wes catches my elbow.

Nyx crumples to one knee, gasping.

"It won't take you," I say quietly.

She looks up at me, something breaking behind her eyes. "Then it's already over."

Wes takes a step forward. "Bree—"

I shake my head. "No."

I don't know why I do it. Maybe because I see myself in her—the desperation, the fear of being cast out, the ache of not belonging.

Maybe because mercy costs me nothing here.

I call the raven.

Shadow forms feathers mid-air, solidifying into wings and talons. It lands on my shoulder, tilts its head, then hops to Nyx's shoulder.

She stares at it, wary. "What are you doing?"

"You wanted to be seen," I say. "You are."

I channel a soft pulse of Ether through the raven. The chamber glows faintly, light rippling outward through the veins on the floor. The Feeders nearby pause, heads bowing instinctively.

The raven dissolves into nothing, leaving behind a single silver-black feather in Nyx's palm.

"It's yours now," I say. "Not as mine—but as proof you were forgiven."

Nyx stares at the feather like she doesn't know how to hold it.

"He'll come for you first," she whispers.

"Let him."

She backs away slowly, toward the archway. The light around her dims as she moves.

Feeders pause their work, watching silently as she vanishes into the outer mist.

Her last words echo faintly: "You don't know what he's become."

Then she's gone.

The chamber feels heavier now. The light subdued but steady. The gathered Feeders begin moving again, quietly resuming their Oaths as if nothing happened.

I exhale shakily. Wes steadies me with a hand on my back. Gray keeps his eyes on the archway, watching the space where Nyx disappeared.

"We keep going," I say. "Every one of them through before nightfall."

Gray nods once. "We will."

The Ether veins flare suddenly—bright enough to sting my eyes—then pulse in rhythm with my heartbeat.

I turn toward the nearest Feeder, ready to help them through it.

Nyx's warning echoes in my head: *You don't know what he's become.*

"He's coming," I say quietly. "Sooner than we think."

Outside, thunder rolls again—the first heartbeat of the storm.

Chapter 46
THEO

I'm halfway across the courtyard when I pass Wes and Gray heading the opposite direction.

Wes grins. "Kitchen's all yours."

Gray smirks. "She's been in the chamber all day. Probably starving."

"I know." I keep walking, but I catch Wes's knowing look over his shoulder.

"Don't do anything we wouldn't do," he calls after me.

"That doesn't narrow it down much," I reply without turning.

Gray's laugh echoes behind me as they disappear into the dark.

The Sanctuary feels different tonight. Charged. The air hums faintly with residual Ether like static after lightning. The Oath Chamber has been running all day, dozens of bonds formed, dozens of lives changed.

And Bree's been at the center of it all.

I tell myself I'm just checking on her.

But I know better.

The kitchen glows with soft lantern light when I step inside. She's at the fridge, barefoot, hair loose around her shoulders, wearing what looks like one of Rhett's shirts—oversized, hanging to mid-thigh.

She's rummaging through shelves, pulling out fruit, bread, a jar of honey.

I pause in the doorway, watching.

Her hand trembles slightly as she reaches for something on the top shelf. Exhaustion carved into the line of her shoulders, the way she leans against the fridge door for support.

She's running on willpower alone.

Then she feels me watching.

She glances back over her shoulder, eyes meeting mine in the glow of the open fridge.

"Theo."

My name on her lips does something to me. Something primal and possessive that I've been keeping buried for too long.

I cross the room without a word, coming up behind her, sliding my arms around her waist. She melts back against me immediately, her head tipping to rest near my shoulder. I can feel her heartbeat through the thin fabric of the shirt, rapid but steady.

"You didn't eat all day," I murmur near her temple, breathing in the scent of her—mist and magic and something uniquely Bree.

"Didn't have time."

"You do now."

I reach past her, taking the honey jar from her hand, setting it aside on the counter. My other hand spreads flat against her stomach, feeling the muscles tense and release beneath my palm.

She huffs a soft laugh. "You always this bossy?"

"Only when you need me to be." I press a kiss to the junction of her neck and shoulder, feeling her shiver. "And right now, you need someone to make you stop."

"Stop what?"

"Running yourself into the ground." Another kiss, higher this time. "Taking care of everyone else and forgetting to take care of yourself."

"I don't forget," she says, but her voice has gone breathy. "I just—"

"Prioritize everyone else." I turn her gently to face me, hands settling on her hips. Her eyes are tired but bright, silver-flecked and beautiful. "You know, I'm starting to think you have something against pants."

Her mouth curves, mischief sparking in those eyes. "What gave me away?"

"Breakfast was a strong indicator." My thumb traces small circles against her hip bone through the thin fabric of the shirt. "I still can't stop thinking about it."

"Good." She reaches up, fingers threading into my hair, and the simple touch sends electricity down my spine. "Because I wasn't asking permission."

That shatters something in me.

I've been patient. Restrained. Watching her choose the others, waiting for my turn, telling myself I could wait as long as she needed.

But the way she's looking at me now?

Like she wants *me*.

Not the careful, measured Theo who keeps his distance. Not the seer who's always three steps ahead.

Just me.

If I don't touch her now, I never will.

I don't think.

I move.

My hands grip her waist and I turn, lifting her onto the counter in one smooth motion. She gasps, legs parting instinctively as I step between them. The movement makes the shirt ride up, exposing more of her thighs, and I have to grip the counter edge to keep from losing control completely.

"Theo—"

I kiss her.

Deep. Claiming. Every ounce of restraint I've been holding onto for months dissolving in the taste of her mouth. She tastes like possibility and power and home, and I can't get enough.

She kisses me back just as desperately, fingers tightening in my hair, pulling me closer. Her legs wrap around my waist and I groan against her lips at the feel of her pressed against me. Even through our clothes I can feel her heat, and it's driving me insane.

I break the kiss, breathing hard, resting my forehead against hers. I Saw you this morning. Kneeling in the Ether. Radiant. Untouchable."

"I'm very touchable," she breathes, and pulls me into another kiss.

"I know." My hands slide up her thighs, slowly, deliberately, pushing the shirt higher. "It terrified me. Because what I saw looked like goodbye."

Her hands frame my face, forcing me to meet her eyes. There's something fierce in her expression, something that makes my chest tight. "Then stay with me now."

Something in my chest cracks open.

I kiss her harder this time, one hand tangling in her hair while the other grips her hip. She arches into me, making soft sounds that drive me insane. I kiss down her jaw, her throat, finding that spot that makes her gasp.

"Tell me what you want," I say against her skin, feeling her pulse racing beneath my lips.

"You." Her breath hitches as my teeth graze her pulse point. "All of you."

I pull back just enough to look at her, making sure she sees the hunger in my eyes. "Once I start, I'm not stopping."

Her answer is to pull me back into another kiss, deeper this time, her tongue sliding against mine in a way that makes my vision blur.

That's all the permission I need.

I yank the shirt over her head in one smooth motion, tossing it onto a nearby chair. She's bare underneath—of course she is—and the sight of her steals my breath.

The lantern light catches on her skin, making her glow. The Ether responds to my attention, silver mist beginning to curl around us both, warm and almost alive.

"Do you have any idea what you do to me?" My hands map her skin, reverent but possessive, learning every curve, every place that makes her breath catch. "How many nights I've dreamed about this? About you?"

Her skin is impossibly soft beneath my palms. I trace the line of her collarbone, down between her breasts, feeling her scars, her heartbeat quickening. When I cup her breasts, thumbs brushing over her nipples, she arches into my touch with a sound that goes straight to my cock.

"Then stop talking," she says, voice breathless, "and show me."

I lean down, taking one nipple into my mouth, sucking gently before letting my teeth graze the sensitive peak. She gasps, hands fisting in my hair.

I give the other breast the same attention, alternating between gentle and rough, learning what makes her moan, what makes her grip me harder.

The Ether pulses brighter with every sound she makes.

"Theo—please—"

"Please what?" I kiss my way down her stomach, feeling her muscles jump beneath my lips. "Tell me what you need."

"You. I need you."

I drop to my knees between her legs.

Her eyes widen, pupils blown with desire. "Theo—"

"Shh." I press kisses along the inside of her thigh, working my way higher, taking my time. "Let me worship you properly."

I can already see how wet she is, and the knowledge that I did this to her—that I make her this desperate—nearly undoes me.

"Look at me," I command softly.

She does, and I hold her gaze as I press my mouth to her center.

She gasps, head falling back, but I grip her thigh firmly. "Eyes on me."

She obeys, and I reward her by dragging my tongue through her folds, slow and deliberate, tasting her. She's sweet and perfect and I could spend hours here.

I work her with my mouth, learning every sound, every shiver. When I suck her clit, her thighs tremble. When I fuck her with my tongue, she moans my name. The Ether responds to every touch, silver mist curling tighter around us, pulsing with her pleasure.

I can See it—flashes of light behind my eyes, fragments of our future tangled with the present. Her magic recognizing mine, weaving us together in ways that go beyond physical.

"Theo—oh god—"

I add my fingers, sliding one inside her, and she's so tight and hot around me that I nearly come just from that. I curl my finger, finding that spot that makes her cry out, and work it relentlessly while my mouth focuses on her clit.

"Please—I'm so close—"

I add a second finger, stretching her, preparing her, and increase the pressure of my tongue. Her hands are in my hair, gripping hard enough to hurt, but I don't care. I want her to lose control.

"Come for me," I murmur against her. "Let me feel you."

She shatters.

Her thighs clamp around my head, her entire body arching off the counter as she comes undone. The Ether flares so bright it illuminates the entire kitchen like daylight. I can feel her clenching around my fingers, pulsing with her release, and I work her through it, prolonging it, until she's gasping my name and pushing weakly at my shoulders.

The glow lingers in the grain of the wood, fading like embers.

When I finally pull back, she's trembling, chest heaving, eyes unfocused and glazed with pleasure.

Beautiful.

I stand, wiping my mouth with the back of my hand, and capture her lips in another kiss so she can taste herself on my tongue. She whimpers against me, hands fumbling with my belt, still shaking from her orgasm.

"I need you," she breathes against my mouth. Her voice trembles, wrecked and certain all at once. "Inside me. Now."

I help her with my belt, shoving my pants down just enough to free myself. I'm so hard it's almost painful, and when she wraps her hand around me, stroking once, twice, I have to grip the counter to stay upright.

"Bree—"

"Now, Theo."

I lift her off the counter, turning her, pressing her forward over the wooden surface. She braces herself on her forearms, looking back at me over her shoulder, pupils blown wide, hair falling around her face.

The sight of her bent over like this, presenting herself to me, nearly makes me lose it before I've even started.

"You're sure?" I ask, even though I'm barely holding on. My cock is pressed against her entrance, and it takes every ounce of willpower not to just slam home.

"Theo." Her voice is desperate, pleading. "Please."

I grip her hips and push inside in one slow, deep thrust.

We both groan.

She's impossibly tight and hot and perfect around me, and I have to pause, breathing hard, giving us both a moment to adjust. The feeling of being inside her is almost overwhelming—not just physically, but magically. I can feel our connection blazing, the Ether binding us together.

Then she pushes back against me, taking me even deeper. "Move."

I do.

Slow at first, pulling almost all the way out before sliding back in, watching the way her body takes me, the way her fingers grip the counter edge white-knuckled. The Ether coils tighter around us with every thrust, silver light pulsing in rhythm with our bodies.

"Harder," she gasps.

I obey, setting a punishing pace, the sound of skin slapping against skin filling the kitchen. Each thrust drives her forward slightly, and she braces herself, pushing back to meet me.

The visions come in flashes—silver light, her face beneath me in a dozen different moments, futures branching out from this single point. The bond between us blazing like a star, permanent and unbreakable.

"You feel so good," I groan, one hand sliding up her spine, feeling her arch beneath my touch. "So fucking perfect. Do you know how long I've wanted this? Wanted you?"

She's making sounds I've never heard before—desperate, needy, completely uninhibited. Each moan, each gasp of my name drives me closer to the edge.

I lean over her, pressing my chest to her back, changing the angle so I'm hitting deeper. She cries out, and I feel her tightening around me, getting close again.

"That's it," I murmur against her ear, one arm wrapping around her waist to hold her steady while I drive into her. "Come for me again. I want to feel you."

My other hand slides around to where we're joined, fingers finding her clit, circling with the same rhythm as my thrusts. She's so sensitive still from her first orgasm that it only takes a few touches before she's trembling.

"Theo—oh god—I'm—"

"I know." I increase my pace, fucking her harder, deeper, my fingers working her clit. "Let go. Now."

She breaks.

Her entire body locks up, a sob tearing from her throat as she comes. The Ether explodes outward, light flooding the kitchen so bright I have to close my eyes. She clenches around me so tight it's almost painful, and that's all it takes to push me over the edge.

I bury myself deep with a groan, my own orgasm tearing through me. I can feel myself pulsing inside her, filling her, and the feeling is so intense it's almost transcendent. The visions flash faster—our future solidifying, the bond stronger than it's ever been.

For a long moment, we just breathe, both of us shaking.

Then I carefully pull out, immediately mourning the loss of her heat. I turn her in my arms, pulling her against my chest, holding her while we both come down.

She's trembling. I press kisses to her temple, her cheek, her lips—gentle now, reverent.

"Okay?" I murmur against her hair.

She nods against me, arms wrapping around my waist. "More than okay."

I lift her back onto the counter, stepping between her legs again, gentler now. She's still catching her breath, skin flushed and glowing with Ether-light.

She rests her forehead against mine, fingers tracing idle patterns on my chest. "You're dangerous."

"So are you."

I retrieve the shirt from the chair, helping her back into it, then pull my pants up, and we just hold each other in the soft lantern light.

"Well," a voice drawls from the doorway, "I'm never going to be able to look at this kitchen the same way again."

We both freeze.

Jace leans against the doorframe, arms crossed, grinning like the cat that caught the canary.

"How long have you been standing there?" I ask, trying for casual and probably failing.

"Long enough." He pushes off the doorframe, sauntering toward the pantry. "You're welcome, by the way."

"For what?"

He grabs an apple, biting into it with a sharp crunch. "Not interrupting sooner. Some of us have self-control." His grin widens. "Well. Most of us."

Bree lifts her head, cheeks flushed. "Jace—"

"Relax, sweetheart. Your secret's safe with me." He winks. "Though you might want to do something about the Ether-glow situation before the others come looking. Pretty sure the whole sanctuary can see it from here."

He's right. The silver mist is still curling lazily through the kitchen, pulsing softly with residual energy.

"Get out," I say, but there's no heat in it.

"Already gone." He heads for the door, then pauses, looking back over his shoulder. "But seriously—next time, maybe pick a room with a lock?"

Then he's gone, his laughter echoing down the hallway.

Bree looks up at me, and we both start laughing at the same time.

"Well," she says. "That was mortifying."

"Could've been worse." I kiss her forehead. "Could've been Rhett."

She groans. "Don't even joke about that."

I help her down from the counter, and she wobbles slightly on her feet. I steady her, pulling her close again.

"Food," I say firmly. "And then bed."

"Bed sounds good."

"Sleep," I clarify, even though part of me is already thinking about round two.

She smirks. "If you say so."

She starts gathering the food she'd abandoned earlier, and I watch her move around the kitchen—my shirt hanging on her frame, hair messy from my hands, that satisfied glow on her skin.

Mine.

Then she stills, head tilting slightly like she's listening to something I can't hear.

"Bree?"

She turns to me, and something in her expression has shifted. Alert. Wary.

Outside, thunder rumbles. Closer than before.

"It's close," I say quietly. "The storm."

"I know." She wraps her arms around herself, and I pull her back against my chest.

"Stay with me tonight, for however long we have," she whispers.

"Always."

Thunder rolls again—closer this time.

The storm doesn't wait anymore.

Chapter 47
SETH

I can't sleep.

Haven't been able to for hours now. Everyone else finally crashed after the long day—the Oath Chamber is still running, Feeders streaming through one after another. Exhausting, necessary work.

But I'm too wired. Too aware of what's coming.

So I sit in the common room, near the window where I can see the road leading up to the Sanctuary. Moonlight filters through the glass, casting everything in silver-blue. The fire had burned down to embers, but I don't bother stoking it.

I'm not cold.

Just watchful.

The Sanctuary feels different than anywhere I've been. There's a hum to it—like the walls themselves breathe with Ether. I've never felt anything like this before. Never felt anything this alive.

Never her.

I shift in the chair, trying not to think about the way Bree looked earlier when she came back from the Oath Chamber—exhausted but radiant, silver mist clinging to her like a second skin. The way she moves through this place like she was made for it.

Maybe she was.

A sound cuts through the quiet—footsteps outside, fast and urgent.

I'm on my feet before the door opens.

A young Feeder bursts in, breathless, eyes wide. "They're coming. Ten minutes out. The Council—" He swallows hard. "And the man with them."

My pulse spikes, but I keep my voice level. "Wake Thane. I'll get Bree."

He nods and takes off down the hall.

I move quickly through the corridors, boots silent on stone. The Sanctuary is still sleeping—peaceful, unaware. I pass closed doors, hearing faint breathing, the occasional rustle of movement.

When I reach Bree's room, I hesitate for half a second.

Then I push the door open.

The space is dimly lit, a single lantern burning low on the bedside table. She's asleep, tangled in blankets, Theo beside her with one arm draped protectively across her waist. The faint shimmer of Ether glows around them both like morning fog.

She looks younger like this. Softer.

I cross to the bed and kneel beside it, reaching out to touch her shoulder gently. "Bree. Wake up."

Her eyes snap open immediately—clear, sharp, fully aware despite having been asleep seconds ago. Theo stirs beside her, already alert.

"What is it?"

"They're here. Ten minutes out."

She sits up in one fluid motion, and Theo follows, swinging his legs over the edge of the bed on the other side. No panic. No hesitation. Just readiness from both of them.

"I'll wake the others," Theo says, already moving toward the door.

I step back, giving Bree space, averting my gaze as she stands and moves toward the wardrobe where her leathers hang.

The white ones.

I've seen them before at Auren's—sleek, reinforced, somehow both elegant and deadly. When she pulls them on, the air in the room changes. The Ether responds, curling tighter around her, brighter.

She's not just a woman getting dressed.

She's armoring herself.

I move toward the door. "I'll help Theo—"

"Wait."

I stop. Turn back.

She crosses to me, stopping close enough that I can feel the hum of her magic against my skin. It's warm, electric, alive.

Her voice softens. "Just in case I don't get another chance to do this."

Before I can ask what she means, she kisses me.

Her lips are soft against mine, tentative for just a breath before she commits fully. Her hand comes up to cup my jaw, fingers sliding into my hair, and I freeze for half a second—stunned by the certainty in her touch, the warmth of her mouth.

Then I kiss her back.

My hands find her waist, pulling her closer, and she makes a soft sound against my lips that nearly undoes me. She tastes like honey and something sweeter underneath, something that feels like home even though I've never had one.

The kiss deepens. Her fingers tighten in my hair and I angle my head, claiming her mouth more thoroughly. She melts into me, body fitting against mine like she was made for it.

And then—

She gasps against my mouth.

The Ether surges between us, wrapping around both of us in a silver blaze that fills the room. I feel the bond flare to life—not new to me, but new to her.

She knows now.

Bree pulls back slightly, eyes wide with shock, her hand flying to her chest like she can feel the connection burning there.

I've known since the Void. Since she said those words—*you were supposed to be mine*—and the bond locked into place while she was unconscious, fighting for her life. Even if I didn't know what it was then. Not until Stellan put a name to it.

But she didn't know.

Until now.

The bond hums under my skin, a pulse syncing with hers, faint but undeniable. The taste of her lingers—salt and static, the kind of heat that feels like it could burn through skin if I let it.

Her hand presses against my chest, right over my heart, trembling. I can see the realization in her eyes—the confusion, the wonder, the certainty all crashing together at once.

"You were already mine," she whispers, voice shaking.

I cover her hand with mine, holding it there. "And now you know."

Her breath hitches. For a moment, we just stand there, the Ether pulsing softly around us like a heartbeat.

Then she steps back, composure sliding back into place like armor. But her eyes are still wide, still stunned.

"We need to go," she says. "Now you can wake the others."

She nods once, breath still uneven, and turns toward the door.

Then we're moving.

The Sanctuary is already stirring as we pass through the halls—doors opening, voices murmuring, footsteps quickening. Rhett's already halfway down the stairs, pulling on a shirt. Jace is cursing under his breath as he buckles his knife belt. Theo's talking quietly to Gray near the common room entrance, both of them already dressed and armed.

We reach the common room where Thane is waiting, Wes hovering near the doorway, tense and alert.

Bree steps forward. "We don't have time. Ten minutes."

Thane nods once. "Then we meet them outside."

Bree shakes her head. "Not yet. They'll come to us."

The group exchanges glances. No one argues.

"Feeders first," she says. "I want them to see what we've built before the Council tries to tear it down."

Rhett crosses his arms. "You think that'll stop them?"

"No." Her voice is steady. "But it'll make a statement."

Thane's mouth curves slightly—not quite a smile, but close. "Then let's make it loud."

Bree moves toward the door, and we all fall in behind her. Not following. Supporting.

The air outside is cool, the sky still dark but beginning to lighten at the edges. Dawn's not far off.

The door creaks open, and mist spills in like a living thing.

Bree steps through the archway first, into the courtyard beyond.

And stops.

The mist moves like breath through the open space, glinting silver in the first light.

I come up beside her, and my breath catches.

The courtyard is full.

Not just a few Feeders scattered around doing late-night repairs or standing watch.

Hundreds.

They line the edges of the space, standing in clusters, sitting on low walls, leaning against trees. Some are talking quietly. Others are silent, watching. Waiting.

Every single one of them stayed.

Bree's hand lifts slightly, like she's reaching for something that isn't there. Her voice comes out barely above a whisper.

"I thought... I thought maybe a dozen would stay."

"They all did," Thane says quietly from behind her. "Every last one."

She takes a step forward, and the nearest Feeders turn toward her. Then the next group. Then the next.

A ripple of movement spreads through the crowd as they all shift their attention to her—hundreds of eyes, hundreds of faces, all focused on the woman standing at the center of it all.

The Source.

Bree's shoulders straighten. Her chin lifts.

The Ether rises around her like wings.

And for the first time since I met her, I see it clearly—not just the power, not just the magic.

The queen.

Chapter 48
BREE

I can't breathe.

My pulse stutters, too much air in my lungs and not enough space to hold it.

Not from fear. From the weight of what I'm seeing.

Hundreds of them.

Every single Feeder who came to the Sanctuary—still here. Standing in the courtyard as dawn breaks over the hills, silver mist drifting between them, alive as breath, silver veins of my Ether glowing at their feet.

They're watching me.

Waiting.

I take a step forward, and the nearest ones shift slightly—not backing away, but leaning in. Like they're afraid I might disappear if they blink.

My throat tightens.

"I didn't expect you to stay." My voice comes out quieter than I intended, but it carries in the stillness. "Not all of you. Maybe a handful. Maybe none."

A few heads tilt. Some exchange glances.

"Some of you have been enslaved for the last five years," I continue, taking another step. The Ether rises around me without me calling it, silver mist wrapping around my ankles, my wrists. "The rest of you taught that safety means staying hidden. Staying silent. Staying small."

I pause, letting the words settle.

"And you stayed anyway."

Silence.

Then someone near the front—a woman with dark hair and tired eyes—nods once.

That's all it takes.

I feel something crack open in my chest.

"You were told you were lesser." My voice grows steadier now, louder. "Tools. Feeders. Shadows in someone else's story. Dangerous because you needed what others freely gave—connection, touch, life."

The mist pulses brighter.

"They made you believe you were broken. That your hunger made you weak. That you deserved to be cast out, controlled, or killed."

A murmur ripples through the crowd. Agreement. Pain. Recognition.

I let it settle before I speak again.

"But look around you."

I gesture to the Sanctuary—the rebuilt walls, the gardens coming back to life, the Oath Chamber glowing faintly in the distance.

"You built this. Not me. Everything we've done here, every root planted, every oath sworn—that was you. Every heartbeat of this place exists because you chose it."

The woman in front lifts her chin slightly. Others straighten.

"The Council calls you dangerous," I say, voice dropping lower but harder, "because you now remember what they made you forget."

I pause.

"Your worth."

The Ether flares.

Silver light spreads outward from where I stand, tracing along the veins in the ground that glow brighter with every word.

"They're coming." I don't look away from the crowd. "Right now. To take this from you. To tell you that you don't belong here. That you never did. That I have no right to offer you sanctuary."

The air thickens, every heartbeat syncing to mine.

Thunder rumbles faintly in the distance.

"And if they try—" My voice hardens. "If they come to tear down what we've built, to take what you've chosen, to tell you again that you are lesser—"

I take one more step forward.

"They'll have to go through me."

The mist explodes outward, silver light flooding the courtyard. The veins beneath the ground pulse in rhythm with my heartbeat—bright enough to see even in the dawn light.

Someone gasps.

But no one moves away.

I feel it then—the bond with Seth humming in my chest, still new and raw. Thane's steady presence at my back. The others close by, solid and certain.

And hundreds of eyes on me, no longer afraid.

Believing.

"No one here is lesser," I say, and my voice doesn't shake. "No one here is alone. This is our home."

The sky darkens. Thunder rolls again, closer now.

I lift my chin.

"And if the world wants to burn it down—"

The Ether rises like wings behind me, silver and blinding.

"—then let it learn what fire really is."

The words hang in the air for one perfect, crystalline moment.

Then the crowd erupts.

Not in cheers—something deeper. A roar of recognition, of defiance, of belief. Hands raise, fists clench, voices rise in a sound that shakes the ground beneath my feet.

The Ether answers.

Light floods the courtyard, brighter than dawn, wrapping around every person standing there like armor. The veins in the ground pulse once, twice, then settle into a steady glow.

I feel Thane's hand on my shoulder. Seth beside me, still radiating that quiet certainty. The others close in, forming a wall at my back.

Not protecting me.

Standing with me.

Thunder cracks overhead, sharp and immediate.

And then I see them.

On the hill beyond the Sanctuary gates, figures appear—dark against the lightening sky.

The Council.

And someone else.

Taller. Broader. Moving with the kind of confidence that comes from believing you've already won.

Phil.

Behind them, hundreds more. What must be five hundred at least—soldiers, enforcers, followers. An army ready to tear us down.

The crowd goes silent.

I don't move. Don't flinch.

Just watch as they approach.

The storm doesn't wait anymore.

And neither do I.

The first drops of rain hiss against the stones as we step forward.

Chapter 49
STELLAN

I've never been more in awe of this beautiful woman.

The courtyard is still vibrating from her speech. The Feeders nearest the epicenter flex their hands, shaking off the residual Ether like static crawling under their skin.

Bree's Ether flares bright enough to leave afterimages burned into my vision, silver light pulsing through the stone beneath our feet like a living heartbeat. She stands ringed by Gray, Rhett, Wes, Theo, and Jace—Thane a step off her shoulder. The Feeders around us are standing taller, breathing deeper, believing for the first time in their lives that they might be worth something.

Bare. Dangerous. Necessary.

And then I see them.

On the ridge beyond the gates, silhouettes appear against the dawn—dark figures cresting the hill like a wave of shadows.

The Council. I recognize their formation, the way they hold themselves above everyone else even from this distance.

Phil. Taller, broader, moving with that infuriating confidence that comes from never having been told no.

And behind them—

My lungs forget the motion.

An army. Five hundred at least. Maybe more.

Soldiers. Enforcers. Followers ready to tear down everything we've built.

But that's not what makes my hands curl into fists.

It's the others I feel before I fully see them.

Feeders.

Dozens of them scattered through the ranks, their emotional signatures pulsing beneath the surface like cords of hunger and compulsion. Even at this distance, their signatures rasp—hunger harnessed to someone else's leash. That specific rhythm—suppressed, twisted, trained into obedience until it calcified.

They taught them to kneel so well they forgot how to stand.

Rage floods through me, cold and immediate. Not the wild, reckless kind. The controlled fury that sharpens every sense, every thought, every breath.

Of course they brought them. What better weapon than the ones they taught to fear themselves?

I watch Bree standing at the center of the courtyard, chin high, Ether still glowing around her like armor. She won't flinch. She won't back down.

So neither will I.

I step to her right, Thane a shadow at my left. Gray, Rhett, Wes, Theo, and Jace hold the arc behind her. The shape of a wall.

I keep my voice low enough that only she and Thane can hear.

"Thane and I have the Feeders," I say quietly. "If you'll let us."

She turns, meeting my eyes. For a fraction of a second, I see the hesitation—the weight of trusting someone else with this. Then her shoulders relax slightly.

"I trust you."

She's never said those words to me before. They settle something in my chest I didn't know was waiting.

I nod once and turn away, already moving.

Thane falls into step beside me without needing to be told. We've done this before—different battles, different stakes, but the same dance. He knows when to lead and when to follow.

Right now, he follows.

The Feeders respond before I even open my mouth. They feel the shift in my energy, the way my focus clicks into place. Some straighten. Others tense. All of them watch.

My voice cuts clear through the rising wind:

"Mothers and children—lower hall, east corridor, the rooms there."

A few women move immediately, gathering children close. Others hesitate.

"If you want to fight," I add, meeting their eyes one by one, "stay. The choice is yours. Not mine. Not anyone's."

Several nod and step back into formation. The rest move toward safety without shame.

Good.

I turn to the rest—the fighters, the ones whose hunger has been sharpened into something useful.

Zira steps up beside me, her presence steady and sharp. She doesn't need to be told what's coming. She already knows.

"Fighters in thirds: northern wall, low gate, gardens."

They move without question, already positioning themselves. Zira's voice cuts through, reinforcing the command with quiet authority.

"Stay low. Stay sharp."

"No one shows early," I add. "You move on my signal."

Thane steps forward, Zira falling into formation beside him, finishing the distribution with that clipped authority that makes people obey without thinking.

"The moment they breach the threshold, you hit from both flanks. Don't give them the chance to organize."

I reach for my magic—not to feed, but to command.

The Ether responds, curling outward from my chest in threads too faint for most to see. It's stronger than I remember. I watch as it weaves through the clusters of Feeders, dampening their fear, sharpening their focus. Amplifying the quiet confidence that comes from knowing you're stronger than they think.

I'm surprised as I feel Wes's magic join mine as I lock eyes with him still standing near Bree—subtler, but just as precise. Learning from my lead in real time. He steadies the nervous ones, the young ones who haven't fought before. I nod once. *I knew he had it in him.*

Then I push outward, toward the approaching army.

I lay a thin field over the approach—boredom, false ease, a whisper to the hindbrain. Not a glamor, just a nudge. Enough to make a watchman blink the wrong second. A soldier who thinks he's safe is already halfway dead.

They may see our numbers, but they won't know our strength. Zira stands at my left, eyes scanning the horizon.

I remember what it was like to be hungry and leashed. To be told I was dangerous, broken, lesser. To watch others like me believe it.

Bree's voice still echoes in my head: *They'll have to go through me.*

Not while I still breathe.

Thane appears at my shoulder, silent for a moment before speaking.

"You take the south flank," I murmur. "I'll keep the heart of it steady."

He nods once. "Try not to kill them all before I get there."

I don't look at him, but my mouth almost remembers how to smile.

Zira's voice is dry. "Save some for the rest of us."

Then the moment passes, and we're moving again.

The Sanctuary hums like a living thing around us—Ether threads glowing faintly beneath the soil, matching the stormlight above. Bree and the others stand near the courtyard center, a constellation of power waiting for the storm to break.

I position myself at the edge of the assembled Feeders, Zira a shadow at my side, every nerve tuned to the distant rhythm of approaching footsteps.

Five hundred heartbeats. Maybe more.

And beneath them, those familiar signatures—Feeders marching toward their own destruction because someone told them it was loyalty.

My pupils dilate, bleeding black from the edges inward. Beside me, Zira's fangs extend.

The world sharpens. Every emotional thread in range snaps into focus like drawn wire. I feel the fear in our ranks, the determination, the hunger barely leashed. I feel the false confidence radiating from the approaching army, the obedience threaded through the enslaved Feeders like chains they can't see.

Lightning flickers on the horizon, illuminating Phil's silhouette at the head of the formation.

I let my power coil tighter, ready to strike.

Thunder cracks overhead.

The air tastes metallic, charged.

The first boot strikes Sanctuary stone.

The field hums against my teeth.

"Let them come."

Chapter 50
BREE

The stillness after Stellan's words isn't silence. It's the breath before everything breaks.

I stand at the center of the courtyard, mist coiling at my feet like it's waiting for permission. The others close ranks around me—Gray at my right, Rhett at my left, Theo, Wes and Jace just behind. Silent. Ready.

Where the hell is Seth?

Theo leans close, his voice quiet but absolute. "You aren't broken, Bree. You're more whole than you've ever been. Cracks and all."

My breath catches.

More whole.

I want to believe him. Looking at the silver veins threading through the ground, the Sanctuary alive and responding to me, the people who've come because they felt my call—I can almost see it.

But wholeness like this feels like standing on the edge of a blade.

The ground rumbles.

Not thunder. Not earthquake.

Marching.

"They're here," Wes says quietly.

I don't need him to tell me. I can *feel* them—Council magic, sharp and sterile, ozone and blood. And underneath, something worse.

Phil.

Through the mist threading across the grounds, figures emerge.

He leads, of course. Smirking like he's already won. Like showing up with an army makes him untouchable.

Behind him, the Council walks in formation—Valdris with flames licking her boots, Marcus cold and pristine, Eris's blank gaze fixed on nothing, Nyx draped in shadows that move wrong, a raven perched on her shoulder.

And behind them—

Five hundred.

An army that stops just outside the Sanctuary boundary, held back by the pulsing silver veins that mark territory that isn't theirs. The first ranks halt instinctively, sensing the hum of power underfoot.

My power.

The realization settles cold in my chest: *They're not here to negotiate. They're here to reclaim.*

Phil reaches the edge of the silver veins—the ones that pulse like a heartbeat through the ground. He stops, boot hovering over the nearest thread, and his smirk widens.

"Hello, Bree."

The Ether *flares*.

Silver light explodes upward from the veins, a warning so bright I see several Council members flinch. The ground trembles. The air crackles.

My voice comes steady. "That's close enough."

Phil's smile doesn't falter. If anything, it sharpens. He spreads his hands like he's being reasonable. "We only came to talk, Bree. Surely you can allow that."

"Talk," I repeat flatly.

"The Council has... concerns." His gaze sweeps over the others, dismissive and calculating, before settling back on me. "About the chaos you've caused. Your scandalous interlude with someone harboring dark magic."

The words land like poison.

He's talking about Ethos. The name I can't hear without tasting blood and lightning.

Twisting everything. Making me the villain.

My hands curl into fists. The mist around my feet darkens just slightly—not corruption, but storm-silver, charged and dangerous.

"The bonds you've formed," Phil continues smoothly. "The power you've claimed without permission. The laws you've broken allowing Feeders to take the Oath. The instability you've brought to our carefully maintained balance."

Carefully maintained balance. He means control. He means submission.

"We can resolve this peacefully," he says. "All you have to do is come with us. Answer some questions. Cooperate."

The trap crystallizes in my mind, sharp and clear.

If I go, they take the sanctuary. They erase everything we've built, again. It goes back to how it was—a labor camp, forcing them to mine Ether, giving up their freedom, their lives.

"I'm not going anywhere with you."

The words come out as hard as I intend. Final.

The Ether pulses once, sharp and deliberate. I reach through it, calling.

Shadows darken as the fox materializes first—smoke and silver, eyes like stars. The snake follows, winding through the air like living shadow.

Find Seth, I send through the connection. *Protect him.*

They vanish without sound, slipping between realms like they were never here.

Phil's expression shifts—just slightly. The mock-gentleness falls away, replaced by something colder.

He steps back. The Council moves with him, forming a line. Behind them, the army begins to ready—not weapons, but *magic*. I can feel it building, pressure mounting in the air.

Phil's smile returns, sharper than before.

"Then perhaps it's time you meet Daddy," he says softly.

And his voice *folds*.

The word echoes—once in Phil's familiar slur, once in something impossibly older. The air bends, sound warps; colors flatten into silver and black.

My breath stops.

"Or perhaps," he continues, and now the second voice is stronger, layered beneath like a current pulling me under, "you remember me by another name."

The world tilts.

His face doesn't change—still Phil, still human—but the thing beneath surfaces. Not transformation. *Revelation.*

The voice in the Void. The whispers in my dreams. The presence that wrapped around me and called me *his*.

The second voice shapes a word I once heard in the dark—*Ethos*.
Daddy.

Not Kevin. Not my father.

Him.

My pulse fractures. The mist recoils violently, silver light snapping back toward me like I've been struck.

"No." The word scrapes out of my throat.

Phil—*Ethos*—tilts his head, and for the first time I see it. The way he moves. The way he watches. The calm, predatory patience that has nothing to do with being drunk or human or anything I convinced myself he was.

He's been here the entire time.

"You've been so close," he murmurs, his voice fully his now—no more Phil, no more pretense. Smooth and deliberate and wrong. "So brave. So determined to protect them all."

He gestures to the people behind me, the Feeders who came because they felt my call. The families. The broken.

"But you couldn't even see me standing right in front of you," he purrs as shadows form at his feet. "Not even when I was inside of you."

The words crawl under my skin like hands.

I can't breathe.

Horror crawls up my throat.

The supply room. His hands on me. *Your father says hi.*

The sanctuary. The corruption threading through my Ether. *Daddy will be so pleased.*

In the Void when I wanted nothing more than his touch, his power to consume me. *Do you feel it? How right this is?*

Every moment I thought I was escaping him, he was *right there*.

The mist lashes outward, striking the ground in silver arcs that hiss like lightning in rain.

Behind me, someone makes a sound—half rage, half devastation. Gray's voice cuts through the shock, raw and broken: "You son of a bitch."

Rhett's heat flares so violently the air shimmers. Wes goes absolutely still, the kind of stillness that comes before violence. Theo's breathing turns sharp and uneven, like he's fighting not to collapse under the weight of what this means.

And Thane—

Thane already knew.

I can feel it in the way he doesn't move, doesn't react. He's known, or suspected, and never said a word.

The ground trembles. The silver veins pulse erratically, light flickering like a dying heartbeat.

"No," I whisper again, but it's not denial. It's rage.

The mist rises, wild and bright, straining against my control.

Ethos smiles—Phil's face wearing an expression that was never his to begin with.

"Welcome home, little queen," he says softly. "We have so much to discuss."

Chapter 51
BREE

The glamour falls.

Not slowly. Not dramatically.

It just *stops*.

Phil's body doesn't twist or transform—it simply sheds pretense like a snake shedding skin. His eyes go black, shot through with silver that moves like liquid mercury. His voice reverberates, layered over itself until I can't tell where one tone ends and another begins.

The air around him hums like a tuning fork struck too hard.

I try to move—try to call the Ether, *something*—but he's faster.

"Don't—" I start.

Too late.

The guys charge as one. Rhett leads with fire blazing around his fists, Gray half-shifted mid-motion, Jace's blades flashing silver in the light. Theo and Wes channel energy behind them.

Ethos barely moves.

A gesture. A pulse.

They're thrown back—not struck, not burned, simply *rejected* from existence for a heartbeat before they hit the ground hard enough that the impact echoes through the courtyard.

They fall like stars pulled out of orbit.

"No!" The scream tears out of my throat.

I lunge forward, but the world *stops*.

Marcus raises one hand, murmuring words I can't hear over the ringing in my ears. My body locks mid-step. The Ether thrashes—wild, furious, *mine*—but my limbs refuse to obey.

My mind screams. My magic rages.

But I can't move.

Ethos tilts his head, watching me struggle with something that might be amusement. "Don't fight it, little queen. You'll want to see this."

Behind him, the army surges forward.

Five hundred soldiers crash against the Feeders and families who answered my call. Ether, fire, blood, and mist explode together. The air fills with screams—raw and primal and *wrong*.

The sanctuary's walls pulse like a heartbeat trying to survive cardiac arrest.

I feel each death through the Ether like a nerve being cut.

The Feeders who came because they trusted me. The families who believed I could protect them. One by one, their lights wink out—bonds severing, magic dying, lives ending.

The world becomes a map of dying lights.

"Look at them." Ethos steps close enough that his breath ghosts across my ear. "Your beautiful rebellion, dying for nothing. Tell me, does it still feel like salvation?"

My eyes burn. The mist around my feet writhes uselessly, unable to reach anyone who needs it.

He points, directing my gaze like I'm a puppet.

Stellan—on his knees in the dirt, chest heaving, hands drenched in blood that isn't his. His perfect control shattered, replaced by something raw and desperate.

Rhett—flames guttering out as a blow sends him sprawling. He tries to push himself up, falls, tries again.

Wes and Theo—collapsed together near the fountain. Theo's eyes are half-closed, blood trailing from his temple. Wes shields him with his body even though he's bleeding from the mouth.

Gray—down but still dragging himself toward me, fingers digging into the earth. His eyes lock on mine even when he can't stand.

And Thane—

Thane fights like a storm contained in flesh. A dozen opponents surround him and he moves through them with ruthless efficiency. But even he's slowing. Even he's bleeding.

"They're dying for you," Ethos murmurs. "Every single one of them. And you can't save them."

Movement catches my eye—Seth, half-hidden in shadow near the sanctuary wall.

He's doing something. I can't tell what. The Ether can't reach far enough through Marcus's binding to sense it properly.

But he's *there*.

"Your newest love," Ethos purrs. "The one you kissed like a promise. The one who bonded to you while you were in *my* bed. Where is he now, Bree? When you need him most?"

I try to speak—to call to Seth, to scream, to do *anything*—but nothing comes out except a choked sound that might be his name.

The battle rages. More lights wink out. More screams cut short.

And I stand frozen, forced to watch it all burn.

Then—

Ethos stiffens.

The change is subtle—just a fraction of tension in his shoulders, a break in his perfect composure. His smirk falters.

Pain flickers across his face.

Not mine. *His*.

I feel it through the air, through the bound Ether—something *hit* him. Something he didn't expect.

In the shadows, Seth's silhouette finally moves. Light flares—or maybe sound breaks through the chaos—but I can't see what he does.

Only Ethos's reaction.

A sound tears from his throat—low, startled, *pained*.

The entire battlefield stills for a fraction of a second, like the world holding its breath.

"What—" His voice frays at the edges, no longer smooth. "What have you—"

Chapter 52
GRAY

Dirt. Blood. The metallic crackle of Ether in the air.

Her scent under all of it—silver and smoke.

I drag myself forward, vision fracturing with every movement. My ribs scream. Something's broken—maybe several somethings. The world tilts sideways, sparks of fire and Ether cutting through the haze.

One thought pulses through the static: *Get to her.*

I lift my head.

Bree stands twenty feet away, but she's not *standing*—she's frozen. Eyes wide, mouth open like she's screaming, but no sound comes out. The mist writhes around her feet, shuddering uselessly.

Marcus.

The realization hits like ice water. She can see everything. Feels every death. And she can't move.

My hands dig into the earth, claws half-formed, dragging me forward inch by inch.

The battlefield spreads around me in ruin.

Stellan moves through the melee like a blade of night, fangs bared, every strike a promise—but even he's slowing. Blood streaks his jaw.

Rhett lies crumpled near the fountain, barely conscious, the air still shimmering with leftover heat.

Theo and Wes—collapsed together, Theo's eyes half-closed, Wes shielding him even though he's bleeding from the mouth.

Thane cuts through soldiers with ruthless precision, but he's bleeding heavily. Too many opponents. Too much ground to cover.

Zira tears through three fighters at once, fury incarnate, but for every one she drops, two more press forward.

We're losing.

I crawl faster, ignoring the pain screaming through every nerve.

Then I see him.

Ethos stands in front of Bree, close enough to whisper. That same predatory calm. That same certainty.

Until something *hits* him.

He stiffens. The smugness cracks.

For a breath I think it's her—some buried surge finally breaking free—but then I see him twist, light in his chest pulled *outward* instead of in.

My gaze snaps to the shadows near the sanctuary wall.

Seth.

On his feet now, arm outstretched, veins lit like cracks in glass. Void energy coils from Ethos's body toward his hand—black threads laced with silver, writhing like living things.

The wrongness of that power slams into me: cold, endless, *hungry*.

He's doing to Ethos what Ethos did to Bree.

Pulling the Void itself out of him.

A shout cuts through the noise.

I turn—

Riley bursts from the treeline.

Her magic hits the ground first—half silver, half black, streaming from her palms like mirrored smoke. The air bends around her, the two colors fighting and then twisting together as she runs straight into the battlefield.

She doesn't slow. Doesn't hesitate.

She slams both hands down.

The black-silver Ether races across the soil like wildfire, reaching the wounded. Some stabilize immediately—gasping, eyes clearing. Others just stop dying.

The shift is instant. Tangible.

She's *healing* them.

I drag myself the last few feet, tasting blood, the earth vibrating beneath me from the Void tug-of-war happening twenty feet away.

Ethos screams.

Not loud—but ancient. A sound that splits the air and makes every instinct I have scream *run*.

I reach Bree's boots. Look up into her eyes—still locked, still trapped—and force the words out.

"Hold on," I rasp. "We've got you."

Her gaze flickers. Just barely. Like she heard me through the paralysis.

The battlefield shakes.

Seth pulls harder.

Riley's magic spreads farther.

And somewhere in the chaos, something is about to break.

Chapter 53
BREE

Breathe.

One of you. Please.

The word isn't mine—I don't know if I think it or whisper it—but it breaks the silence between screams.

Movement on the ridge.

A cluster of Feeders surge toward Marcus—three of ours who were supposed to be retreating. They hit him before he can react, teeth bared, Ether sparking wild.

His concentration shatters.

The binding on me *snaps*.

The world slams back in all at once—sound, heat, pain. My lungs drag in air like I've been drowning. The mist surges around my feet, wild and uncontrolled.

But it's already too late.

Ethos feels it at the same time.

His head jerks, silver bleeding out of his eyes. He turns toward the wall—toward Seth—and realization twists his face from calm to fury.

"No," he snarls, and the word hits like an earthquake.

He charges.

Seth doesn't run.

The Void is still coiling from his hand, black threads laced with silver dragging Ethos's light with it. For one heartbeat it looks like he might actually win.

Then Ethos reaches him.

One hand closes around Seth's throat and lifts.

Effortless. Like he's nothing.

The sound Seth makes isn't fear—it's defiance—but it's cut off fast. The Void flickers. The silver dies.

My knees hit the ground.

The Ether tries to rise with me, to fight, to do *something*—but it scatters, wild and useless. The mist writhes around my feet, reaching toward him, but it can't cross the distance.

I can't move.

Can't breathe.

I've spent every moment since the crown swearing I'd never be powerless again.

And now I'm watching the two of them—light and shadow, both mine in different ways—destroy each other.

There's nothing I can do to save them.

Chapter 54
BREE

The battlefield is quiet now—too quiet. The kind of silence that follows a scream.

I'm still on my knees. The earth is warm beneath my palms, veins of Ether pulsing faintly like a heartbeat on life support.

Around me, the world is ruined.

Smoke. Ash. Blood soaking into silver-veined ground.

And the people I love.

Rhett—holding me in the rain outside my apartment, promising I'd never go back to that place alone.

Theo—whispering *"You don't have to be whole to be worthy of being seen,"* when I needed to hear it most.

Wes—calling me beautiful like it was the only truth that mattered, even when I couldn't see it myself.

Jace—making me laugh in the garden when the weight of everything felt too heavy to carry.

Gray—saying *"Love"* like it was the simplest thing in the world, like I'd always deserved it.

Thane—kneeling in front of me, silver eyes holding mine, making me feel seen for the first time in my life.

Stellan—staying with me that night when sleep felt impossible, asking nothing, giving everything.

And Seth—bonding me in the Void when I was too broken to understand what it meant, staying when everyone else was gone.

Maybe this isn't about winning.

Maybe it never was.

Maybe it's about giving everything I have left to the people who remind me why it mattered at all.

My hands dig into the veins of Ether beneath me.

They pulse once—weakly—before answering.

The mist rises, silver and bright and endless. It burns through my skin, through my heart, through every scar I've ever carried.

And I push.

Everything.

All of it.

Through the haze, Riley meets my eyes and nods, doing the same—hands pressed to the earth, black-silver Ether spilling from her like a mirror to my own. Her magic threads into mine, shadow and light twisting together until I can't tell where one ends and the other begins.

The Ether splits into rivers of light.

One by one, they find their marks—threads connecting to every bond, every scar, every promise we made.

Rhett's chest rises first. Fire flares around him, not wild but controlled, deliberate.

Theo gasps, his eyes snapping open, silver light threading through his irises.

Wes shudders, warmth flooding back into his limbs, hunger replaced by something steadier.

Jace's fingers twitch, then curl into fists as air spirals around him.

Gray's breathing deepens, his eyes locking on mine even as strength returns to his body.

Thane straightens, blood drying on his skin, his silver gaze sharp and alive.

And Seth—

The Void flickering around him steadies, brightens, *fights back*.

They breathe.

The Sanctuary breathes with them.

The light in my chest flickers, smaller, softer.

The Ether hums like a lullaby.

I feel it leave me, spilling into the world, into them, into everything I love.

My vision blurs. The edges of the world soften, dissolving into silver mist.

The last thing I see is their eyes opening—one after another—light returning where there was none.

And then...

Silver turns to white.

The world exhales.

Thank You

To My Readers

You are the reason Bree keeps fighting.

Thank you for following her into the void—for staying when the battles got brutal, when the losses felt unbearable, and when she had to choose between saving everyone and saving herself.

Your messages about these characters amaze me. The way you've adopted this chaotic, beautiful found family as your own. The way you argue about who deserves more page time (I see you, Stellan stans). The way you tell me these books have helped you feel less alone in your own complicated relationships and messy healing journeys—that's everything.

Thank you for loving Bree even when she burns too bright. For understanding that sometimes the bravest thing you can do is give everything you have, even when you don't know if you'll survive it.

Thank you for believing in Riley's redemption—for recognizing that people who've been used and hollowed out still deserve the chance to become whole. That being someone's shadow doesn't have to be your forever story.

To anyone who has ever given too much of themselves for the people they love: Bree's sacrifice is for you. Your worth isn't measured by what you have left to give. Sometimes the people who love you need to carry you for a while—and letting them isn't weakness.

To everyone who has ever faced impossible odds and chosen to fight anyway—this one's for you.

And to anyone learning that love isn't just about the grand gestures, but about showing up broken and being held together by people who refuse to let you shatter alone—Bree sees you.

Here's to the wars we survive, the people who fight beside us, and the terrifying, beautiful truth that sometimes you have to empty yourself completely before you can discover what you're truly made of.

The void doesn't get to win.

Zora Stone

About the Author

Zora Stone writes romantasy with teeth: fierce heroines, protective men who'd burn the world for them, and enough emotional wreckage to keep things interesting. When she's not plotting betrayals or steamy chaos, she's drinking iced coffee, dodging laundry, or daydreaming about enchanted forests.

You can find her online at:

Website: ZoraStone.com

TikTok | Instagram: @ZoraStoneAuthor

And on Amazon and Goodreads.

Want behind-the-scenes chaos and sneak peeks? ZoraStone.com/Influencers

ALSO BY ZORA STONE

The Ether Chronicles

Crown of the Mist
Into the Ether
Ashen Oath
Veil of Echoes
Shattering the Void
To the Final End

Arcanum Academy

Shadows of Change
Shadows Rising
Shadows Found

ZORA STONE

Shadows Revealed

www.ingramcontent.com/pod-product-compliance
Lightning Source LLC
LaVergne TN
LVHW041655060526
838201LV00043B/437